Savage Ancestors

Savage Trilogy, Volume 1

Leo Chosa and Donald Chosa Jr

To: Linda Lapine

Donald L. Chosa Jr

SAVAGE ANCESTORS

First edition. August 6, 2017

Written by Leo Chosa and Donald Chosa Jr

Preface

One day at work I was sitting at my desk in my office at the Bois Forte Tribal Government building doing my job duties as the Bois Forte Language and Cultural Coordinator. My desk phone rang so I picked up the receiver and answered. It was the curator at the tribal heritage center and museum. She told me that she had a trunk that contained my grandfather, Leo Chosa's personal papers. The trunk had been delivered to the heritage center by the granddaughter of Bill Trygg Sr who ran a land office in Ely Minnesota and had been a good friend of my father Donald Chosa Sr and my grandfather when they were alive. I had vague memories of visiting Bill Trygg Sr at his land office, a log structure surrounded by tall pines, as a young boy with my father. My memory of Bill Trygg Sr was of a kindly man who during our visits had, on several occasions, offered me pieces of highly prized maple sugar candy.

The next day the trunk was delivered to my office. I opened the lid and looked inside and found it full of documents of land allotments, receipts, personal memorabilia, old picture calendars from the 1940's, newspaper clippings, letters received from his children while attending boarding schools, postcards, and some large legal sized envelopes that contained manila folders overfilled with yellowed typewritten papers.

The large envelopes were postmarked from various publishers, addressed from places like New York, Massachusetts, California, etc. I closed the lid because there was too much to look at in the time I had. It would require a few days to go through the trunk. It wasn't until almost a year later I had enough time to sort through the trunk. All of the papers in the trunk were yellowed with age and crumbling a bit on the edges. Most of the articles were written by my grandfather during the time from between the 1920's to the early 1950's. The articles had been addressed to the local newspapers in Ely, Winton, Tower and Virginia

Minnesota. The articles were concerning conservation of the natural resources in what would later become the Boundary Waters Canoe Area.

I decided to open the large old fashioned faded brown envelopes that were of legal sized paper or 8 ½ inches by 14 inches. I carefully removed the manila folders and slid the thick pile of papers out of the folders. To my surprise they were fully typewritten manuscripts with title pages. The number of pages was included and even the estimated number of words. One contained a manuscript no less than 207 pages in length and the other two were more than 400 pages. There were three manuscripts and two copies of each as well. I carefully read first few pages of each manuscript expecting to read perhaps some badly written or maybe monotonous writing that was written by an inexperienced and amateur writer. To my amazement I found that the manuscripts were well written and upon reading the first paragraph, each caught my interest as any bookstore novel would. I am not a critique by any means, but during my life I have always been an avid reader and have read many classic fiction novels. I have also been an adjunct university instructor at various colleges and universities for over twenty years teaching various courses on Native American studies with ample experience in correcting thousands of term papers and essays.

All of the manuscripts were fiction novels with powerful Native American women as the main characters, each in different time periods. I conjectured at that time during the 1920's to the early 1950's there was little interest in Native American authors who wrote about Native American women, so all of the manuscripts had been returned to my grandfather unpublished.

I had no idea my grandfather Leo Chosa was educated to that degree. What I knew of my grandfather was that he had always been an Indian guide, fisherman, avid outdoorsman and resort owner in the

5

Boundary Waters Canoe Area. Leo Chosa was a Native American from the Ojibwe tribe with some French ancestry who originally came from the Keweenaw Bay Indian Community in the Upper Peninsula of Michigan.

His father, Joseph Chosa Sr and my great grandfather, was a French Canadian Ojibwe Indian who owned the first trading post and general store in the Keweenaw Bay area. My great grandfather Joseph Chosa Sr had nine sons. Three of his sons stayed in the Upper Peninsula of Michigan, three settled in northern Wisconsin in the Lac Du Flambeau Indian Community and three came to the Boundary Waters Canoe Area in Northern Minnesota. The three brothers who came to Minnesota including my grandfather, married three sisters who were members of the Ojibwe tribe in Minnesota.

My grandfather eventually came to own the land, which was a part of what would eventually become known as the BWCA or Boundary Waters Canoe Area, surrounding the Prairie Portage north of Winton, Minnesota. Leo's brother eventually came to own the Four Mile Portage and Leo's third brother also came to own a land allotment on the shores of Basswood Lake as well. My grandfather and my great uncle charged a fee for boats to be transported across each of the portages. They used flatbed trucks designed from Model T's to transport the boats. After a time my grandfather built a series of nine log cabins that he rented to tourists and hunters and opened a general store in another log cabin he built that serviced the other resorts in the Boundary Waters Canoe Area. The store cabin is now considered a historical site and is maintained by the U.S. Forest Service.

My grandfather and grandmother had eight children. My father Donald L. Chosa Sr or in Ojibwe was named "Gaa-gaa-giishabaad" or the Cormorant, was the youngest of them. My father was also the youngest of my grandfather's nieces and nephews born of his other two aunts and uncles. In later years my grandmother Annie

Dufault Chosa left my grandfather and moved to the Vermilion Sector of the Bois Forte Reservation so she could work at the Vermilion Boarding School that was also an orphanage for Native American children on the Vermilion Indian reservation. My father attended the school as a day school until he went the high school in the town of Tower. My father spent summers with Grampa Leo on Basswood Lake working at the resort and winters with my Gramma Annie on the Bois Forte Reservation to attend school. My father Donald Chosa Sr joined the Army at the age of 17 and served during World War II. When the United States Air Force came to be, my father then served in the Air Force for a total of 22 years. He married my mother Martha Durant who was also Native American, an Ojibwe from Keweenaw Bay, Michigan. My dad was stationed at an Air Force base in Houghton Michigan and, hearing stories from his father Leo about Keweenaw Bay, visited there and met my mother, who he married. My father took her with him to Newfoundland where he was stationed and my mother followed him throughout his travels during his military career. I was born on a U.S. Air Force base in England and my three sisters and one brother were born on different Air Force bases in Europe and the United States. An elderly aunt, who was a fluent speaker of Ojibwe, gave me my name in the language from a dream, "Bayba-waywetung" or Wolves Howling All Around You.

Eventually my father was stationed in Duluth Minnesota and, before I could remember ever meeting my Grandfather Leo Chosa, he had passed away. Leo Chosa was an activist and wrote many articles to the local papers about protecting the natural state of the forest in the Boundary Waters area of Northern Minnesota and the wastefulness and carelessness of the loggers. My Grandfather Leo Chosa set precedence and an example with his ideas which were before his time for environmentalists to come.

Leo Chosa's name in Ojibwe was "Gaagaa-nonaquet" translated in English as "He who has long hair". When he was young, Leo Chosa did wear his hair long and was quite proud of it as well as his Native American ancestry. His wife, also my grandmother, Annie Dufault, whose name in Ojibwe was "Daajige-binesiik" which translates to English as "Bird who dwells there". Both were considered mixed bloods at that time, of Native American and French descent, but living in the lifestyle, beliefs and traditions of the Ojibwe.

I decided that I would like to see his manuscripts published and I believe he would have wanted that. In them, there are references to ideas and a mindset that was prevalent in that era of time. There are also references to things that were popular at the time that aren't spoken of or written of concerning that area in remote far northern Minnesota. My grandfather Leo Chosa was a popular and well known Indian guide. He has been written about in other books during the early 1900's such as a book titled "Wilderness Days" written by Sigurd Olson.

I began the monumental task of editing and typing the manuscripts with my computer into an editable electronic document. I found that there was not too much to edit as they were well written. It is hard to imagine how much time it must have taken my grandfather to type the manuscripts with the typewriters available for use in the 1940's and I admire the work and perseverance he must have had.

I hope that you find this book, and the others, when available, as interesting as I have and I hope you learn how things were viewed through the eyes of a Native American.
Miigwech!

Grandfather: Leo Chosa

Grandson: Donald Chosa Jr

Prologue

Late in the afternoon, in early autumn, I walked into our family home after a busy day. I closed the door behind me and slipped off my shoes. I looked up and noticed the oil painting that hung on the wall in its usual place, where it had hung for the last decade. The familiar painting was tall, perhaps five feet from top to bottom, and three feet wide, fitted into an old heavy oak frame, carved in bas relief with patterns of leaves and stems. It was a painting that I had painted in a college art class many years previous. I painted a young Native American man with long flowing black hair standing in the hull of a canoe. Kneeling in the bow was a young attractive Native American woman, who also had long flowing black hair, facing forward in the same direction as the man. The man held a brown deer hide, which was acting perhaps as a sail, before an oncoming storm. Both had a focused look, as if completely absorbed in their situation. The entire painting was a wild figment of my imagination, and, when I painted it I remembered opening my mind and letting my creativity flow. The painting actually seemed to have painted itself.

As I stood looking at my creation critically and thoughtfully many years later, after raising our children and now, enjoying our grandchildren, I realized that my painting had come to life. I painted the work of art only a year before I met my wife and married her. Every year since our marriage, we harvested wild rice together, on the Bois Forte Chippewa Reservation in Northern Minnesota. All those ricing seasons, I, like the painting, stood in the rear hull with a push pole while my wife knelt toward the bow knocking the ripe grains of wild rice into the canoe with a pair of hand carved cedar knocking sticks. I realized at that point, almost a lifetime later that the painting was us, had always been us. Not knowing my grandfather, I never could have imagined how I would share his legacy and imagination so uncannily, like the painting in his story, in the future.

Chapter one

With the coming of daylight, the great storm had subsided. Giant waves, like angry wolves sweeping the shores in search of food, continued to dash themselves with thunderous abandon against the low cliff-like shore of sandstone, where throughout the centuries the ceaseless wash of the waves indented cavernous caves into the soft red rock.

Little pillars stoutly defying the continuous onslaught of the crystal, clear water, stood upholding the forest floor above. Over the violence of sound, a roof composed of masses of interwoven roots of giant maple, pine and hemlock, deeply imbedded in a thick soil, muffled the turmoil, softened and modified its density until it sounded like a continuous rumble of distant thunder.

A short distance eastward, a deep ravine, its sides sharply inclined, cleft the landscape like a notch in a wood-choppers log, shielding the fast-moving stream that tumbled along its bottom from the slowly rising hills. The ravine, like a line purposely drawn by nature across its scenic beauty, marked the end of the rocky shore and the beginning of a broad, sandy beach that spread its wave-washed sand, ribbon-like into the distance where the forest jealously spread over its leaf burdened branches.

Inland from the beach, where the hills, at nature's whim moved their thickly forested slopes back from the pebble strewn beach leaving a broad patch of flatland, the hemlocks stood in park-like array.

As the first streaks of dawn in the east turned the dark to gray, "out there", the reflected light from the few remaining stars in the west peeping in and out of the passing clouds, undulating with the roll of the waves, while persistent white caps spread their foamy crests over the transparent crystal-like blue of the great Lake Superior.

The great storm that had struck with hurricane fury, whipped the water into a seething boiling mass of foam, also kept the Natives whose teepees and wigwams clustered in tiny village-like formations along the shore, huddled within their flimsy circular shelters. For three days and nights, the incessant sound of rain and sleet beating against the thin bark shelters, was broken only by crashing sounds of falling trees that having withstood the fury of the elements for a century would seemingly relax its struggle for survival with the inevitable result. At such moments, convenient woodland gods were called upon for protection, and each family steeped in age old tradition and superstition would delve deep into meager food supplies or some little sacrificial offering.

The storm, with the same suddenness as it approached, subsided, leaving the morning still, save for the incessant wash of the waves over the beach, and the distant thunder-like roll within the cave-washed cliffs to the west. Nature once again settled down to its customary peace and quiet.

Among the Natives, audible reaction was apparent. The high pitched childish laughter, the friendly barking of a pet dog found a ready echo in the scolding voice of a worried mother as she retrieved her favorite large flat bark basket commandeered for the moment as a make-believe sled for the transportation of firewood. The customary early morning sounds of village activity in hurried preparations for the morning meal mingled with the distant cry of a gull as it sailed gracefully on motionless wings.

The crooked little foot path wound snake-like around various obstacles along its torturous way, a boulder here, the rotted stumps of shattered tree trunks there, mute evidence of storms of yesteryear. A close-knit cluster of white birches that stand united against the elements is blocked off by a freshly shattered giant of the forest that lay twisted and splintered. Farther along the little path, a stately maple, still clinging desperately to its upturned roots, lay defiant and proud. Near its tormented branches partly hidden by a thick screen of fluttering foliage, a girl twisted and turned among the many leaf laden branches while keeping a precarious footing along the trails narrowing top. She moved catlike and noiselessly. The thin buckskin of her moccasins gave her ample warning of a dry twig under foot as she hastily changed to a quieter step. Scantily clad in a one piece sleeveless, sack like dress of grayish woolen "trade goods", its belt of the same material, dyed a lighter shade of gray gave the illusion of a two-piece garment. Her black hair, unkempt and disheveled, left two scraggly braids protruding from her shaggy head from whence stray locks of varying lengths tried the girl's patience by persistently obscuring her vision and tickling her nose. With both hands fully occupied for the moment, her left firmly grasping a bow, three arrows, and two freshly killed partridge, while clinging with her right to one of the upright limbs of the fallen tree. Not unlike a wild cat stalking its prey, the girl moved with an ease born of sureness. At a slight toss of her head, the offending loose strands of her hair parted, revealing a clean, frank expression emphasized by large almond shaped, dark brown eyes. Eyes with a faint hint of an Asiatic slant that spoke an age in advance of her years. Having followed atop the tree to a point where it lay across the path, she sat on the trunk and lying her bow and arrow aside, proceeded to strip the feathers from the birds.

While thus occupied, the sounds from the widely-scattered village increased in variety and volume. In a distance towards the deep ravine and its noisy little stream came the sounds of creaking wooden hinges as the heavy wooden door of the Trading Post swung open, lazily, to the cool morning air. The girl smiled unconsciously at the variety of sounds, recognizing the origin of each in turn. The smile revealed white, even and well-formed teeth set in an attractive mouth with full rounded lips. With the Latin classic lines of forehead and nose of her French father and not too prominent cheek bones, straight coal black hair, a legacy of her Indian mother, Paulette DuCharme was more than passingly attractive despite her meager attire and unkempt hair. Tall for her 18 winters, her athletic figure swayed as she moved about with a steady unassuming grace, the birthright of those who lived and struggled in that forested empire where, at the time of this narrative, every person was a law unto himself and conscience the only guide to human behavior.

Suppressing a yawn, Paulette prepared to continue her journey although sleepy having been up since the first gray streaks of light appeared along the eastern rim of the horizon. She had hunted diligently, her flashing eyes taking in every tiny space that might harbor a rabbit or a partridge among the tangled undergrowth along the path she followed. She had been unsuccessful until she came to the giant tree that lay across the path. Knowing the partridge's fondness for the seeds of the maple, she moved cautiously to within easy range of the two birds greedily devouring their morning meal. In rapid succession, she had killed them both. "Now we can eat", she muttered to herself as she gathered the fruits of the chase. She said to herself quietly, "For a while I thought our breakfast would be late." Arising quickly from her seat on the tree trunk she thought, "I must hurry back.

Grandmother must be up and about by now waiting until I get back with our breakfast." She smiled at the pleasant thought of having, for the time being, plenty for morning repast.

As she gathered her bow and arrows she was rudely and forcefully shoved to the ground. The suddenness and force of the attack sent her sprawling. Releasing her bow and the two birds that she might break the force of the fall with her hands, she immediately sprang to her feet. She recoiled as she recognized the leering maniacal grin on the face of Napoleon LeChance, the trader's only son. Dressed in tight fitting knee breeches of blue velvet, black stockings and low shoes adorned with silver buckles, a black chapeau of beaver sans le plume served to emphasize the little piggish eyes set widely apart, apparently to make room for the beak-like nose that all but reached his thin bluish lips. Contrary to his own opinion of himself, the trader's son would present a pretty picture in any attire. The grinning ego-maniac eyed his victim closely and waited until she spoke. For one trembling with rage, the girl spoke rather mildly, hoping she might at least regain her game. "Please Napoleon, don't do that", she said, her voice trembling with emotion. "Give me back my birds, they are for my grandparents, we have not had anything to eat since yesterday morning. I couldn't yesterday on-account of the storm." Napoleon, giving no sign of either relenting or releasing his hold on the birds said, "Aw go on, you can get more, I want those," and with that he started to pass Paulette who stood blocking his path. In passing Napoleon spied the girl's bow and arrows lying on the ground where she had dropped them and while purposefully stepping on the bow, thrust his entire weight upon it until. with a resounding crack it snapped in two. Paulette, wide-eyed at the sight of her favorite bow being broken, stood as one totally devoid of powers of expression. Napoleon, after committing the dastardly little trick, turned to the girl and in his best leering and grinning manner said,

"Just in case you get any notions, after all for a Native girl you a good archer."

"Yes, yes, I am a Native for which I thank the Creator, and I pray that some day, somehow, I can get rid of the cursed white blood that runs through my veins, you...you dog! You, you dirty snake!" Shocked to the point of distraction, Paulette, overcome with rage, snatched Napoleon's bow and arrows and before he realized fully what was happening, the girl had leaped over the fallen tree trunk and with eyes blazing in fury slipped an arrow onto the sinew, whirled to face the young man as he started to follow her menacingly.

"Stand where you are!" she managed to say, "I am going to kill you...you...dirty snake!" Raising the arrow to a level with his chest she drew it back with all her strength. On the verge of letting the arrow fly on its deadly mission she was taken with a sudden fear that unless it pierced him clear through it would not kill him. Gathering all the strength that her fingers and right arm could command she drew the arrow back, back until the bit of flint at its tip and all but reached the bow. In the meantime, Napoleon realizing his predicament stood as one frozen in his tracks. Stutteringly he managed to say "D-o-n'-t, don't Paulette, take your birds." Amidst the ever-rising tumult of emotions within her, Paulette but vaguely heard his words. What she did hear conveyed but little meaning to the girl. She had decided to kill a human being. The girl raised the tip of her arrow a little, pointing it straight at his breast, she couldn't...she must not miss. "Only another little bit," she thought as the stiff bow resisted her every effort to draw the stubborn arrow to its very tip. With a loud crack, the bow snapped in two and a half fell and dangled uselessly from her hands. The sudden reaction left the girl pitifully speechless, while the color slowly returned to her cheeks. She was not afraid. From childhood, she had grown accustomed to fighting her own battles and win, lose or draw it had never once occurred to her to shift her troubles to anyone else. At a

18

loss for the moment, she stood eyeing her tormenter, a feeling of helplessness crept over her, the desire to kill still uppermost in her mind. She hissed, "I am going to kill you Napoleon, and when I do, it will be a little at a time, not quickly, that would be too easy for you, your moans and cries will sound like little bird calls."

During the girl's outburst, Napoleon had advanced stealthily until he came within reaching distance. With the suddenness of a snake striking its prey, his hand shot out and grabbed the girl by the arm. Jerking her viciously towards him, she stumbled over the tree trunk that lay between them. "You, you little savage," he hissed, "you would dare talk to me...me, Napoleon, son of the trader, like that. I'll teach you to be more careful what you say to me!"

In the sudden and unexpected attack, Paulette had fallen on her face and before she could spring to her feet, Napoleon seized her dress collar and placing one foot on her back, ripped the garment to its belt. The loss of the birds and her bow, Paulette might have withstood without too much show of outward emotion, but the loud ripping sound of her only cloth garment was more than the poor girl could bear. Like a wounded pantheress at bay, with claws and fangs bared, the girl backed by the inherited ferocity of a thousand years of savage ancestry, sprang to her feet and fell upon her assailant with a fury that could come only to one of her sex. Blinded by rage, she sank her teeth into his right arm, the first part of his anatomy she could reach. With a howl of pain, the youth grew limp with fright at the sudden turn of events. Harder and harder the girl's jaws closed...down upon the muscle of his arm until she thought her teeth must come together through his flesh.

"Paulette! Paulette! He howled, "Let me go, let me go, I say..."

Unmindful of his cries, she hung on lest she lose the advantage she had gained. Her savage desire to kill mounted higher and higher with each passing moment. The feel of his cold hand on her naked back, as he thrashed about with his free arm in a vain effort to free himself, inflamed her savage passion to kill. She was weaponless, if she let go her hold, he would get away, her jaws were tiring fast, she had to act quick or he would escape. Her fingers found his throat, yes, that was it, his throat, if she could only sink her teeth into his throat, and hang for a little while, he would die. Lack of food for one day and night, the emotional strain of the last few minutes, began to tell on her strength and the girl knew that she must let go while she still had some strength left with which to defend herself further if need be. Reluctantly she let go and made one last wild effort to shift her hold to her victim's throat. Napoleon was free, jerked away and still howling, sped out of sight along the well beaten path. Paulette turned to look for the birds, hoping that in the excitement, Napoleon might have dropped and left them, but they were nowhere in sight, he had taken them with him. After searching in vain for the missing partridge, she picked up the pieces of her broken bow and removed the precious sinew bow string, winding it carefully around her two unbroken arrows. While doing this, she appeared unmoved. She felt a cool wisp of air on her bare back. A sudden recollection came over her, much as one would remember fragments of a forgotten dream. Quickly reaching around to her bare shoulder and back, she felt the tear in her dress. For a moment, she stood unmoved then sank slowly to the ground. Burying her face in her arms, she broke into violent weeping, sobbing bitterly, her naked back bent beneath an emotional strain she was finding hard to bear. As her bitter tears flowed unrestrained, she did not hear the sound of approaching footsteps. Not until a heavy thud on the ground beside her did she suspect the presence of anyone. Hastily wiping her eyes with the back of her hands, Paulette sat up and looked into the wondering kindly eyes of Little Eagle, a noted hunter from the village.

Lying on the ground beside the fallen maple where the Indian had dropped it was a medium sized deer neatly trussed into a convenient pack. "My daughter weeps. Why?" the Indian asked as he tried to decipher for himself the puzzling signs about him, two broken bows and several arrows, partridge feathers scattered about, a girl with hair disheveled and clothing torn, sobbing bitterly. Shaking his head slowly in bewilderment, he again asked, "Why does my child weep so?" Paulette straightened up and turned her tearstained face towards the man towering above her. Little Eagle, belying his name, was big and tall, with sharp black eyes that could, at will, mirror his every mood, eyes that could flash dangerously, soften in deep sympathy or twinkle mischievously in response to a well-developed sense of humor. The girl loved the big kindly man, ever since early childhood, he had all but adopted her for his own. But knowing that she was all her grandparents had to comfort them in their old age, he was content to call her "My daughter".

Paulette felt her strength returning fast as she recounted her morning's experience in detail. Little Eagle remained silent all through her narrative while his eyes, always so open and frank, narrowed to two tiny slits. Only when she told how she had hung on to his arm with her teeth did his eyes flash a merry approval for an instant. In a reproving voice, he said, "Why did you not tell me that you had little food, can you not see that I am big and strong, have you not heard many, many times that I am one of the great hunters of this village?"

"Because I can get the food we need if, if he would leave me alone," she answered rather timidly and continued, "I do not like to ask for food, I, too, am strong," pointing to Napoleon's broken bow, "I broke it with my two hands." She had arisen to her feet and looking into the hunter's eyes, said pleadingly, "Little Eagle, take me with you some time when you hunt for deer, I am tired of hunting for small game, always partridge or rabbits and the next day the same thing over, more partridge and more rabbits. I want to use the flint tipped arrow." Then more demandingly asked, "Will my father take me with him?"

Little Eagle looked at the girl for a few moments, his concern for her having disappeared, in its place a look of amusement as he said, "Your father goes far and travels fast, you would get very tired, and hungry too, for a good hunter never eats before a kill."

"I could do that and more," said Paulette excitedly. "See, I haven't eaten since yesterday at day break and I have hunted all morning."

Turning to his pack, the Indian loosened the thongs that bound the feet and head of the deer and deftly stripping the hide from one of the animal's hind quarters, expertly severed it with his hunting knife and laid it on the matting of dead and dried leaves beside the girl, remarking, "Take that home and feed your grandparents." Slipping the knife back into its sheath, he immediately untied the strings that fastened it to his belt and handed it to Paulette saying, "It is time my daughter had more than her teeth and claws to protect her, take this knife, it is old and worn, you may need it before you learn to use the flint tipped arrow." Coming nearer to the girl and lowering his voice continued, "I must warn you, never draw it in anger, in defense, in fear, yes, but never in anger. Does my daughter understand?" After a moment's hesitation, continued, "Always carry it where you can reach for it easily with either hand, it may save you many bitter tears." Swinging his heavy pack on to his broad back and adjusting the "tumpline" over his head, Little Eagle strode off as if nothing had happened to interrupt his journey homeward.

Chapter 2

When Napoleon, in abject fright escaped the infuriated girl, he sped hurriedly along the winding path. Holding tenderly the spot where Paulette had bitten him, he had but one thought, to get back home as quickly as possible. Dodging overhanging branches and small dead trees leaning crazily over the path, the youth paid scant attention to several snarling, half wild, little dogs that came snapping at his heels. Several families, camping along the trail, looked up in wondering surprise at the "heir apparent" to the LaChance Trading Post. Never before had he been known or seen to pass in other than a leisurely pace, patronizingly condescending to let the Natives feast their eyes on the latest model of what the well-dressed young man should wear. Then as now, he looked neither to the right or left. Clinging tightly to Paulette's two birds, he reached his parental roof, somewhat out of breath and without further mishap. Not until the heavy door made of split logs closed behind him and the sound of the wooden latch dropping into place, did he feel secure from pursuit. Hastily glancing about the room, he quickly regained a semblance of composure, he was, for the time being, alone. Tossing the birds under the built-in bed-like bench that ran along the length of one wall, he hastily undressed that he might better examine the damage to his now useless right arm. Tenderly and carefully drawing his wounded arm from the sleeve of his jacket, the youth all but shouted with joy upon discovering that the wound consisted of nothing more than two rows of well-defined teeth marks. Though bruised and swelling rapidly, the heavy material of his garment protected the arm from more damage. Hastily dressing again and whistling gaily, Napoleon busied himself about the room doing nothing in particular.

The LaChance Trading Post consisted of two log buildings. The larger housed the store and living quarters of the owner, the other was used as a warehouse and fur storage. Except for the little clearing where the buildings stood, the forest was untouched. Great trees of maple, birch, and pine shaded the thatched and bark covered roofs from early sunrise to its setting. In the distance, southward, through the parklike growth could be seen the lazily rolling waves of the great "Superieur" the greatest lake of them all. The crystal blue-green of its waters reflected the morning sunlight, as rising and falling gracefully in perfect rhythm, each wave marking off the brevity of time in man's troubled stay on earth. Westward, beyond the little ravine, from whence came the timed and muffled roar as of growling and grumbling giants far beneath the earth, tall pines registered each incoming wave in the slight quiver of its wide spread branches. Back from the post, where the ground rose not too quickly to break the symmetry of the landscape, many smaller log cabins stood, each facing in its own direction, while preserving their own individuality in the general picture. Running parallel with the broad sandy beach to the east, Native wigwams of birch bark, their circular framework of saplings arising cone shaped seemingly out of the earth clustered in little village-like formations.

A broad well beaten path joined the group of log cabins, generally known as the "French Quarter", to the humbler abodes of the Indians known as the "Native Quarter". Though fraternizing without thought of hindrance and intermarrying without restraint, a marked class distinction arose simultaneously from both quarters. In between the two self-defined groups, divided only by their self-appraisal of rank, the half-breeds or the lawful or unlawful offspring of both red and the white formed a third though weak link in the chain connecting both. Tolerated by the Indian and the White man, an undercurrent of feeling that they were neither white nor red, set them apart from both factions. Arising alone and above all three factions in this forest society was the Trader LaChance and his son Napoleon. How and where he came from nobody knew and none seemed to care. Trader LaChance lived for himself and his son, and this occupied most of the thoughts of and all the activities of the Trader. He spoke perfect French, but a swarthy skin, beady eyes in a round full face and short curly black hair gave rise to many a conjecture as to his nationality. One of the French inhabitants made vague mention of some little known Mediterranean tribe and the subject was soon forgotten. When the Trombley Brothers had vacated the buildings some eight summers past to relocate at another point some two weeks distant by canoe, Monsieur LaChance opportunely happened upon the scene and moved in. With less than fifteen canoes of merchandise, thirteen to be exact, appeared one calm day as if from out of the skies and calmly announced that the LaChance establishment was open for business. Besides several Algonquin Indians and their families, Monsieur LaChance was accompanied by his only child, a son, aged about eight, and his nursemaid, an Indian woman from some strange eastern tribe. Excitement rose to a high pitch that day as the heavy canoes were carefully beached by many willing hands both Native and French.

When the Trombley Brothers had moved away, nearly all of their runners, packers and Native trappers remained behind. Through intermarriage, strong family ties and developed between the French and Indians, ties that the women and children refused to break thus keeping intact an entire village of experienced workmen much to the advantage of Monsieur LaChance. In the years that followed, the Trading Post prospered and Monsieur LaChance's heavy freighter canoes multiplied rapidly. He was seldom, if ever, seen outside of his store and except for the periodic fashion parades of Napoleon, they took no part in or displayed any interest in village life other than was necessary to further his trading interests. When Napoleon arrived breathless from his adventure with Paulette, Monsieur LaChance was busy with his accounts. Seated on a high stool before a sloping shelf-like desk pegged into the wall, the dim light filtering through the square of white cloth serving as a window, cast queer square shaped shadows over the ruled paper of his account book. Paying little if any heed to the goings and comings of anyone, he was surprised, very much surprised, even slightly alarmed, when the door to his store was violently thrust open and Henri LaClair, his head packer and all around lieutenant stomped into his presence. Monsieur LaClair, a big man, or rather a black bearded semi giant whose will, by right of might, was law among his companions, now stood before his employer glaringly mad. Monsieur LeChance, outwardly calm, regarded his most valuable employee with an inward feeling that something was wrong, for never had he seen Monsieur LaClair so thoroughly upset.

"Where is that young snake you call your son?" asked the irate man.

Around matters pertaining to his family life, Monsieur LaChance invariably drew a curtain and so raising his eyebrows in surprise, he in turn asked, "My son Napoleon?"

"Yes, your son, the little rat! If I had caught him in the act, I would have twisted his little neck around until his long nose stuck out from between his shoulder blades!" By emphasizing his remarks with suitable gestures, closing his hairy fists until his nails dug deep into his palms and the tips of his fingers were white and bloodless, the big fellow relieved himself of some of his pent up anger. The brisk walk from his cabin, where he had left his brother in law Little Eagle, to see what could be done about LaChance Jr.'s attack, did much to cool him off.

Monsieur LaChance, fast becoming apprehensive, yet like a disturbed porcupine with quills "en garde", stood ready to defend himself and his son, right or wrong, against all odds, said in a forced, matter of fact tone, "Now, Monsieur LaClair...please calm yourself, enough, at least enough to tell me what this is all about."

In a voice still trembling with rage, Henri related what Little Eagle had learned from Paulette. "And now" he added "unless you teach that little devil a lesson, I, me, Henri LaClair will do it for you!"

"Now, now...Monsieur LaClair I am sure you are worked up over something you heard. I shall speak to my son Napoleon and learn from the boy's own lips just what happened and if, from what he tells me meets with my disapproval, I shall tell him so."

"Yes, I understand Henri, and I can assure you and your friends that if my son has done anything that I cannot approve of, I promise that we shall make proper amends, you may tell your people that."

With every action intended to convey utter disgust for his employer, Henri LaClair turned, stomped out, slamming the heavy door behind him.

The Trader turned to his desk, and continued arranging his accounts. After a few moments concentration on the book before him and without looking up, Monsieur LeChance raised his voice and called, "Napoleon." Not getting an immediate response, he tried again, a little louder. "Na-po-leon!" The sound of a faint, very faint shuffling footstep in the adjoining room, the creaking of hinges as the door to the store opened, a faint voice saying, "Yes, Father, I am here," responded to the Trader's vocal effort.

Laying his quill aside and turning deliberately on the high rustic stool addressed his son with equal deliberation. "Napoleon, what is this I hear about you engaging in a brawl with some Native girl this morning?"

Napoleon raised his eyebrows questioningly, "A brawl, Mon Pere? with some Native girl? I do not understand."

Monsieur LaChance eyed his son sharply, raised his voice and said rather sternly, "You heard Henri LaClair's accusations plainly. You were by the door listening attentively. Now tell me what this is all about."

Napoleon, having long since prepared his defense, proceeded to lay the entire matter openly and truthfully before his parent, or so he planned. "Oh that," he smiled condescendingly, "I thought you were referring to something serious."

Monsieur LaChance all but smiled his approval of his son's approach to a difficult situation.

"You see father," the boy continued, "it was like this, I was walking along the path, as you often recommended I should do in the early morning, when, all of a sudden this, this, Native girl sprang out of the thick bushes and attacked me."

The trader interrupted, "You mean to say that a girl attacked you?" Shaking his head slowly said, "That is unbelievable my son, why should a Native girl attack you?"

"I don't know, father, but she did and I have the marks of teeth on my arm, where she bit me."

Monsieur LaChance slid off the stool and strode quickly around the long table of bark covered saplings and confronted his son.

"You say she bit you! Show me at once where! I will have to see for myself." Napoleon quickly removed his jacket and bared his arm, now swollen and red but still bearing the telltale marks of Paulette's teeth. The trader examined the bruised arm carefully and with some misgiving said, "This is unbelievable, and what happened after that?"

"Well, after that I got away from her as gently as I could so as not to hurt her too much, she attempted to shoot me with her bow and arrow. I had to break her bow to protect myself after I dodged one of her arrows aimed directly at me."

"Was that all?" asked the elder LaChance in anticipation of further account of his son's chivalrous behavior.

Napoleon with well feigned hesitation continued, "I made one mistake, father, in my anger at her sudden and unreasonable attack, I, without giving thought to what I was doing, took the two partridge she had, as a punishment for her behavior."

"What did you do with the birds?" questioned the trader with some solicitude.

"I have them."

"Bring them here, to me." The trader examined them carefully, noting the arrow marks and the thorough way in which they were plucked. "Well, well," he remarked giving voice to his thoughts, "the girl who got those must be a good archer, both birds were hit each in exactly the same spot, and quite neat too, who did you say she was?"

"Paulette DuCharme," answered the boy quickly.

"Paulette DuCharme?" The trader was shocked. "Why that is the half-breed girl who lives with her grandparents, I cannot believe it." Handing the two partridges back to his son said, "Take those to the cook and tell her to prepare them for our supper." Returning to his stool muttered to himself, "Those Natives are queer people. Oh well, we will soon get rid of them, another year, perhaps two."

Monsieur turned to his account book while his son hurried away to the kitchen.

Chapter 3

The name given a white man by the Natives as oft as not, grew
into custom from repeated first impression due to an outstanding
peculiarity of appearance or behavior or from marked accent of speech.
These names or nicknames, if you will, once established by use,
however, brief, clung to its owner for life. In the case of Monsieur
LaChance, his lop ears being the most outstanding peculiarity of his
appearance, large, round and set well back at the sides of his head,
quite naturally and with popular acclaim earned for him the title of
"Ma-ma' ki-ta-wug", or "Big Ears". It followed naturally that his son
who resembled him so completely in the minutest detail should be
called "Ma-ma' ki-ta-wug-ens", "Little Big Ears", or "Big Ears, Jr.".
The appellations thus established were in no sense used in a spirit of
ridicule or criticism, but were honestly, in some cases, a
characterization or designation; one might say quite often a
classification due to some special ability. A good traveler would this
earn the title of the "deer", an industrious collector of fire wood, in all
probability, would be designated, as the "beaver". Apart from readily
acquiring a name for himself and his son, the trader gave the Natives,
both French and Indian, little else by way of information about both
Big and Little Big Ears. Short and stocky of build, heavy black

eyebrows forming a line, without a break, clear across his forehead accentuated a rather forbidding mien. His eyes set close to a roman-ish nose never reflected "Big Ears" inner emotions, but remained cool and passive. Whether or not he was ever sufficiently impressed by the behavior of the Natives to create an emotional tension, was never known. Perhaps a wide and varied experience, with peoples in other lands, had over shadowed the deportment of the inhabitants around him to an extent beyond his notice. A firm believer in fate, his optimism was unbounded and from his experience, amply justified.

Leaving Montreal, against expert advice, at the break of day, his small flotilla of canoes sailed peacefully on amid tribes of hostile Indians. On portage after portage along the Ottaway River, signs of recent battles and ambushes by hostile Natives were everywhere in evidence. Hastily constructed barricades of recently cut timbers, blood stained and pockmarked with musket slugs, like sign posts along the trail of "White Man's progress" served but to guide them on to their destination. Amidst all this, his little party traveled on like one successfully braving swarms of angry bees. From members of his party was learned that upon reaching the mouth of the Ottaway River, he called his little band about him and showed them a crudely drawn map. Tracing, with his finger, the flow of water to the Northern-most bay of Lake Superior, he quietly informed them "That is where we are going." To his party's murmur of disapproval, some voicing the dangers of such an undertaking, the hazards of crossing the little known "Gitchi Ga-mee" in their frail bark canoes, he paid not the slightest heed. Traveling without the customary scouting precautions of the time, they were, not only in constant danger, but an easy prey to any one of many hostile bands of roving Indians.

Unhurried beyond the usual pace of adventurers, never looking backward, always moving forward, impelled by an irresistible inner force, a desire to know what lay over yonder hill or beyond the

31

next point jutting so boldly out into the lake, a restless spirit of adventure, whetted by the, too often, fantastically exaggerated tales of those who had lived to return, overshadowed and minimized their sense of immediate dangers, this passing them safely where the timid and more cautious met with disaster. In answer as to how he had managed to come through without mishap, "Big Ears" had merely shrugged his shoulders, he didn't know, didn't know there were any dangers, and why worry about it all now?

Setting up shop in the recently abandoned log buildings, Monsieur LaChance and his son proceeded to live, not as gregarious human beings, en famille, but rather within a self-created little circle. Living thus, with his private life completely enclosed outside the environment of village activity, he soon became as a thing apart and inanimate, at least, insofar as the villagers were concerned, a convenient place to get needed equipment, as a stream from which to draw water, or a lake for necessary food fish. With a faraway dreamy look that never left his half-closed eyes, the trader carried on his business honestly yet with a degree of casual shrewdness that bespoke a long line of sagacious tradesman ancestry. Village life ebbed and flowed about his establishment without so much as causing a lift of his bushy eyebrows, a birth, a tragic death, unlike an exceptionally large catch of furs, was something to be looked for as ordinary in the course of human affairs. At any rate, such matters didn't concern either him or his son.

In the years that followed, the trader's business grew both in volume and profits. His large freighter canoes, multiplying in number, shuttled back and forth across the great lake without mishap. Along with the business, his son Napoleon grew into young manhood, physically, and mentally into a selfish, deceitful overbearing snob. Cloistered by self-appraisal within the narrow confines of the Post grounds, the youth grew up in an atmosphere of uncorrected self-centered imaginary importance that grew into a wall between him and the children of the village. Like their elders, the younger generation soon forgot that Little Big Ears existed. In their rough noisy games, they could get along without him and the mere mention of his name was usually sufficient to bring on a sudden hush even among the noisiest.

Among the many children, both Indian and half-breeds of varying ages, Paulette was perhaps the only one who developed a strange curiosity concerning the youth. On days when she could get away from her many duties or the insistence of her many friends that she join in some playful expedition along the sandy beach, she would quietly wend her way and loiter near the trading post. With more than ordinary imagination, she would construct in her mind the probable interior of the log rooms. Standing hidden from view by one of the many huge pine and maples, the girl was consumed by a burning desire to see what was inside the buildings. She wanted to be friends with the youth who was of her age. Peeking through the chink less seams between the logs of the warehouse, her curiosity was heightened by the piles of baled merchandise. In one end of the great room were the dog sleds and toboggans, along the wall, harnesses for the sled dogs hung in orderly array on pegs driven securely into the timbers. Tools of various kinds used in the construction of cabins, canoes and equipment were stored on a wide bench. While thus immersed in the wonders of another world, she didn't hear the catlike approaching footfalls of Little Big Ears and did not become aware of his presence until she was rudely and forcefully kicked. Skinning the bridge of her nose against the rough bark of the log where, but a moment before, she leaned so restfully, Paulette turned and stood facing the grinning Napoleon.

"What are you doing here?" he asked, and without waiting for a reply, continued, "Don't you know you can't come sneaking around here?"

The girl always slow to anger, stood silent holding her injured nose, "I'm not doing anything," she ventured in a muffled nasal voice, "and you didn't have to kick me."

"Well, what are you going to do about it?"

"Nothing, I guess," she said while groping for something expressive of her feelings. "Nothing, I guess for now."

Then springing into action like a young pantheress, she slapped his face, once, twice, three times in rapid succession, then before Little Big Ears could recover from his surprise attack, she fled and like a young deer went bounding through the forest and out of sight.

After their first encounter, the two, as if by expressed arrangement, avoided one another. In the years that followed, Paulette DuCharme grew into a beautiful young woman embodying the best traits and characteristics of both her Indian and French ancestors. Her straight black hair glistened with a blue iridescence and bounced in the sunlight with each saucy toss of her head. Always happy in company with her aging grandparents, carrying sweet sap of the sugar maple during "iskigamizige-giizis" or "the month of maple sugaring", picking and drying blueberries for the long winter ahead, tanning deer and caribou skins for clothing, smoking and drying fish and meat to fill the big "Makuks" in defense against the blizzards and deep snows of winter. Despite her busy days, Paulette found a little time to play with other children. Her keen sense of humor and ready laughter made her a welcome visitor in both the French and Native quarters of the village. From Henri LaClair, the good friend of her deceased father, she learned to speak French fluently. "No! No-no, Mon Cheri," he would say teasingly. "I do not understand one word when you speak the language of the savage. Ah-ha, but the French, that is the language of the Gods, you ask the good Pere Daniel when he comes again."

Paulette believed every word he spoke, the stories of the glories of Old France, her beautiful women that were the models for the very angels, fantastic legends of strange little people and ferocious giants mingled in her fertile imagination with the stories of the prowess of "Nanaboozhoo" the mythical God of the Ojibwe; Nanaboozhoo, the mighty creator of the Earth and all things on it.

In the wigwam of Little Eagle, beside a cheery little fire that showered sparks into and beyond the intricate cluster of pole-tips, Paulette absorbed legends of brave and mighty hunters of her tribe; of men and women who fasted in their youth, fasted until the Spirits carried them far beyond the rim of the horizon, to the wigwam of Nokomis, the grandmother of Nanaboozhoo, and came back with gifts, gifts of wisdom, of knowledge of medicines and the arts in hunting and in the taking of the bounties of the Earth.

As the years rolled on, Paulette came to view life and its intricate pattern with a clearer understanding than most young people of her age. From her vantage point, she recognized the narrow perspective that encompassed her only enemy and pitied Little Big Ears in his environment of wealth. He had no "little people" like the ones who inhabited the caverns where the waves sounded like thunder and shook the earth above, the little old men with flowing hair and beards to match the color of the wild flowers, and no taller than a rabbit sitting on its haunches. Grandmother had taken her one night when the moon was full and taught her the song that put her to sleep beside the great pine. The little men had appeared as if by magic, each near the stem of a wild flower. With robes ankle length and tiny sandals that somehow clung to little feet as they danced, wrestled, and turned somersaults in the golden light of the moon. She remembered, from later visits to the little men in blue, red, yellow, and crimson robes, how, after sitting in a circle about a tiny wisp of smoke and lighting tiny stone pipes, they would spring lightly to overhanging branches and like the birds, swing gracefully up and down. What did it matter if on awakening they had all disappeared into the caverns below leaving only the wild flowers to mark the place where they entered the earth? She would come often, they were her people, and some day, maybe they would take her to their homes to watch the thunderous roll of the waves.

Chapter 4

Above and beyond the swiftly moving veil of autumn clouds, the sun, a ball of pale amber, shone dull and cold. In and out of the varying density of snow laden vapor, momentarily casting its pale light through a rolling rift, like the parting of curtain only to be quickly obscured, in turn, by a thickly flying wall of darkening mist, the light giving orb floating midway on its daily journey across the blue above gave warning of approaching winter. Among the inhabitants of the village, the cold brisk northern breeze stripping the last crimson leaves from the stately maples and birches created a current of suppressed excitement.

The time had come, as it had every Autumn, to lay aside all thoughts of indolent summer days, of berry picking, waving fields of wild rice, the midsummer festival, lazy red coated deer that carelessly gamboled with their fawns among the rushes of inland streams and lakes, the excited laughter of boys and girls along the cool trout streams, tender young partridges and rabbits, white fish, lake trout, and herring from the great lake itself. In its stead, the uncertain future with its cold, bitter biting cold, deep snows, long starless nights and days when the sun would barely arch into the gray sky and shyly return into its nighttime hideaway.

Inhabitants of the village passed one another on the path without stopping for the customary comment or latest bit of humorous gossip at some villager's expense, for each was intent on his errand, an errand as important as life itself. In every villager was manifest, each in his own way, uncertainty and wondered on the possibility of a return in the following spring, for some of their number was busily preparing for that last long journey from whence none ever returned. This was the day that fate busily spun fortune's wheel, the prize, all knew too well.

Every spring when the Natives returned to their summer encampment beside the shores of their Gitchi Ga-mee, the question uppermost in all minds was "Who was it this time?" Youth and brawn did not count in fate's selection. The winters in the vast inland were rugged and exacted its toll of lives. The ever-present threat of famine and sickness accompanying each family across the lakes and portages of des Pays d'en Haut hovered like a shadow across the prows of canoes and deeply indented snow paths alike. Lengthy or lingering farewells at the parting of relatives and friends, lest they be interpreted as an ill omen, were discreetly avoided. In their stead a quick wave or nod, as each canoe was forcefully launched, would suffice as a cover for an inner feeling that it might be the last.

And so, this day, as if by common consent or some ruler's decree, inhabitants of the little village, both French and Indian hustled about, each intent upon his or her mission. Bark canoes were portaged from the beach and carefully laid beside an outdoor fireplace of a wigwam or log cabin to be made ready for a journey, its upper seams pitched and sealed against the water that would reach its gunwales under a heavy load. The careful inspection of pack straps or "tumplines", those indispensable strips of raw deer or caribou hide, used in portaging heavy packs, lest a hungry mouse had nibbled a weak spot served but a momentary check on the lamenting of a mother over a daughter's decision to load, for better or for worse, her belongings into the canoe of the village swain.

The wind and falling leaves, the exposed bared branches pointing stiffly upward, also brought busy days for the LaChance Trading Post. Outfitting its trappers and advancing goods against the catch of furs, warm woolen cloth for clothing, small blanket squares for footwear, knives, muskets and ammunition, copper arrow tips, woolen blankets to the best and deserving hunters. Children in their own little ways caught in the fevered excitement of preparation scolded half wild pets lest they be left behind. Toy canoes and outgrown snowshoes of yesteryear were gathered and put away in the "cache" high up on the platform atop posts securely set deeply into the ground where birch bark "Makuks," of wild rice, maple sugar, and dried blueberries were stored against the lean days of midwinter. Soon the Native quarter of the village would be deserted leaving only the many clustered wigwam framework of saplings standing skeleton-like in a ghostly blanket of white.

In the midst of all the preparation, Little Eagle, at the insistence of a thoughtful spouse, laid aside his carving knife with a brisk walk, along the path leading to the wigwam of Paulette and her grandparents. Stopping near its entrance, the hunter, with a puzzled expression, searched the surroundings for signs of activity. With, the exception of one or two families, who had decided to remain near the post for the winter, the wigwams were empty. Paulette should be busy making ready for the annual migration to the winter hunting grounds. Neither she nor her grandparents had ever missed a winter. Unceremoniously lifting aside the curtained entrance, Little Eagle stepped within the abode and casually sat down on a mat of fragrant boughs. Beside the little fire that sent a few wisps of smoke rising into the opening at its peak, Paulette busily and expertly removed the hair from the hide of freshly killed caribou. Little beads of perspiration dotted her forehead, her eyes, now half closed, narrowed as tiny wrinkles formed about them in evident pleasure, as she welcomed the only father she ever knew.

At the opposite wall of the wigwam, the elderly couple sat side by side. The old lady, puffing contentedly on a well blackened stone pipe while her spouse diligently scraped the inner bark from red willow twigs, welcomed Little Eagle with the customary "Boozhoo" and "Aaniin ekamiguk noongom?" or "What is happening today?"

"There is everything happening today, we are all moving out," and turning to Paulette asked anxiously, "And why are not you ready too? Soon winter will come, deep snow, there is no good wood for your fire nearby, why are you not ready, my child?"

As the girl looked frankly into the eyes of the kindly man, her long lashes fluttered slightly, her well-developed bosom rising gently in response to gathering emotion. "We have nothing to prepare, you see our wigwam in almost bare, all we have is wild rice, maple sugar and dried berries to load in our canoe." With a wry smile that brought out a nod of understanding from Little Eagle, she continued, "Why should we be in a hurry when the others have gone perhaps?"

Little Eagle, however, knew the real reason for her delayed departure. He knew that Paulette was too proud to let the others see their meager belongings piled on the beach beside the rest who were more favored by the Trader. He knew too, of the merciless jibes of the youngsters, their embarrassing questions, and so he sat long and waited while Paulette turned back to her work. The Indian marveled at the industry and skill of the girl at her task. He recalled the days when, as a youngster, instead of playing with the other children of the village, she would insist on helping the older women in their customary tasks. He nodded approval of her foresight in acquiring the skill she was now putting to good use.

"Have you been to see the trader?" Little Eagle asked.

Paulette shook her head slowly, "No, I know they don't like me, neither the trader or his son" once more flashing that little smile, that could mean anything, "it matters not how much they dislike me, I detest them more."

"But, my daughter is wrong," the Indian said slowly, measuring each word carefully. "It is not the trader or his son that matters, it is what you and your grandparents need and must have. Many times when I am hunting, I have to wade or even swim in icy water. That is not easy to do on a cold morning, but if I would have the game that is beyond the water, I must forget my own feelings and look only to the results of my effort. I have seen many traders come and go, all they mean to us is what we can get from them and," he smiled a little derisively "all we can ever mean to them is what they can get from us. What we think of them or what they think of us matters not. Hate them as much as you wish, that is for you alone, keep it to yourself, until someday, perhaps," his voice died away in deep meditation.

Paulette laughed loudly, "So my father hates the trader too, and waits patiently for that day when."

Little Eagle smiled, "I got everything I wanted from them and when the Spring comes, I will pay them, and…"

"And wait for that day," Paulette teasingly added.

Little Eagle remained pensive behind stoical features. The girl's grandfather added wood to the fire remarking as he did so, "When I was a young man, we did not know what a trader or his goods were, I never saw one until I was a grown man, we seemed to live all right, we took what we wanted out of the forest, it did not require much for one family to live well. Now, you get goods from a trader and it takes many, many times as many skins of fur animals to pay for them as we ever used. The Traders are never satisfied. They want more and more each year. We used to kill a few beavers for our own use, now it

41

takes a canoe load of beaver skins alone to pay for a gun and a blanket."

"But Grandfather," said Paulette, "everything is different now. We could not go back to using a stone ax or a stone knife, those things are too slow, it takes nearly all day to cut down a small tree with a stone ax and from morning 'til midday to skin and cut up a deer with a stone knife."

"True, my grandchild speaks well, but it takes all winter to take the many colonies of beaver skins to pay for a Trader's iron ax. It takes many fox, otter, and other furs to pay for a blanket that is…not either as good, or as warm as one made of rabbit fur."

"But, I need something to wear grandfather, all this summer I have worn only this one dress," pausing in a downcast mood, the girl continued, "Other girls not as strong or as good with a bow and arrow have two and three dresses. I get tired of this one color, I want something to wear, something besides buckskin. I want warm clothing for the cold winter. I want nice clothes, clothes with many colors, like other girls.

A deep hush fell over the little assemblage as Paulette finished. Little Eagle sat toying with his hunting knife, sticking its sharp point deeply into a piece of firewood as he said, "Go and talk to the Trader, my child, he may let you have some of the things you need, maybe not all you want, his warehouse is full to the roof, what little you need."

Paulette interrupted her friend, "He refused us last year because Grandfather and Grandmother are too old to hunt much. They are older now than they were then."

"Did you ask him for anything for yourself, you get some beaver fur too," Little Eagle persisted.

Paulette smiled, "He said if I was married and had a good hunter for a husband, he could let me have all I wanted, but because I am a girl and alone," her voice died away as her eyelashes fluttered dangerously near the brink of tears.

The Indian leaned nearer to Paulette, better to emphasize his words, "My child, I am known as the greatest hunter in this village, I did not get that reputation by sitting on a rock ledge crying because I thought there was no game beyond the next hill. I got to be the good hunter because I went over there and found out for myself. Only the brave, the one who is not afraid ever gets to be good at anything."

While Little Eagle spoke, Paulette had turned and listened attentively, so attentively that a slight frown creased her brow, her eyes usually partly open, now all but closed in deep meditation. At the end of his talk, the Indian arose, pushed the door curtain aside and without another word stepped out and strode back to his wigwam. As the weighted curtain clattered to its place, Paulette arose, arranged the loose strands of her black hair and followed Little Eagle out into the crisp autumn air. The girl shuddered slightly as the sudden change from the warm sheltered atmosphere of their abode gave way to the chill of a north wind. Along the path she followed, crisp dry leaves rattled under foot, a veritable garden of crimson and gold blended with pink and yellow. She stopped and gathering up a handful of the colors, tossed them into the air letting them scatter over her head and shoulders, again her eyes brimmed with tears as she noted the beautiful colors in contrast to her soiled and worn dress of drab gray. Gathering several of the brightest colored leaves and holding them in a cluster by their long stems, fashioned them into a bouquet and placed them securely in her hair. Smiling a little and wondering what she looked like, if the colored leaves made any difference in her appearance, she strode along bravely towards the Trading Post.

Chapter 5

Within the store room, several Natives were awaiting their turn to point out to "Big Ears" the things they wanted while a steady muttering conversation was carried on, not always complimentary to the trader. The one large opening in the wall covered with a square of white cloth and serving as a window admitted but little light. It was for some moments after she entered before Paulette noticed the stranger standing quietly leaning against some bales of merchandise piled on the long table serving as the counter. Not used to curbing her curiosity, she stared in open eyed wonder at the well-dressed man. Clean shaven and dressed in blue velvet, a white shirt with crimson ruffles barely visible beneath a cape of gracefully flowing blue velveteen. The lining of the cape held the girl's attention, its colors, orange, crimson, brown, changing with the wearer's every movement, its smooth texture, its seemingly inexhaustible color patterns held her fascinated. He was not a Native, a stranger, she was sure. Taking in every detail of the man's attire, she noted that he wore a ring with a setting that glittered, whatever it was, it was beautiful. She caught herself wondering why she couldn't have nice things like some people.

The other customer's wants having been taken care of, Monsieur LaChance, with his hands resting on his counter in an attitude of impatience, eyed the girl curiously. Suddenly realizing that the trader was waiting for her, she strode boldly up and before she could speak, he said "I am sorry Mademoiselle Paulette, I cannot help you. I told you why last year."

"But, I gave you all the furs I caught last winter, I did as well as some of your hunters, you said I did." Lowering her voice and adopting a more pleasing attitude, continued, "We need so little Monsieur LeChance, my grandparents are old it is true, that is why I need some things for them."

But the trader continued to shake his head while she talked. "Come next spring, Paulette, and bring your furs, then you may have the things you need, if you have enough furs.

The girl thoroughly discouraged, continued, however, "Your warehouse is full, Monsieur LeChance, you have so much and we have nothing, can't you spare just a few things? I will pay you well. I am not asking you to give me anything."

The trader had by now held up both hands with palms outspread as if to ward off further pleading. "You are wasting my time, my girl. I cannot let you have anything." With those words spoken, in a tone of finality, he turned away and busied himself with his goods.

Paulette turned and with a heavy heart, started to leave the place. In the excitement of her pleas, she had completely forgotten the stranger who had retreated deeper into the shadow of the darkened corner made by the piled bales of merchandise. Sick at heart and eyes smarting with the tears that could not, flow, she groped, rather than saw, her way towards the heavy log door. She had reached it and was about to lift the latch when she felt a light touch on her arm and the voice of the stranger spoken so low as to be almost inaudible.

"You speak good French, Mademoiselle."

Momentarily forgetting her troubles and startled, Paulette saw that the stranger had thrown back a part of his long cape and his left hand rested, with what seemed to her, caressingly over the hilt of a broad bladed knife tucked beneath a woolen sash while his right fingers lazily twirled one point of a small mustache. Engrossed, for the moment, by the flashing colors of his cape's lining, now fully exposed to view, she reluctantly raised her eyes until she met his squarely. Taken aback, she started visibly at the cold gray of his eyes. Beneath the outwardly dull and listless appearance, the girl detected a cold glitter like one gloating over a victim's anguish. Turning his head slightly away, Paulette was struck by the position of the man's eyes. He was cross-eyed but not in the usual way. While one eye was looking straight ahead, the other was raised or slightly lowered. Forgetting herself for the moment, Paulette stared rudely at the man's strange appearance, which reminded her of an unpleasant experience while berry picking. The memory of a snake that had poked its head from among a thick cluster of vines almost at her finger tips, is how she had become momentarily fascinated by the cold glitter of its beady little eyes. Becoming suddenly apprehensive and nervous over the stranger's appearance, she let her gaze wander once again to his cape and its lining, it was beautiful, never in her wildest dreams had she ever visualized anything so lovely. When her gaze returned once again to his face, he was smiling and the glitter in his eyes had all but disappeared, they half closed in evident amusement.

Reassured somewhat, she remembered his remark and said, "I am part French Monsieur."

"And very beautiful," he added.

Paulette blushed as she suppressed a faint trace of a smile. "You must be mistaken. I am sure you do not mean what you are saying."

A thought as startling as the eyes of the stranger struck her. From the days of her childhood, when she toddled along the path to the "French Quarter", she remembered oft repeated tales of fairy princes in search of beautiful maidens, tales brought by the "Voyageur" and "Courier Du Bois" from their native France. How in the long winter nights, tucked snugly in her own little rabbit fur blanket, she watched the fantastic antics of shadows that played across the circular ceiling of their wigwam and pictured in her childish mind a fairy prince.

Was, was she standing in the presence of a Prince? Paulette glanced down at her only torn and soiled dress. With a slight quiver in her voice she haltingly asked, "Who, who are you? You don't belong here. Where do you come from?"

He smiled broadly and did not answer at once, but seemed to be listening intently at approaching voices barely audible through the thick log walls of the building. "Have a little patience, Mademoiselle. In a short time, you will know who I am, and, I hope to know you better too."

Paulette frowned, she didn't understand. Well, she must be on her way, grandfather would be waiting, and she had work to do. As the girl stepped towards the door, she felt his hand on her arm and instinctively pulled away, she didn't like the stranger, prince or not, it made no difference, she had, on the spur of the moment, acquired a dislike for him and proceeded to show it by moving resolutely towards the entrance. Paulette had taken but one step when she felt his grip on her arm tighten unmistakably as his voice so soft and purring but a moment before, now carried a note of command.

"I said, Mademoiselle, have a little patience. I want you to know who I am, and the trader here also must know." In a quite different tone, asked, "Where are your grandparents? They must be nice people to merit such a lovely granddaughter. If, during the day's excitement, I seem to forget them please remind me, they must be taken care of, for your sake," he added as an afterthought.

Paulette, now thoroughly puzzled, stood as one drawn to the brink of a precipice by an invisible force, a mixture of curiosity and a growing premonition of impending events.

The stranger now turned and raised the latch, swinging open the heavy door, the loud creaking of its dry hinges attracted the trader's attention and he turned to see who the customer must be. The stranger nodded to three men who stood outside the door as Paulette's eyes widened in evident surprise. The three were dressed alike, all in black velvet-like material. In contrast to the stranger whose clothes were of blue and hatless, the others wore broad brimmed chapeaus of beaver ornamented with a jet-black plume that curled gracefully around the crown.

Monsieur LaChance, with hands resting lightly on the counter, his round eyes usually half closed in a sleepy mood, now cocked his head sharply at an angle and asked with an unmistakable note of apprehension in his voice, "My friends, is there something I can do for you?"

The stranger ignored the question, if he heard it, and asked the others in crisp commanding tones, "Plans carried out, Pierre?"

"Oui, Monsieur, all the white men and their families are safe in two cabins under guard. The Indian scouts have scattered among the Natives with the news."

"Bien," nodding curtly towards the trader, continued, "tie him securely, and, Jacques search the building."

As two of the men stepped quickly towards the trader, one of them extracted from somewhere within the folds of his long black cape, a handful of buckskin thongs while the third, a larger man and the only unshaven one of the little party, stopped in front of Paulette and roughly tilted her head back and said gruffly, "Well, Mon Petit, what have we here, a pretty little half-breed, a prize for me, maybe I shall…"

He didn't finish whatever he intended to say, for the crisp cutting voice of the stranger startled him as though he had been struck with the lash of a whip. "Jacques! Hands off! She is mine, do as you are told!"

Paulette glanced up quickly and instinctively shrank toward the log wall. The stranger's eyes were wide open and again, little lights danced devilishly within their orbs as he glared at the man he called Jacques. Seeing Paulette's apparent fright and surmising the reason, he quickly smiled and closed his eyes to their normal peaceful appearance.

Jacques, about to enter the adjoining room, turned, spoke coldly, "If I were you, Monsieur, I'd cut her throat, and save yourself a lot of trouble."

"And if I were you, Jacques, I'd mind my own business and live to be a nice old man." This time the stranger spoke without a trace of temper.

With a slight bow, Jacques said simply, "Yes, Monsieur," and passed on into the living quarters of the post.

Monsieur LaChance, on being securely tied hand and foot, was laid, not too gently, on his long table or counter, where, seemingly resigned to his fate, he lay quietly, his round eyes partly closed.

With a puzzled look, Jacques returned to the doorway and said, "There is no one in here, Monsieur, I have looked carefully."

"But, there must be," said the stranger impatiently, turning to Paulette and asked, "Tell me, young woman, how many are there in this man's family?"

"Three," answered the girl quickly. "Big Ears, I mean Monsieur LaChance, his son Napoleon and their cook."

The stranger advanced laughing, said playfully, "The Indians named you well. I should take one of your ears home for a souvenir, tack it on the wall over my fireplace." As an afterthought, he continued, "I don't think I will, Monsieur, you will need it much more than I, and, we will have plenty to remind us of you." At this the trader closing his eyes in evident pain, mental pain, said nothing. Turning again to Jacques, the stranger said curtly, "Search again. Has the back door been guarded?"

"Yes, Monsieur, ever since we landed," answered Jacques.

Paulette surmised that Napoleon was hidden somewhere in the room and in spite of growing fears as to her own fate, anticipated a certain amount of satisfaction in "Little Big Ears" treatment at the hands of the big ruffian Jacques. Paulette could not resist venturing the information that "He must be in there, Monsieur. He is very good at hiding. I am sure I could find him."

With a clever shrugging motion of his shoulder, the stranger threw back the other half of his long cape and with a slight nod towards the door that he had evidently been guarding. One of the other men took his place. Paulette marveled at the quick precise movements of the man, when their tasks were completed, they stood about listlessly as though there was nothing else to be done. At a word or a nod from their master, they sprang into action. Except for the few words spoken by Jacques, the others were silent.

The stranger strode brusquely into the adjoining room from whence a shuffling sound and the loud whining voice of "Little Big Ears" caused the trader to open wide his eyes and listen attentively. Paulette felt a tinge of pity for the man as he lay helplessly trussed. She sensed that he felt not the slightest fear as to the outcome of his own fate, but for that of his only child he was worried, deeply worried. With a slight motion of his hand, he summoned Paulette to come nearer. The girl, more out of curiosity than pity, came quickly to his side.

"What are they doing to my son?" he asked.

"I don't know, I didn't see," replied Paulette.

"Tell that man to come here, the one dressed in blue."

"Monsieur, the trader wishes to speak to you," Paulette told the stranger.

The man whirled at the sound of Paulette's voice. She noted how his hand tightened over the hilt of his knife. "The distance from him to me, is exactly the same distance as from me to him, if he wants to see me, he comes to me." He did not raise his voice and spoke in a matter of fact tone.

Jacques laughed, "Monsieur forgets that the trader is in no position to move about.

With a deep bow and a forced sardonic smile, the stranger said, "I am grieved, Mademoiselle. I had forgotten about the gentleman. I shall place myself at his service immediately." With a flourish, he motioned to the girl to precede him, "After you Mon Cheri."

As Paulette passed on into the store room, the stranger, with mock concern, placed his right hand over his heart and cast a meaningful glance at his man Jacques. Jacques, knowingly, shook his head slowly…a thin smile hovered about what was visible of his lips. He turned his attention to Napoleon whose clothes were covered with an accumulation of the dust and dirt that he had gathered beneath the wide bench or bed. The youth now sat in a luxuriously fur covered rustic chair beside the fireplace. Like his parent, he was carefully tied.

"What is the girl doing here," he asked. "I know she is to blame for this, she brought you here, didn't she?"

"Why do you say that?" Jacques smiled.

"Because you don't tie her up like us, she is helping you. I suspected her I knew she would do something like this. Someday…and someday I'll…"

"You'll what?" Jacques interrupted, drew his knife and felt its edge.

Napoleon's round eyes bulged "You wouldn't do anything to me."

"No?" Jacques asked, apparently amused, and continued, "If I had my way, you'd never get the chance to ask." Little Big Ears stayed quiet.

In the other room, the stranger stood beside the trussed man on the table. "Monsieur," he said mockingly "you sent for me. Why? It is not often I obey a summons, except, perhaps, to his Majesty's Court."

Monsieur ignored the remark. "I know when I am beaten, Monsieur, and I might say you are clever, very clever, but what I want to talk to you about is my son, he is all I have, Monsieur. Promise you will not harm him.

"Well, our intentions were different, Monsieur, much different, but, since you request, we might say, bargain a little. What will you offer me for his life Monsieur?"

Paulette got a glimpse of the stranger's eyes and again they glittered like, one could easily imagine the eyes of a wolf, on the verge of a kill.

The Trader smiled, an ironic little smile that barely moved the muscles about his mouth. "You, you would ask me to bargain? You are kind, very kind Monsieur, if you will remove the thongs from my hands and feet, Monsieur. I can do no harm now, we can, as you say, bargain."

The stranger nodded to his man who stood nearby. The fellow very obviously reluctant, untied the trader, who relieved, sat up and slid to his accustomed place behind the table.

The stranger evidently amused at "Big Ears'" appearance, studied his victim for some time, and then condescendingly remarked, "Monsieur LaChance, I hope I speak your name correctly. I would buy some of your merchandise, if you were to sell me some."

The trader, annoyed at the stranger's attitude and pretense, said, "Let us stop this charade, Monsieur" he paused, but the stranger shrugged his well-formed shoulders at the implied question, answered, "Does it matter, a name is only a sound that is forgotten before one is cold in the grave. If I told you my real name, you wouldn't believe me. So let us pass that by as more nonsense, and get down to business."

"What are your terms for mine and my son's safety, Monsieur?"

"For your life, Monsieur LaChance, or would you rather I called you Big Ears"

"A name, my friend, is only a silly sound. A sound that once its purpose is fulfilled matters not."

"Quite right, Big Ears, I am glad you agree with me. We should get along well, you know, I rather like the name Big Ears. It fits you well, and your son, has he a name too?"

"Napoleon, Monsieur," answered the trader proudly.

"No, no, I mean, what is his real name, the one the Natives gave him?"

The trader hesitated, then finally with some effort, said, "Little Big Ears."

The stranger laughed loudly as the door opened and another one of the stranger's men entered hurriedly. "We are ready, Monsieur, your orders have been carried out."

"Not quite, Henri," said the stranger. "Follow me," and he led the way out the door.

Paulette, having intensely watched the drama being enacted before her eyes, again remembered her grandparents. With a start, decided to go home, home with news that no one would believe. Reaching the door, much to her surprise and dismay, she found the guard blocking her exit. With a smile and a bow, the man said, "Your pardon, Mademoiselle, but you cannot leave now, soon perhaps, but not now."

"But, I must go home to my grandparents."

"I am sorry, Mademoiselle, but you must wait just a little while. Patience please, it will be better. I assure you."

"But you don't understand, Monsieur. My grandparents are old and I am all they have, please let me pass."

The guard shook his head resolutely, "If I could obey your orders, Mademoiselle, it would be an honor and a pleasure but," and the fellow shrugged his shoulders slightly. "Please be patient and stay a while. I am sure you will see your grandparents soon."

Upon entering, the stranger in blue strode directly up to the trader and said, "I have good news for you Big Ears. You and your son will be spared. I detest bargaining, so I have taken the liberty to collect what merchandise we can use and as many of your best canoes to transport the goods and our little party safely. I regret," the stranger continued, "having to leave you, I wish I could have enjoyed your hospitality for a longer period, perhaps another day we shall have the pleasure of meeting. Au Revoir, Monsieur Big Ears." With a deep bow and flourish, the stranger turned to his men and commanded, "Come men let us go." In answer to the questioning look of the guard at the door, he answered with a slight motion of his head, "Take her to the canoes."

With a man on each side of her, Paulette was forced to accompany them towards the ravine and its noisy stream where the trader kept his freighter canoes. The girl pleading tearfully for her release at every step of the way knew that, neither her sobs, nor any resistance she might attempt, would be of any avail. She walked along steadily. Arriving at the brink of the steep depression, she stopped involuntarily and wiped the tears from her eyes that she might better verify the sight before her. Yes, it was true! There at the bottom of the ravine and comfortably seated amidst a colorful array of warm woolen trade blankets, amidships of one of the trader's large canoes, were her grandfather and grandmother. With a bound, the bewildered girl broke away from her captors and all but flew down the steep incline, grasping and dodging, with reckless abandon, in and out of the clusters of birch and poplar. "Grandfather, what are you doing here?" she managed to gasp.

The old couple looked at one another curiously, "Didn't you send for us? The strange Indians told us that you wanted us here."

Fearful of alarming the old couple needlessly, she decided that come what may, she would give herself up in sacrifice for the welfare of the only ones she had to love on the Earth. Hesitatingly, but enough to make her decision, Paulette stepped resolutely into the frail craft and settled herself comfortably beside her aged grandmother.

The stranger, standing on the bank with one end of the long paddle he held resting lightly on the canoe, gave instructions to the four men beside him "Have the others gone on?" he asked.

"Yes, twelve canoes, Monsieur!"

"Did you see to the items I wanted in particular?"

"Oui, Monseiur! Dress goods in many colors, jewelry, necklaces and threads to match."

As their canoe drifted out in the fast-moving water of the stream, little waves lapped at its sides until rising gracefully over an oncoming rolling wave, it veered westward and skirted the low murmuring grumble of the waves as they swirled in and out of the cavernous depths in the low cliff-like shore of the great Superior. Paulette's heart trembled at the sound of the waves and the sight of the only home she ever knew disappeared from view amidst the giant pine and stately maples. With no little effort, the girl held her tears in check as she grasped her grandmother's wrinkled hand and patted gently.

"We will be better now, grandmother. You will be cared for."

"But, where are we going, did the trader, Big Ears, send us on this trip?"

"Oh, yes, didn't I tell you. I'll tell you all about it some time, not now. Don't worry, we will be all right."

The stranger, sitting atop the after thwart hearing every word the girl said and evidently understanding enough Ojibwe to know what she was saying, released the clasp of his cloak, placed it gently around the girl's shoulders saying, "For you, my child. Keep it, it is yours."

"Oh no…Monsieur, I could not accept it. Please take it back. It is much too good for me." Raising the garment lest its beautiful lining become soiled by coming into contact with her, not too clean and only, garment, continued, "Please Monsieur, this blanket will be more than good enough should I need it."

"Paulette, listen to me, no one ever questions what I do with what is mine. My orders are always obeyed without question. It is my wish that you have my cloak."

Paulette drew the garment snugly over her shoulders. She drew a paddle that lay along the gunwale and facing the prow of the canoe that rose and fell gently with each wave that passed beneath it, she would paddle, help to push the canoe over the water to a new land somewhere towards the sun that now neared the rim of the horizon. She raised her head resolutely as the water swirled at the tip of the paddle blade. Her aged grandparents were safely and comfortably wrapped in warm woolen blankets, at least for the time being, that in itself, was sufficient. For tomorrow, she was unafraid. She would meet it bravely, somewhere "out there" to the West, where it, lie waiting. Unconsciously she tightened her grasp on the paddle until her finger tips were bloodless. Whatever it was, she would meet it bravely. For a moment, her mind wandered back to her grandparent's people, her savage, proud and noble ancestors, they were a people unafraid. The shame of fear could overshadow anything that fate held in store, even death itself.

Chapter 6

Realizing that her grandparents were virtual hostages held to compel her behavior in accord with the wishes of the raider, Paulette became, for their sake, more and more resigned to whatever fate had in store for her. On the evening of the third day, after leaving the LaChance Trading Post the heavy canoes, with sails furled and stowed along the gunwales, swung into one of the many tiny bays or coves that indented the otherwise straight shore line. At each such landing, the canoes remained loaded and tied securely to some makeshift dock out of the reach of the turbulent waters from the lake. Upon entering the little harbor-like cove, their canoe was met with a current of fast moving brownish water that disappeared into the crystal blue-green of the great lake some distance from the shore. With some misgiving, Paulette watched the men unload the canoes and pile the heavy bales high up on the bank. That could mean but one thing, they had come to the parting of the ways. From now on, the cargoes would be transported overland on the backs of the men, to some point where the canoes could be used for further travel.

That evening, by their camp fire, grandfather said in a reminiscent mood, "I remember this place, it is many winters since we were here, your grandmother, I and some others spent the winter inland, over the hills."

"Then that must be where we are going," Paulette remarked more to herself than to the old man.

"It is the only place within many days travel either way along this shore that one can get into the country beyond the hills by canoe, not far from here, about two suns travel, it is the beginning of a long chain of lakes that lead one into the great valley where the water runs towards to the land of Ke-way-din, the North Wind and many strange people.

"Did you see any of them?" the girl asked curiously.

"No, we didn't, but everywhere we found signs of their summer camps. They had left for the north before we arrived."

"How far inland did you go?"

"Many, many lakes, to where the water runs the other way, it is far with many portages," interrupted grandmother.

"Was there much game, beaver, caribou?"

"Oh, yes. There were many colonies of beaver on most of the lakes, their dams made travel easier by raising the water along the streams. Caribou and deer were everywhere" grandmother answered patiently.

On into the late evening, the old couple recounted their experiences beyond the great divide as the girl weighed her chances of survival should they get an opportunity to escape. Up to now, she had built up the raider's confidence in her intention of staying with her grandparents come what may. Later that night, after the old couple slept peacefully beneath the canvas shed-like shelter leaning protectively over them, Paulette sat by the remnants of their little fire pensively watching the embers die slowly, each in its own turn. She had drawn the cape, with its lining of many changing colors, closely over her shoulders. The night breeze from the lake was cold, as the great horned owl broke the night stillness with its muffled "Whoo…whoo…whooh". The constant swish of little rollers breaking noisily over the rocky beach, and long since became as one with her very existence. They were a part of the great stillness of the Forest.

The sharp crack of a dry twig underfoot, brought the girl sharply to attention as she involuntarily reached for her knife always within reach of either hand. "Your pardon, Mademoiselle, if I startled you, you seem so lonely by your fire that I could not resist coming to talk with you." The voice of the raider was low and, if it not for his appearance, his voice might have been considered pleasant much like the purring of a well-fed kitten.

Paulette released her hold on the knife and quickly concealed it beneath the folds of her cloak. "Lonely, Monsieur, what did you expect…that I should be happy?"

"Why not Paulette, you have more here than you had back there? Your grandparents are well cared for, much better than they were."

"Stop, Monsieur, don't make me hate you any more than I do. You think I should love you for charity's sake. Oh, I know I am only a creature of the forest, but as such, I also know that love has no trade value, something you would have for a couple of blankets and the flesh of a few rabbits."

The trader, seated at the opposite side of the dying fire, stirred impatiently, his whitish eyes glittered dangerously. For some moments, he sat quiet as one weighing a momentous question, then spoke slowly, "Paulette, listen to me."

"I have no choice, Monsieur," Paulette reminded him.

Ignoring her remark, he continued, "I, too, am lonely."

"Strange," the girl thought but withheld any comment.

"In the many years that I have traded here…"

"With other trader's goods" again she thought but remained quiet.

"I have been a lonely man. In all these years, I have never met the woman that I would walk the length of a canoe to see the second time. Not until the moment I saw you pleading with that trader, not for yourself, but for your grandparents, did I realize that at last I had met my fate. Yes, Paulette, in you I saw the girl I was going to love. I want you, Paulette. I want you for my wife."

The little flame that darted up from the pile of dying embers, revealed the contemptuous curl of the girl's lip as she said, "I will still have my choice, Monsieur."

"It is because of that fact, Mademoiselle, the fact that you have no choice that I am giving you one."

The girl looked up suddenly. "Monsieur is very kind, the choice of being your wife, or, what?"

"There are many things, Paulette, that I could place before you from which to choose. Please remember that I am the only and absolute authority here, our good King Francis I, has no more power in his France than I have here. I hold not only your life and well-being in the palm of my hand, but that of your grandparents as well."

Paulette's eyes opened wide as the full implication of the raider's words dawned on her. "You wouldn't, Monsieur, not to a helpless old couple who could do nothing to harm you or defend themselves, surely you are human enough to have a heart!"

"A heart…" with a slight toss of his head, "I didn't have a heart until I saw you at the trading post, and, if I was sensible, I would have done what Jacques told me to do, cut your pretty throat and leave you where I first saw you."

As if in echo, somewhere up in the long gently sloping hills, a lone dismal wolf call drifted in on the night air. Paulette turned slightly to listen as the mournful cry died away. The troubled girl seemed to sense in that lonely cry of the wilderness an echo of her own feelings as her long slanting eyes, with their hint of Asiatic origin closed momentarily in response to an inward emotional turmoil. She said, "You could not have hurt me very much, Monsieur, and, who knows, it may have been best for you and me."

"But, I can hurt you, Paulette."

"How?" he saw the raider's eyes wander slowly over the old couple, blissfully unaware of the scene taking place. Again, Paulette started in dismay, "Monsieur, if you are thinking of harming the helpless old couple, I promise you that I shall find a way to die with them, yes die, and curse you with my last agonized breath." With her face flushed, her eyes sparkling in evident earnest decision, she trembled at this seeming amusement at her outburst.

"Paulette, believe me, you are beautiful," and in a reminiscent mood, continued, "I once saw a wolf kill and devour a fawn while its mother looked on. The look in that beautiful creature's eyes shall remain with me as long as I live. The sheer beauty of her agonized expression was something that only God could have painted. I have tried many times to record it on canvas, but, I am not a God."

"What happened to the doe?"

"I killed her."

"Why?"

"Because, I alone, wanted to carry the memory of that moment of sublime beauty…something that was meant only for the savage life of the forest."

Paulette paled under the inference. "Then, you, you…"

The raider's voice lowered slightly, "If you would wish it that way."

The girl added fuel to the embers and coaxed them into a blaze. Her hands trembled, "Is that the choice?"

"No," his answer was crisp. "You love your grandparents, Paulette. You love them with a love that is not pity, but something that borders on passion. I know for I too, am French. If I harmed them, you would hate me with a hate many times as intense as your love for them. Why then, Paulette, if I were good to them and provide for them in their old age, why could you not love me, not as intensely as you would hate, but, I'd be satisfied with so little."

The kindly girl's eyes brimmed with tears as she listened to the man's earnest passionate plea. "I believe you are sincere, Monsieur, at least with me. I thank you. If love were something that I could capture like a rabbit and give away at will, I do not know of anyone, at this moment, I would rather give it to than you. You say you are French, then, you know that love is not like a bolt of cloth that a trader gives out in pieces to anyone in exchange for furs. Are you sure, Monsieur, that you do not mistake respect and admiration for love? If that is what you want, first you would have to earn it. How much of my respect you deserved is the exact measure of what you would get, but love, Monsieur, is something I cannot trade for.

With hands outstretched in a pleading gesture and trembling with emotion, Paulette, in a few brief moments, had evolved from a thoughtless and somewhat irresponsible young person into a serious woman fighting for her age-old right to choose the man she would love.

The strange raider, with a sigh of resignation, stared into the little blaze between them. When he spoke again, it was in a different tone. "In a week, Paulette, with good weather, we shall reach the "height of land", Pays d'en Haut…our people call it, where more of my men will meet us. From there we will be home in two days. I want you and your grandparents to come with us, if you will. I promise you that with every means at my command, you shall be protected. No harm will come to either you or the old couple. You shall be provided with food and anything else we have to offer."

The girl hastily weighed her chances of getting back to their home. Alone she had an even break, but, she was not alone. Coming quickly to a decision, she said, "I do not need any of your food, Monseiur, if you will kindly provide me with a bow and a few arrows, I can easily provide our food."

The raider had arisen to his feet and evidently satisfied, said, simply, "As you wish, Mademoiselle, command me. I am your servant." With a stiff little bow, he quickly strode into the dark, the long black cape he wore blending into the night.

Chapter 7

Back and forth, from early dawn until dusk, French, half-breed, and Indian packers shuttled across the long portages. Great bundles of merchandise, each weighing eighty to ninety pounds, kegs of rum and powder, sacks of shot, muskets and axes in crates and lighter bundles of trinkets consisting of squares of polished tin for mirrors, strings of many colored ornamental beads, sewing needles and spools of thread and strings of glass beads colored to imitate pearls flowed in a steady stream along the winding foot path that led from Lake Superior north over the hills to des Pays d'en Haut, the mecca or "promised land", if you will, of the intrepid Voyageur and dauntless Courier du Bois, adventurers in search of wealth and adventure. A thick carpet of rotting leaves muffled the footsteps of the packers whose silent, ghostly disappearance into and among a thick growth of balsam and spruce left little trace for any but the expert to follow.

Somewhere along the path, a "repose" selected by the "head packer" gave needed, if only momentary rest while sweating bodies retraced the path for another load. Since the last camp on the shore of Lake Superior, the raider paid scant attention to Paulette and her grandparents. She moved about on short hunting trips without restriction. Keeping his part of the bargain, gave the girl much needed assurance, perhaps, after all, her apprehension was groundless. Every day she found new scenes that spreading out from some hilltop in panoramic splendor held her breathless and spellbound. On their fourth day since leaving the shore of Lake Superior, Paulette climbed a hill that rose from the very edge of their campground, and the stream that grew smaller as they neared its source. Stopping to rest on one of its many step-like plateaus, the girl stifled an ecstatic cry as she turned her attention southward towards the giant lake.

Far, far away across the "big water", where the heavenly blue of the sky met the pale green of the lake, a thin line of darker hue extended part way along the horizon. "Surely this must be the rim of the world," she whispered softly to herself. It was the first time she had ever seen or even realized that there was another shore beyond the great water. She had heard many Native stories about Superior lying at the edge of the earth and as many more from the French to the contrary.

"I wonder what it is like, do people live there too, I wonder what they are like?" Many thoughts, mostly questions, raced through the girl's mind as she stood in awe at the handiwork of the Creator. Lost, for the moment, in the spectacle that spread out before her, she was startled by an unmistakable footstep behind her. Schooled in the art of self-defense by her grandfather and Little Eagle, Paulette slipped an arrow into place with scarcely a perceptible motion and turned quickly. Her action was so accurately timed in its speed that, the raider started in surprise, then stood motionless as he stared at the pointed arrow, drawn back almost to its tip and aimed directly at his breast. Paulette immediately released the tension on her bow. "Oh, Monsieur, you startled me, I did not know who or what it was."

The man let out a sharp breath, "That was close Paulette. You might have killed me."

"Killed you, Monsieur? I do not understand."

"You might have shot me, Mademoiselle."

"Non...non, Monsieur! I do not make mistakes, not like that. I know what I am doing all the time."

"But tell me, where did you learn to be so fast with a bow and arrow?"

Paulette laughed, "My grandfather lived many, many years. Why, because he was good with the bow? I want to live too, Monsieur...so."

"I understand, Paulette, but what are you doing here?"

"And you, Monsieur?" her eyes twinkled. Somehow, she felt more at ease in his presence today than at any time since they left her home.

"I came to tell you that we must be moving camp soon."

"You didn't have to do that, Monsieur."

"I wish you would not call me Monsieur. It does not sound well. I...I don't like it Paulette."

The girl shrugged her shoulders. "But what else shall I say? Maybe you don't have a name? I don't know."

The raider looked surprised. "You don't know my name?"

"I never heard it, how should I know?"

"Strange...but my name is Francois."

"Francois...Francois" she repeated "You are named like the King of France."

He nodded. "I am not having the trouble keeping my name as he has luck."

She looked puzzled, "Oh, tell me, Monsieur, I mean, Francois, what is over there?"

"Where," he asked.

"Over there," pointing to the thin dark line across the lake. "Come stand here beside me, you can see it better."

"Oh, that," he said moving beside the girl. "That, Paulette, is part of the other shore of the lake."

"When you came, I was wondering what it was like. Do people live there too?"

"Yes, the same as here, Paulette, we came along that shore and crossed over to this side, way over there where it is narrower."

"I wish I could go there sometime, ever since I was a child, I wondered if there was land there."

"Someday, Paulette, you and I, Paulette and Francois, people will say, will go over there and beyond."

Paulette's eyes narrowed, "I don't know, Francois. I don't know."

"Don't know what, Paulette, what is it you don't know?"

"That is it. I don't know many things, like one walking over a trail in the dark, you wish for light, you can't see, you just don't know where you are or where your next step will be. It is like that."

Taking her hand lightly, he said, "Maybe I could help you, Paulette. Help you to know, bring you light so you can see the path ahead. Why don't you let me, if you will be my wife?"

The girl shook her head slowly. "Not yet, Francois, not yet please."

"But why not...are you afraid of me?"

She raised her eyebrows quickly. "Afraid of you, Monsieur, why should I be afraid of you?" Lowering her voice, continued earnestly, "I could have killed you many, many times since we started, just like today. I held your life at the tips of my two fingers, like you hold mine in the palm of your hand, but no, I wouldn't kill you because I am not afraid of you. I can trust you, Francois."

"Thank you, Paulette. That is the nicest thing I have heard in many years, but why can't you be my wife?"

Her eyes followed the skyline across the lake, traced the water's light green to where it blended into the darker shades of pine and spruce of the forest below. She spoke slowly. "When you are near,

Monsieur, I feel heavy in here," placing her free hand over her heart, "and when I am alone, I am so light and free I want to laugh and sing."

"Do you feel so badly now, Paulette?"

"Not…today, for the first time, Francois, I do not feel so when you come near."

He smiled, "Maybe tomorrow you can say yes."

"Yesterday I would have said no and told you never, today, I don't know, I am not sure. Tomorrow only le Bon Dieu must know. Let us wait and see, Francois."

"You are a good girl, Mon Chere, and soon we will be home, tomorrow we reach the first of the lakes. Two days after that we will be home! It will be good to get back."

While the raider spoke of home, Paulette turned her head away. A sudden longing for the only home she had ever known came over her. The incessant wash of the rollers over the sandy beach, the sound as of distant thunder coming from the caves beneath the trembling earth was her world…reality, peopled by her unlimited imagination, inhabitants of the underground caves whose stature and fantastic shapes and habits grew and kept pace with her years. She felt the hot tears blurring her vision, the thin brown line dividing the blue and pale green along the far horizon, now danced queerly into a jumble of odd shapes and colors. Somehow, she didn't want Francois to see her crying and keeping her head averted, tried to wipe the tears away unnoticed.

Francois, carried away by thoughts of home forgot, for the moment, the beautiful girl standing beside him. "You are going to be happy there, Paulette, I am sure…you will be the queen of my people. Anything you want for yourself or your grandparents, I will get for you."

"How can I be happy here? Monsieur? Can anyone be happy anywhere not of their choosing? I am of the great lake where there is sound, sound that never ends, but here, this terrible quiet. The dreadful stillness that presses down from the very sky itself, even the trees stand still and naked like so many ghosts waiting for the dark. Oh, I know I can have all the clothes and blankets I need to keep warm in the cabin of logs. I will have all the food we need, but the price? The sound of washing waves over the beach, my little cave people where the rumble of distant thunder never ceases beneath the forest of living trees, the stare of someone peering in through the smoke of a wigwam fire, cold and hunger? Yes, with the life of one's choice. The price, Monsieur, is high very high," her voice died away in a whisper. Paulette had turned to face the man, unmindful of the tears that by now streamed down her cheeks. "In your haste, Francois, to get everything you want, you forget that I am half savage, with a thousand years of savage ancestors. You can't buy off the savage blood that someday must run through the veins of your children and they, too, will want to live with the wild storms, the sound of distant thunder, the stars that dance to the howls of the wolf pack. Don't ever forget that it is I and my mother's people who will shape the lives of your children, they, too, will be savage for it is only a savage who lives, who knows life as the Creator intended he should. Yes, Francois, I will be your wife, but first pray to your God that you escape the price you too must pay."

"Mon Chere, you speak strangely, what price do you mean? Tell me and if it is in my means to pay, I shall gladly do so."

At the man's last word, a long low dismal wolf howl arose from the foothill. Deep throated at first, then rising higher and higher, before sliding slowly into a dying mournful end. Both the girl and the raider listened attentively. Francois spoke first, "What is there about the howl that makes my blood run cold every time I hear it?" Paulette forgetting her tears, laughed at the man's evident dismay. "Doesn't it affect you too?"

"A wolf's howl…yes, but not that one."

"Do you mean to say that…that was?"

Paulette interrupted, "He is getting good. Soon, he will be able to fool a real wolf. That was one of your Indians."

"I think we should go back, Mon Chere, and please don't worry. I will do everything under heaven to make you happy. We will move to Lake Superior if you want me to."

"Please, Francois, don't talk about that now. Tell your men that I am your wife. When the Missionary comes again, he can bless our marriage, but pray that God will spare you the day when you must wish that I, this day, had not spared your life."

"I promise you anything you wish, Mon Chere," he spoke unthinkingly as one in grave doubt.

Slowly they turned to walk down the hillside, each deep in thought. The naked white birches standing stiffly at attention while the broad palm-like branches of the spruce and balsam waved gently in the light breeze, as the couple moved on slowly over the rock-strewn ground sloping downward…ever downward.

Chapter 8

A glad shout of recognition and welcome rent the otherwise peaceful quiet of midafternoon as the head packer, Jacques, dropped his heavy load to the ground with a thud. A deep voiced and unenthused, "'ello, Pascal, you alive yet? Where are your men? Get 'em together, we got lots of work," brushed aside all formalities of the gladsome reunion.

Pascal, gnome-like creature, darted about the cleared campground excitedly attempting the impossible by trying to tell all that happened and ask questions at one and the same time. "My men?" waving his long arms in disgust, "loafers, chase rabbits all day and eat all night...you have a good trip? Nobody can find them now...Francois all right...what did you get, eh?"

The packer, Jacques, on one of his rare humorous moments, stood and grinned at the stubby man, "If you will shut up, Pascal, I got big news for you."

Pascal stopped, in the midst of his excitement, and let his well-muscled arms drop at his side where they hung listlessly as he looked up into the face of the black bearded giant Jacques, his red hair cut shoulder blade length and held in place by a narrow strip of checkered white and red trade goods in the shape of a head band that did double duty, holding the hair in place and as a marker of sorts showing where the flaming hair ended and the equally flaming whiskers began.

Pascal's whiskers were his pride and the joy of the entire post. Cut square, paint brush fashion, when he stood upright, the whiskers in front were of exact length as the hair behind. Little round blue eyes that sparkled in continuous good humor, gave the instant impression of a jolly good fellow.

"For me…you got news? No, you tease me again…always you tease, nobody ever have news for Pascal."

"This time, Mon Ami, I have the news for sure. Francois got a wife!"

Pascal cocked his head, disproportionately large for one so short, at several crazy angles in quick succession. "No-o!" he almost shouted. "No! I don't believe that. Francois never going to get married. He tell me himself. Why do you always tease me Jacques, because I am not big like you?"

"But, Mon Pascal, I tell the truth. Come, you will see for yourself."

The Packer, without further comment, started back on the portage trail. Pascal, like an enthusiastic hunting dog, immediately sprang in front of the big fellow and blocked the path. "Tell me Jacques, are you sure what you say is true, what kind of woman he get, a Native? It must be because there are no white women around here."

"Come, come little man, get out of my way. The others should be here now. Can't you see we are busy?"

Pascal placed both his hands against Jacques sash that came level with the short man's nose, and looked up pleadingly. "Tell me…tell me quick, my friend, is it true?"

"Pascal, you are shaking all over, are you cold? Run along and see for yourself. You don't believe me, so go and see."

The unmistakable sounds of branches, told of approaching packers. Pascal listened but a moment, and then bounded off at a fast run along the path.

In evident sympathy, Jacques muttered, "Poor little fellow. He is going to take it hard."

Pascal, Francois' childhood playmate and life-long companion in Old France and all-around handyman and confidante in this their venture in quest of fame and fortune, was not deformed or a cripple. Nature had, merely in her inscrutable ways, forgotten to develop a long body on a good, but short, pair of legs, and in compensation for its oversight, placed an unusually large head on a pair of broad and well-muscled shoulders. To further offset its discrepancy in Pascal's makeup, it had also endowed the little man with an actively keen brain along with a well-developed sense of humor thrown in for good measure. Pascal, though short in stature, was long on generosity, with a pleasing personality what, combined, placed him in characteristic contrast to the general runoff of the white men of his day.

Pascal dodged past the oncoming packers without his usual cheery greeting. The little fellow's heart bounded in, a mixture of fearful anticipation and excitement. Nearing the point where, in his judgement, the "pose" or rest with its camp should be located, he slowed to a walk. Undecided, for the moment, on a procedure and hoping against hope that Jacques was only teasing, he suddenly realized that were he to unceremoniously break into the camp in search of Francois' mythical wife, he would be the butt of all jokes for the rest of the season. So that was it! A predetermined plot to make a monkey out of him! No doubt Francois was waiting for him now. He could see that sly assumed air of injured innocence. "My wife," he would say with that blank stare he could adopt so readily and convincingly. "Are you feeling well Pascal? Did you sleep well? I am afraid this country is getting the better of you." The little fellow almost laughed out loud.

Why hadn't he thought of their little scheme sooner...but, on the other hand, suppose it were true? Shaking his head in perplexity, he stepped off the path and prepared to wait, well hidden among the thick growth of evergreens.

At the camp, a short distance from the spot where Pascal waited patiently for his friend to pass with or without his bride, renewed activity was everywhere. Tents and crude shelters, cooking utensils, muskets, bows and arrows, sacks of dried meat, and wild rice were carefully gathered into convenient packs so that the packers would lose no time in moving everything across the portage.

This being the last "rest" or relay before embarking on canoes that Pascal and three selected men had been left to guard near the first of a long chain of lakes, created added excitement and impetus to the activity. As usual, Paulette and her grandparents were the first to be ready. As was her custom, she sent her grandmother on ahead. The old lady, though perfectly capable of taking care of herself, walked on leisurely, resting at intervals. Paulette busied herself and arranging the many bundles of camping equipment while grandfather made himself usable by seeing that nothing was forgotten. Since deciding to become the wife of Francois, the girl immediately took an active interest in the management of the trip. Circulating freely among the men and sitting by their campfire in the evening, she immediately wound her way into their affection. A fluent command of both French and Indian, won her a place especially with the Indians who marveled at her exhibition of a marksmanship in archery. The men soon began to show their esteem and admiration for Paulette in many little ways. They left the choice spot in the camp for her crude shelter with a few extra packs of dry wood piled handily. If water was hard to get or carried any distance, a large bark container was invariably found nearby ready filled. In vain, the girl pleaded with the hired men not to do these things for her. She had nothing to do but get a little game each day, on every occasion her plea was met with blank stares. Why no one had done anything. "Don't blame us" was the usual rejoinder. The little attentions surreptitiously showered upon her made Paulette work harder. She packed, in turn, while the men were busy on the trail. When the hunting was a good, she got an entire dinner of partridge and spruce hens, plucked, cleaned and hung them on the racks over the fireplace. Among the plentiful supply of rabbits, an occasional caribou or young deer neatly dressed and quartered found its way to the smoke frames in time for the return of the packers.

As from a distance, Francois' prideful love for the girl grew hourly. Where, in the whole wide world, could there be another as beautiful and industrious, yet walks so humbly among men, he mused as he watched the girl cleverly lash a canvas wrapped bundle of the miscellaneous items of camp equipment into a convenient pack. As Paulette looked up from her struggle with the bundle, her face red with the effort in getting the heavy pack in the proper shape for portaging, she laughing, met the eyes of Francois who had been watching her unaware.

"Does my lord approve?" she asked in mock solemnity.

Francois frowned. "Tell me, Paulette for a girl born and raised in the wilderness, how did you pick up the many surprise expressions you use such as 'my lord'"?

"From the French quarter of our village, and you know we had a few serious and intelligent Frenchman. They took on an active interest in teaching me."

"Remind me someday that, we, both of us, Paulette, owe them a debt that will be hard to repay."

"I often wonder, Francois, which is more important, the art of living, protecting and providing for one's self in the forest that I learn from my grandfather and Little Eagle, or from the French, the use of nice words so many of which have no more meaning or use then a bit of west wind?"

"Oh, or that is only part of it, Mon Cheri, to know which and when to use the ones, as you say, have no use for meaning, is more important than their use.

She studied his words, frowning slightly, replied, "I never thought of them that way."

"That, my pretty Paulette, is the beginning of your education. The use of the bow, by one who knows how to use it, is very important in its place, while the use of pretty French words under proper circumstances is equally important."

"I don't think I'd ever learn too eat nice French words my lord," and Paulette flashed her even white teeth.

"Ah, but in France, my dear, many people live and eat solely by the use of "nice" words, not a thing else, to talk and talk, very carefully so as not to shorten their supply of food and clothing.

"But you are fooling, Francois, who could live by talk alone?"

"Politicians can, my dear."

"Will you show me some day, have I very much to see what you call them? They must be skinny."

"On the contrary, they are most always big and fat like an old porcupine. Maybe someday I'll call catch one for you," adopting a studious attitude, continued, "They are not easy to hold after you catch one, they are very slippery, some are quite slimy."

"But what do they say?" Paulette persisted.

"Anything, my dear, anything they think will please whoever listens to them."

"There must be many strange people in the world, maybe our Indians were right, after all, when they tell stories of the many queer people in every part of the world."

Francois smiled, "If they only knew how near the truth they speak they would be astounded indeed."

Several of the packers, with perspiration glistening on their naked shoulders arrived for the last of the merchandise bales. "Have you seen Pascal?" Francois asked one of the men.

The fellow looked around. "Yes, he should be around here, we met him on the way over."

"He didn't show up here, he will be around presently, did you see any of the men we left with him?"

"No, the camp seemed deserted, probably out hunting."

"Oh, then Pascal is out looking for them."

The packer turned to a companion, "Give me a lift with this one it's heavy." Having tied the bundle securely with the loose ends of the "tumpline" leaving a loop long enough to reach his hip as he stood beside it, the packer now faced the bale and grasped the line where it was knotted at either end of the pack. With a mighty heave and a half turn of his body, with the added help of his companion, the bale settled snuggly on his back just above the hips. Adjusting the wide strap over his head, he motioned his helper to add another lighter bundle atop the one he had. With an involuntary grunt as the second bale settled atop the first, the packer started off at a trot while leaning slightly forward to relieve the tension on the strap extending over the top of his head. With his neck bowed at an exact angle, his hands grasping firmly the rawhide thongs holding the bales in place, the packer continued his evenly timed pace until he reached the other end of the portage. Francois never ceased to marvel at the strength and endurance of the men who moved his merchandise and heavy canoes into the wilderness.

As the last of the group disappeared along the trail, Francois picked up his light pack and proceeded to follow the others saying, "Paulette, dear, I am going on over, will you see that everything is taken care of here."

Paulette smiled, "Yes, my lord, you go on, we will be along. We will be the tail."

"If you say, 'my lord' again, I'll leave you here alone."

"Try it, Monsieur Francois, and I'll beat you to your post."

"I believe you would, but please, Paulette, say 'our post' not 'your post'."

The girl flashed him one of her meaningful glances, one that emphasized the slant of her eyes. The raider, with the self-satisfied smile of a man enjoying thoroughly an event that could happen but seldom to one human being, stepped briskly along the portage trail.

Chapter 9

Peeking through the tangle of overlapping boughs that hid him completely from view, Pascal stiffened to attention at the approach of slowly moving footsteps. From his vantage point, he had kept close count of the packers and knew that there was no one left at the "pose" but his friend Francois, and perhaps his bride, if he had one. When Paulette's grandmother came into view, with her little pack nestling snugly against her bent back, Pascal's vision became blurred as he strained his eyesight in incredulous astonishment. Trembling, as one with the ague, the little fellow experienced considerable difficulty in keeping his foot from tapping loudly on the ground. He swallowed hard, his lips dry, he knew somehow it would be of no avail to try and speak, his mouth had become suddenly very dry. The old lady coming to the fallen tree trunk that lay parallel to the path, decided to rest for a while and enjoy a few puffs on her little well blackened stone pipe. With some effort, she swung her pack to the ground and delved deep among its contents. Bringing up a long tasseled decorated pouch of soft caribou skin, she proceeded to prepare the tobacco and load the pipe. From the depths of the pouch, the little old lady extracted first a piece of flint, then a square of dry punk. Placing the flint carefully on the punk so one edge protruded slightly, with a slight glancing tap with the back of a knife against the flint, a tiny wisp of smoke miraculously appeared from the dry punk. Breaking off the smoking piece of punk, she nonchalantly let it fall to the ground. After loading her pipe, she stooped, gathered the bit of fire now smoking briskly and placed it carefully on the well filled pipe. Seated on the log, the old lady proceeded to puff away contented, filling the air with the sweet pungent scent of burning Ki-ni-ki-nik and trader tobacco. In the meantime, Pascal feeling a bit dazed and weak stood watching the old lady with an increasing misgiving fast turning into fright. The rapid approach of other footsteps accompanied by the steady humming of a well-known ballad sent the blood gushing through Pascal's veins at an intoxicating rate.

Francois stopped and smiling watched the old lady puffing on her pipe in perfect contentment, said in French, knowing that the old lady did not understand him, "Well, my dear, enjoying yourself?"

The little old woman mistaking his jovial words, quickly arose from the log and started to pick up her pack, but Francois, with traditional French chivalry, assisted her remarking as he did so, "There, sweetheart, now you can run along. Soon we will be home and no more packing for you. I'll see to that."

Pascal could stand no more, appalled, placing his hands before his eyes to shut out the sight of his friend and his wrinkled bride, he stole quietly away into the forest. Finding a seat on a low boulder, he sat rocking back and forth alone with his misery. If lightning had shattered the log walls of their trading post, scattering ruin and devastation about him, the little fellow could not have been more dismayed. He sat dumbfounded and alarmed. How could he, Francois, his friend and confidante, who had never made a move or even planned without his, Pascal's advice and approval, forget himself and his friends so completely? In turn, he became alarmed and his little blue eyes stared beady and fixed, was it, could it be…that the man had lost his reason…his sense of shame…loyalty to his friend? If the woman he chose, as he must someday, was young, beautiful and on a level with his station in life, someone that he, Pascal, could welcome with open arms, well and good, but no…no… this wrinkled, decrepit, antique Native woman…his fears again arose as to his friend's sanity. Flanked on either side by several small shrub-like balsam trees, their wide leafy green branches waved gently in contrast to the emotional turmoil surging within the little man, Pascal grew with each passing moment, more and more apprehensive that his world had come to its ignominious end. He might go on living, yes, but where and why? Certainly not under the same roof with that…that…and her smelly stone pipe. Gradually his troubled and exaggerated emotional spree calmed somewhat, enough so that his usual reasoning powers returned to quiet equilibrium. He couldn't leave. There was no other place to go. After all, Francois was still his friend and it might be to their advantage that the make the best of his friend's bad bargain. Certainly, it could not make matters worse were he to put on a bold, if false, front. It was his friend's choice and who was he to question Francois' choice of a bride. He might comment on it…no…no…he wouldn't do that and he'd defy anyone to make one disparaging remark out loud about either Francois or his choice of a wife. Summoning all of his willpower, he immediately proceeded to carry out his resolution. Arising quickly from his bower-like retreat, the little fellow started resolutely back.

When the last packer had left camp, Paulette and her grandfather, after taking one last look around, lest anything should be left behind, in turn, disappeared among the forest growth along the narrow portage trail. Somewhere along the way from Lake Superior, Paulette had lost all fear and hatred for the trader and in its stead a calm approval of the man that had crept into her consciousness. She liked Francois, not as a wife should regard a husband, but more as a friend and wished he would remain just that, but realizing, that in the final analysis, she would have very little, if any, choice. She moved along at a brisk walk towards what she knew was her fate and whatever it held in store for her and her grandparents.

It was midday when the two reached the little clearing where Pascal and three companions had been left by Francois to guard the heavy freighter canoes. Stretching far into the northern distance, the glassy smooth surface of the lake, broken only by the departing heavily laden canoes, sending little waves scurrying shoreward as stout paddles churned the clear water into tiny swirls at each stroke, mirrored the lofty branches of pine, birch and spruce that lined its shores. Canada Jays flitting from branch to branch, resting but momentarily while sharp little eyes search the abandoned campgrounds for scraps of food, caught and held Francois' attention while he impatiently waited for Pascal's return.

"I wonder what became of him...he should be back by now."

"Became of who, Monsieur?" asked Paulette as she reached the water's edge and deposited her pack beside the canoe moored to the hastily constructed dock of saplings.

"Oh, Paulette, did you see a little man with red hair and red beard? He is very short, about so high," holding his hand out waist high. "He is around here somewhere."

Paulette regarded Francois through ever narrowing eyelids. "A little red man about so high? I've seen and heard of most everything else, Monsieur, but a little red man about so high is something new, I am feeling quite well and wide awake, so I didn't see your little red man."

"Oh, here he comes now."

Paulette instinctively stepped quickly to the trader's side where she stood hidden from the approaching Pascal.

Walking slowly, like one in a dream, the little red man, oblivious of anything or anyone about him, approached his friend.

"Well, well, my friend, where have you been? We have been waiting for you. What happened? You do not look well, tell me Pascal. What is it?"

Pascal, unable to speak, merely shook his head and with averted eyes, said in a loud whisper, "I missed the trail back there and was lost for a little while."

Francois laughed, "Was that all? That is nothing to feel so badly about, that happens to all of us. Come now, we must be off, the other canoes are far ahead of us."

Pascal stood with his eyes fixed on the ground at his feet while Paulette excitedly peeked over Francois' shoulder.

"Oh, say, I almost forgot, you will pardon me, my friends, Pascal, I want you to know my wife, Paulette."

At the words "my wife", the little man winced and closed his eyes tightly, at the moment his good intentions disappeared into thin air as Francois continued, "Paulette, you didn't believe me when I told you of 'the little red man'. Well, here he is. I want you two to be very good friends."

Paulette quickly stepped from behind the trader and said, "C'est mon plaisir, Monseiur Pascal."

The little fellow, with his eyes still tightly closed, started visibly at the sound of the girl's soothing tone, the fluid notes of her voice disturbed the mental picture of the old woman he was sure stood before him. He must go through with it, and tremblingly he opened one eye cautiously, prepared to close it again quickly should he feel himself unequal to the ordeal. At first, the eyelid opened only enough to admit but a tiny blurry picture of the vision of loveliness that smiled upon him so friendly.

"Vien, mon ami…you are afraid of me?"

At the sound of a gentle young voice addressing him again, his other eye opened to its utmost capacity almost before the first. As was his custom, speechlessly he cocked his head from side to side much s a friendly dog begging for food.

"Well, Pascal, why not say something?" Francois enjoying his surprise announcement to its utmost, laughed gleefully. "Come…come, mon Ami, it is not so startling as all that."

"But…but…I thought…" The 'little red man' checked himself, none too soon, to guard his secret, a secret that he carried to his grave.

Chapter 10

The sounds of hustling, bustling activity, of chopper's axes, crackling fires, an occasional bit of song or laughter, the cry of the woodsman's "timber!", followed by the crash of a dead and, long since, dried pine tree; its naked limbs broken to bits in the fall, quickly gathered for firewood, meant the end of another day's toil and rest for weary packers. The sun, all but obscured by a rim of grayish clouds hovering near the horizon turned their ragged edges to crimson and gold, a fitting gesture of welcome at the approach of another night. Tents and lean-to shelters sprung up like tiny growths from the very ground where great pines stand majestically in proud rebuke to the intruders, whose campfire smoke ascending to their topmost branches, lingers on the still air before disappearing into the upper atmosphere.

Amidst the chain of small islands on the lake to the south, Francois' canoe, with Pascal perched proudly atop the forward thwart paddling industriously, hovers into sight. A few minutes later, willing hands are rudely brushed aside as the 'little red man' disdains any assistance in beaching and unloading the craft. Jacques, the "head packer" or foreman of the crew, saunters casually to the water's edge and watches the proceedings with an air of slight concern and displeasure. "What kept you so long?" he inquired, while with his broad bladed hunting knife, he savagely cut the limb of a balsam obscuring his vision.

"Is it necessary for you to know?" The trader was evidently vexed at the fellow's question.

"No-o," Jacques drawled trying to think of some way out to save face. "I think I know the reason," he laughingly remarked and strode away.

"I don't think I like that fellow," Paulette said to Pascal as she handed him various small bundles from the canoe.

"Jacques is not a bad fellow, Madam…if you watch him closely."

"I don't like people that have to be watched," insisted Paulette, "and Pascal, please call me Paulette, I am not old enough for 'Madam'."

Pascal flashed an ironic smile, remembering the old woman he thought was the wife of his friend. "Very well, Paulette, it shall be…Madam," and they both laughed.

Jacques sauntered over to the French packer's fire, before sitting down on the ground covering of balsam and cedar boughs. He looked towards the group of young Indians at their fireplace set some distance away. "I see our half-breed, Batiste, spends most of his time with the savages. I suppose our company is not good enough for him."

"The company he keeps is of his own choosing," said one in the group.

"Which is more than the little lady can say," snapped Jacques with a touch of sarcasm.

The others around the fire became suddenly interested at the implication.

"She seems well content," retorted another, "and just where do you fit into the picture?"

Jacques picked up a piece of dry pine wood and started whittling nervously. "I don't fit into the picture…none of us do. We are just so much bone and muscle and I am getting tired of it."

"Why didn't you stay down at Lake Superior? I don't think you would have been missed so very much. You could go back now."

The big fellow becoming increasing agitated, said, "Yes? After I packed twice as much as my share over the hill…that would please too many people, I have other plans."

"Have you told Francois about your 'plans'."

All joined in the general laughter, all except Jacques who said rather darkly, "When I have something to say to Francois, it will be to Francois and not to you bunch of jackasses."

The voice of Pascal calling for Batiste cut short the discussion for the time being, as the half-breed suddenly sprang from his position on the ground. Without apparent effort or delay in answer to the summons. "Seems like the 'little red man' wants me," he said in fluent Ojibwe, to his companions.

"Maybe he wants you to cook for the new woman," remarked one of the Indians.

Batiste had taken several steps in the direction of the summons, then stopped for a moment as though undecided, then hastily retraced his steps. "Did someone say something about a woman?" he asked the assemblage.

"Yes," one answered. "I did…didn't you see her? The chief brought a woman from the 'big lake', young too and nice to look at."

"I didn't know that. Where was I all this time?"

"They just landed…newly weds always travel slow."

Without further comment, Batiste hurried on to Pascal's incessant calls. The half-breed stepped along quietly over the uneven ground as only one born of the 'Wilderness' can. Tall and muscular, with features of his Indian mother predominant, carrying his weight lightly, at each step he searched the surroundings wonderingly for a glimpse of the young woman. At one of the rare intervals, when he looked at the ground at his feet, he stooped suddenly and picked up a small pearl handled dagger. Wasting no time in inspecting his find, he tucked the toy quickly beneath his broad woolen sash while continuing on his way.

"Batiste, come help me please, soon it will be dark and we have not yet eaten."

"Sure, Pascal, why didn't you call me sooner?"

"I don't know, maybe because I'm all excited today. You hear the news?"

"What news?" Batiste asked.

"About Paulette…she come with Francois."

"What Paulette, why did she come?"

"Don't know…going to be his wife…they don't tell me yet. I just make a guess."

"What is she, French?"

"No-o…I think half-breed…speaks with the Natives and very good French too…just like you."

Pascal darting about the camp gathering wood and preparing the fire while Batiste erected the shelter for the old couple asked, "What is this for, surely not for the bride and groom?"

"No, no, no, Batiste. That is where Paulette stays with the old couple, her grandparents. I think Francois had to bring them along too."

Batiste smiled as he spread the canvas over the framework of saplings. "That is one way to get a wife, take the whole family along. Where are they now?"

"Down by the lake preparing fish for supper. Monsieur Francois is there too, he don't get very far away from Paulette."

"Is Francois cleaning the fish?"

"Oh, no…Paulette wouldn't let him do that, he just look and smile all the time."

The thick black smoke rolled up from the burning birch bark and pitchy wood, as Pascal arose from a kneeling position where he had been blowing the borrowed embers into a flame, and as Batiste busily searched the ground among the leaves, beneath the canvas shelter, for stones and protruding roots preparatory to laying the bed of boughs. While thus engaged, he failed to hear the approaching footsteps. Not until the voice of the girl gave the customary Ojibwe greeting to a stranger, "Boozhoo Anishinaab" did he become aware of her presence. Turning as he quickly rose to his feet, he got as far as the first word of his reply, "Boozhoo" then further speech failed him. For standing before him, was the nearest thing to a vision he had ever seen.

Noting the young man's evident embarrassment on her account, Paulette blushed and for the next moment, they stood silent, the girl, with narrowing eyes, taking in every line of the young man's figure of perfect manhood. His black eyes, a legacy from his mother, sparkled wide in bold admiration, while Paulette, in evident distress, said, "Vous parlez francais aussi?"

"Oui, Madam." For once in his life he was glad he spoke French. "Where are you from, if I may ask, Madam?"

Paulette laughed and relieved the tension by answering in Ojibwe. "From down by the 'big water', I was born there. Where do you come from?"

Batiste studied her for a moment, then, answered evasively, "Oh, no place in particular. I was born in the wilderness and I know no other home. Someday, I am going to see the 'big lake'," then shyly added, "maybe there is another one there, like you."

Paulette moved about uneasily and said, "My husband, Monsieur Francois, should be here any moment. I must prepare these fish for our supper."

Batiste, hooking his thumbs into his sash, felt the little dagger he had picked up and holding it out to the girl, said, "I found this as I came over…is it yours?"

Paulette merely glanced at it and said, "No… it is not mine." Extending the thinly worn knife she carried, added, "This is the only knife I have ever owned, it was given to me by a good friend, Little Eagle, many years ago and I have carried it ever since."

"Perhaps it were better you carried this one too. I would have no use for it. It was probably made for a beautiful lady, so it is yours by right?"

Paulette flashed her prettiest smile as she accepted the dagger. "Je vous merci, Monsieur. I shall carry it always and remember you kindly, now please go."

Batiste bowed and Paulette watched his deliberate strides as he disappeared into the forest where sparks from the fire of the Natives showered skyward. As Paulette busied herself with preparations for the evening meal, Pascal arrived with a pack load of firewood that covered almost the entire length of his body. Despite his lack of height, he was very powerful and carried as much weight as any of the packers.

"Who is that young man? The one you call Batiste," Paulette questioned Pascal.

Pascal, while adding fuel to the already brightly blazing fire, said, "I don't know who he is, a very nice boy that came here in the summer. No one knows anything about him, except, perhaps, the Indians. He does not talk much, never about himself, a willing worker and good hunter. I guess that is all, Madam."

"That does not tell who he is."

"I can find out more if Madam wishes."

"Please, Pascal…I am not interested in knowing more about him. I should not have asked."

Pascal came quickly around the fire and speaking in a confidential tone, said, "Anything you say or ask of Pascal is locked in here forever." Suiting action to his words, he thumped his hairy chest and continued, "You can trust me, Paulette, I do not talk too much."

"Thank you, my friend. I am sure I can trust you and whenever I need your help, I shall come to you."

The "little red man" had arisen to this full height at the girl's words. "Ah, it is me, Pascal, that is grateful for those kind words and I shall never fail you, never!"

Later that night after Batiste had moved his blanket and cape to the Indians campfire and arranged a bed of boughs, he sat staring pensively into the glowing logs as they fell into a bed of coals.

"Did you see the woman?"

The half-breed was somewhat startled by the query. Not wanting to seem rude, but he wished people would mind their own affairs. Scarcely nodding, he replied, "Yes, I saw her, she is young, almost too young for this kind of life. Strange how she ever consented to come."

One of the Indians laughed silently. "I was there when she made up her mind. Her grandparents were in the canoe first before she was asked to come along."

Batiste sat bolt upright. "You mean to say that she was forced to join the Chief?"

"My son," the Indian continued, "The white man has many ways of forcing his kind to do as he wills. What matters which way he uses, she came willingly. She didn't fight. Her grandparents are very happy in their new life…she is a good girl."

The thinly crescent shaped moon rode high amidst the galaxy of stars; and somewhere westward, among the timbered hills that rose row upon row, seemingly without end. A pack of wolves mingled their wild cries and howls with the more subdued night noises of the Great

Forest, answering calls from other directions, causing one of the Indians to remark, "It is not well when the wolf cries so when the moon gives no light."

Each, in turn, nodded agreement. Batiste let down his long black hair that reached well below his hips. Running his fingers speedily through the coarse strands and working patiently over a few knots and snarls, he re-braided it carefully while his friends looked on in admiration and approval. They knew that the young man wore his hair long in deference to their custom and not short, as was the practice of his father's people, he was one of them. The continued howls of the wolves, now joined by the eerie cries of an owl, broke in upon the night stillness with the foreboding feeling of ominous things to come as the Indians edged nearer to the fire.

"It is strange how the wild things that roam the forest at night foretell of impending happenings," one remarked.

"What do they speak of tonight?" Batiste asked quietly.

The Indian listened attentively until another round of howls had subsided, then said casually, "A death, perhaps."

Batiste remained silent and pensive, he knew of the deep rooted convictions handed down, not by "on the spot" conclusions, but gathered through generations of studied experience. He, too, wondered what the day ahead would bring and wished the wolves would stop howling. He was tired and growing sleepy, the morning light would soon show in the east. He spread his blanket carefully, and thoughtfully laid down to rest.

Chapter 11

Dawn, with its promise of another bright and sunny day, found Batiste and his Indian friends up and about, their campfire crackling loudly in the still morning. Snuggling closer into the comfortable circle of heat, like a duckling beneath sheltering wings, the scantily clad Indians, with frequent yawns, each silently engrossed with his own thoughts, gradually adjusted themselves to the sudden exposure to the chilly morning air. Batiste, as was his custom, sat munching on a blackened piece of dried venison. He was about to reach for another morsel, when it happened. A sharp piercing woman's scream rent the stillness. Before the sound had time to reach, the young half-breed was well on his way to Paulette's shelter. Without so much as a guess as to the probable cause of the loud alarming cry, he sped on, twisting and turning among the trees blocking his path. Holding securely his hunting knife lest he drop it on one of the many leaps over low lying windfalls, the youth stopped short at the shelter of the girl and her grandparents. The old folks were still asleep. Searching frantically for sight of Paulette, his attention was attracted by a low wailing sound a short stone's throw in the direction of the lake. Once more bounding with renewed energy towards the sounds, he all but stumbled over the lifeless body of the trader Francois. Born and reared in a land where caution was one of the first requisites for a long and healthy life,

Batiste stopped and searched the surroundings with practiced eyes. The dead man had been killed within his tent and dragged out afterward, a bloody trail through the dry leaves showed that very plainly…but who…who?

With the unfinished question still lingering in his mind, the youth approached Paulette who was seated on the ground near the entrance to the dead man's tent and sobbing quietly. "What happened…how…who killed him? Why?" he asked in quick succession.

"I don't know, I found him like that when I came over here. I stayed with my grandparents last night. Grandfather was not feeling well and didn't sleep until early this morning. When he did, I came here and found him like that."

Batiste opened the flaps of the tent. There was no sign of a struggle. The body had been dragged from the bed immediately after the deed was committed. "Did you drag him out here?" Batiste asked.

Paulette shook her head decisively. "No, I didn't. I told you I found him just as you see him there. I didn't touch him."

The youth rolled the dead man over and examined the body closely. "Stabbed," he said simply and added, "I'll go and tell the men." He walked away a few steps, then quickly returned and stood before the girl, he spoke in a low voice as though fearful of being overheard, said, "Death always brings sorrow; that is to be expected. But one must look ahead to the time when that sorrow fades into the past. Somebody killed your husband for a reason, and I think I know why. That person must not be allowed to gather the fruits of his cowardly deed. Before we leave here, you, Monsieur Francois' widow, will claim all of his possessions, they are yours."

The idea startled Paulette and springing to her feet, exclaimed, "I can't do that, Batiste. I…I…"

"Do you want the killer to get everything and you too? Maybe you are the reason why Francois was killed. You know what will happen to your grandparents if you are taken captive again…their throats will be cut just as easily as your husband was stabbed."

Paulette paled and trembling uncontrollably leaned against a birch sapling for support. "But I can't do this alone," she cried. "Can you…could you help me?"

"Every man of us will help you, except the killer. I'll be around if anything goes wrong, but, please do as I say. It will save you many bitter tears."

Paulette looked up sharply at the youth as he spoke. For the second time in her life she was warned against "many bitter tears". Did those words mark a milestone along her life's pathway?

"Go back to your shelter and stay there. Pascal will look after everything."

The mention of Pascal brought on a new flood of tears as Paulette knew of the bitter sorrow that must overtake the kindly little man. Batiste, too, felt deeply, for he knew that Francois embodied everything that Pascal held dear on earth. Shrugging off any personal feeling he might feel in the death of the trader or its immediate consequences, he strode off towards the packer's camp.

On the morning following the tragic death of the trader and raider Francois, the packers, both French and Indian, moved about their respective campfires with subdued mien, sans their usual good natured bantering. Pascal slept pitifully after the long night's vigil; throughout the long hours, he sat staring open eyed into the fire. The little man's deep suffering drew sympathetic gestures from the most hardened of the "Courier du Bois" or woods travelers; some of them taking turns in keeping the fires replenished throughout the night. Now, at short intervals, he tumbled and with deep moans, tossed restlessly. Even sleep could not dull his aching heart. Of the two people closely connected with the trader, out of necessity and survival, Paulette was the first to overcome the shock and return to a normal state of mind.

Mustering all her courage, she determined to carry out Batiste's instructions and claim for herself the late trader's possessions. Acting on her determination, she donned the silk lined cloak he had given her and carrying her thinly worn knife within easy reach, she started towards the camps of the packers. Stopping some distance away, she searched the faces of the men in hope of seeing Batiste. Momentarily losing courage at the half-breed's absence, the thought of her grandparents immediately restored the girl's wavering resolution. Raising her voice that somehow seemed weak and inadequate for the occasion, she said, "My friends, I have come to tell you that I, Paulette, as the widow of Francois, will from now on conduct this party. I claim possession of all his property wherever it may be. If any one of you has any objections, you have a short time to state them."

At the girl's last word, Jacques sprang to his feet, trembling excitedly and livid with rage, shouted, "I have many objections. I object to this…this Lake Superior squaw taking over what we have rightfully earned. I will not submit to being robbed by a young she-savage, a stranger who never did anything to earn what she now wants to take from us. It is I and I alone, Jacques, who will conduct this party." Stopping momentarily to wet his parched lips, the irate man continued, "I should have done what I intended to do before she left the shore of Superior, cut her throat and left her there. It is I who shall take Francois' place, not only in the possession of his property, but in his bed as well, beside his pretty wife, and I defy anyone to try and stop me."

Taken by surprise at the sudden turn in the tide of events, the men remained silent though some involuntarily reached for their knives. Paulette felt her heart sink at the ruffian's words and was about to turn away, when she noticed her friends, the half-breed and Pascal, standing together beside a pine tree. Batiste was smiling and nodded to her while pointing to his knife. Thus encouraged, Paulette quickly drew her knife, saying, "I stand by everything I said and if I never do anything else in this world, I shall at least die defending what is mine. If Monsieur Jacques is coward enough to fight me, a "she-savage", let him step out here now and not wait until it gets dark when I am asleep."

Several of the young men sprang to their feet and drew their knives, but Jacques, with a loud laugh, sprang ahead of them and rushed towards the girl. With arm upraised, he advanced quickly towards Paulette, who bravely stood her ground. Nearer and nearer the oncoming black bearded giant strode, all the time laughing at the ease with which he would dispatch the girl. To Paulette, everything about her began to swirl madly and she wished it was all over when a shiny object whizzed through the air catching the morning sunlight as it sped straight to its target. Jacques stopped, the fingers of his upraised hand loosened from the handle of the knife and it fell with a rustling sound among the dry leaves…his arm still upraised…his head tilted back slowly…back…back…until his wide unseeing eyes stared at the sky above. Then with a slow swaying motion, he fell headlong to the ground where his head rolled back to its natural position. Jacques was dead.

The half-breed, Batiste, walked towards the body and slowly withdrew his knife from where it had entered, a little below Jacques' left shoulder blade. Gathering up a handful of dry leaves, he carefully wiped the blade while looking over the men standing en masse before him, and said quite casually, "Anyone of you want to join Jacques, let him speak up quickly. No? Very well, from now on, you work for Madam Paulette." Nodding in approval, the men sheathed or tucked their knives beneath wide and many colored woolen sashes.

Pascal, with quavering, emotion choked, voice rushed to Batiste and grabbing his hands kissed them adoringly.

"Batiste...Batiste, my friend, what can I say?"

"Say nothing, 'little red man' it will be better that way. Look after Paulette, you have much work to do, she needs you.

Incredulously the little fellow frowned. "Paulette need me? Me...Pascal? You make a mistake Batiste. No one ever need me."

"Oh yes she does. She may not know it, but she needs you now more than she ever needed anyone in her life."

"If you tell the truth, Batiste, I shall go to her quickly." With that he was off like a wood sprite, his short legs beating the ground is swift little strides.

Paulette staggered rather than walked back to her tent...staggered under the emotional impact of seeing her "would be" slayer die before her eyes. Spiritually endowed with a heritage of ancestry, whose predominating ambition to be included and be worthy in the company of the brave, the girl quickly recovered both physical strength and mental stability. Before reaching her grandparent's shelter, she had completely regained equilibrium and her usual composure. She recounted to the aged couple everything that happened.

While thus engaged, Pascal arrived breathless and excited. "Madam...Madam Paulette, what do we do now? You tell me and I make them loafers work."

The girl, at first amused at the "little red man's" seriousness, thought for a moment, then said, "All right, Pascal, from now on you see that my orders are carried out and the men do as you say. You will report to me any man who refuses to obey you. Now go tell them that we are moving on to the post at once."

Paulette's last words had barely been uttered before Pascal was off like an arrow, with his round blue eyes blazing with excitement and the long red hair spreading fanwise over his broad shoulders. After the Indians had gathered together their belongings, Batiste, out of sheer curiosity, walked quickly back to the spot where Francois was killed. Standing where the outline of the dead man's tent showed plainly, the young half-breed spied what at first resembled a piece of brightly colored quartz rock. Uncovering the shining object with his moccasined foot, he picked up the little dagger he had given Paulette on the evening of their arrival. Examining the small weapon closely, the youth staggered back as though he had been struck and holding a hand before his eyes to shut out the sight…the sight of a picture that rose up before him. The pearl handled dagger was crusted with blood. Quickly tucking the thing out of sight beneath his wide sash and looking neither to the right or left, he strode quickly back to where the men were moving the heavy packs across the short portage to the next lake.

The sun was scarcely treetop high when the flotilla of heavily laden canoes was ready to shove off one by one. With subdued excitement over his new duties, Pascal assigned the men to their posts.

Stopping beside Batiste, the little man said in a low voice, "Madam requests you to take charge of our canoe."

"Batiste frowned deeply and replied, "Give my compliments to Madam and tell her I wish to be excused. Tell her that I feel I have done enough for today."

Pascal listened attentively with his head cocked slightly to one side. "My friend, you are right. Shall I?"

"Yes, if you will," Batiste interrupted, "take one of the Indians instead."

While the last canoe with Indian paddlers was being recalled, Pascal hurried to his new mistress with Batiste's refusal to accompany them. The girl showed her disappointment. "I shall go talk to him," she said. "I am sorry, Batiste. I only wanted a chance to thank you for what you did for me and the old folks. Thank you, my friend." Changing from French to Ojibwe, she continued, "Maybe someday if the spirits will it, I shall find an opportunity to repay you."

Batiste turned toward the girl more energetically than the occasion demanded, and holding up his hands with palms spread towards her, he said with obviously suppressed feeling, "Please, Madam, I would have done as much for your grandmother or anyone else. I do not want either pay or thanks." While he spoke, the young man gazed upon the girl with a studied indifference that was not lost upon her.

Turning back towards her canoe, the little path she followed became suddenly misty and blurred with the tears that she was finding hard to control.

Chapter 12

Far...far beyond the reach of the sound of Superior's waves, washing thinly over its sandy beaches, or the rumbling, as of distant thunder, where the great lake incessantly battered deep caves into its walled prison, another lake, tiny by comparison and in marked contrast, rested quiet and glassy smooth under a lowering sky of gray. The great forest of pine clad hills and valleys that surrounded it, stood deathly still amidst myriads of its little echo-less noises. Like one of a chain of silver beads flung carelessly over the land, the lake, a thing of quiet beauty, hidden away in a setting of the Creator's own choosing amidst age old pines, that providing shelter for the chickadees, flitting recklessly among its branches, and food for the nimble red squirrel sitting jauntily on its topmost branches that lean protectively over its waters. The great hawk, soaring gracefully over the hills, jealously guarding its castle of dried limbs of the pine and moss from the very rocks upon which it rests atop the highest cliff, no doubt, viewed with curious alarm the columns of smoke arising from mud plastered chimneys midway along its shore of otherwise untamed beauty. On a point of well-timbered land, jutting boldly into the lake midway its length, the trading post of the late Francois squatted amidst the forest like a thing affrighted in mid chase. Several small low log-walled buildings surrounded a larger one and at various angles not unlike the remnants of a covey of young partridge within the circle of mother care, housed the white inhabitants of the place. At intervals of various lengths along its shore, in either direction and on the several islands, clusters of little brown circular habitations of the Natives stood as a part of the unblemished forest and well within its sheltering atmosphere.

Within the larger of the grouped buildings of the post, Paulette stood excitedly breathless amidst the strange surroundings. At one end of a large room, a great fireplace radiated comforting heat. Scattered about the smoothly hewn and polished timbers of the floor in planned confusion, were rugs of fur and mats woven of many colored reeds and cedar bark. The low walls and high pitched ceiling crisscrossed in a seeming confusion of timber rafters and braces, surrounding a sky light of transparent material curtained with heavy velvet hangings. Along the seamless walls of expertly fitted timbers, the girl moved along slowly, oblivious of all else save the panorama of the great forest with its lakes and timbered hills in endless array portrayed in all its' natural splendor. The great outdoors, its lights and shadows, faraway hills melting into the cloud banked horizon beyond the rim of the earth itself, had been transferred in miniature to the walls before her. The Natives, their wigwams, naked children playing at the water's edge, brought back memories of her own childhood and tears of happy emotion.

Pascal in evident glee over the girl's occasional emotional outbursts, and expressions of wonder, hovered about in happy anticipation of more to come. Above the fireplace, a large painting of a wolf devouring a fawn while its mother looked on brought from Paulette an angry outburst. Paulette covered her face with her hands for she too, loved the wild things of the forest. Yet, again and again she uncovered her face and returned to gaze upon the scene, each time discovering some little detail that, in its portrayal of reality, brought on a new sense of disquiet and uneasiness.

The girl looked about the room as though lost in some strange land, finally asking, "Tell me, Pascal, where did all this…" with a slight sweeping gesture indicating the paintings. "I don't understand where…"

Pascal noting the girl's evident lack of words to express her thought said, "But do you not know, Madam?"

Paulette shook her head mystified. "Know what, Monsieur?"

"Monsieur Francois was a great artist. I dare say one of the world's greatest painters."

"But, I thought he was…a…trader," Paulette ventured hesitatingly.

"But, Madam, Monsieur was first and always the master painter. A trader…yes…let us say only after a fashion."

"I remember now," Paulette said. "He mentioned that scene about the wolf and the fawn." Recalling the incident of Francois' veiled threat, she quickly added, "I don't like to think of it, I want to remember him in his better moods."

"No one ever understood Francois," mused Pascal. "He really lived as two different men. When he was busy with his painting, he was the most kind and generous of men, so considerate of others, so sincere and honest." At the mention of the word "honest", Paulette raised her eyebrows questioningly. Pascal continued, "But, when circumstances forced him to lay aside his brush and devote his time to worldly affairs," here the little man stopped and shook his head in unhappy reminiscence, "he became as one possessed of the devil himself, crafty, mean, cruel and dishonest, with an absolute disregard for the suffering of others. It was at such a time, when our trade stocks were low and demands for more became insistent, that he would lay aside his brush and don his blue uniform of velvet…it was then that he could set his fertile brain to work on some of the most cruel and diabolical plots to rob his fellow man that none but Satan himself could invent.

"But," Paulette asked "how did he feel afterward when he returned to his other self?"

"Just as though nothing unusual had ever happened, it seems as if he could forget some things completely at will."

Pascal now turned his attention to the end of the room opposite the fireplace where a wide couch-like bed with an overstuffed mattress of feathers stood high and invitingly fluffy beneath its covering of light woolen blankets. Between the bed and wall, wide double drapes of pale green velvet hung gracefully swaying gently at each movement within the room. Filled with expectant curiosity, Paulette stood in a state of near apprehension, as the little man, with hands trembling slightly, grasped the cords that drew back the drapes slowly.

"Oh, Pascal, look!" Wide eyed and frightened by the vision of loveliness that looked down upon her with a half wistful smile, Paulette raised her hand to her bosom to still the excited beating of her heart while, in wild expectancy, she waited for the beautiful creature to speak. Enveloped only in a gossamer-like mist that floated in off the lake when she knelt among the rushes was a girl approaching womanhood…perhaps a woman loath to release the charm of youth, turned slightly as her eyes, long and with a hint of Asiatic slant, partly closed in evident amusement or viewed from a different angle…a look of disapproval at an unwarranted intrusion.

Beyond the sheet of water where it caught their reflection, the hills rose row upon row invading the blue of the sky. A gull, on motionless wings, turned its head towards the beautiful creature unmindful of its presence. Paulette stood enraptured, not daring to move or speak lest the vision disappear into the mist that seemed to enfold her in ever varying density. Her hair, now long and black, hanging loosely down her back, all but disappeared into a thickly moving mass of vapor in obedience to the shadow of a tree playing through the skylight from without. Paulette, unable to longer withstand the emotional strain brought on by her first view of the work of a master artist, motioned for Pascal to draw the curtains.

Turning back towards the fireplace, the little man beckoned the girl to follow him. In a corner of the room by the fireplace, another pair of drapes hung listlessly, their folds weaving slightly as the pair approached. Like one preparing for a ceremony, Pascal surveyed the girl's position with reference to the room before drawing the drapes apart. Taking the girl gently by the arm, he said, "Will Madam stand here please? Now I think it will be all right." Slowly…very slowly the little man drew the drapes apart revealing three mirrors at least twice Pascal's height, and cleverly arranged to reflect into one composite picture all the paintings of that room. A panoramic landscape of a great Wilderness spread out in all its simple grandeur; lakes, rivers, forested hills and their shadows extending beyond the range of human sight, truly the land of the Voyageur…des Pays d'en Haut.

While Paulette was completely engrossed in the reflected scene, Pascal had quietly returned to the farther end of the room and had drawn back the drapes covering the "Lady in Mist". Paulette gasped, the scene, though lovely in its simple scenic beauty, now assumed an illusion of life. From far up on a hill, the "lady" looked down upon the scene below. With the faint shadow of an approving smile playing about her fully rounded lips, she gazed in lazy admiration upon the picturesque panorama spread out before her.

From the place where Paulette stood, she could not see her own reflection in the mirrors. Stepping into the full glare of her own image, the girl gasped in horror. For the first time in her life, she had seen herself as she really looked from head to foot. Pascal, in alarm, quickly drew the curtains covering the painting and rushed to the girl's side. Paulette, with both hands covering her flushed face, stood with an intense desire, yet not daring to look at her image again. With hair disheveled and wearing the same ragged and soiled dress, the only one she owned, when they left Lake Superior, she made a sorry sight amidst her beautiful surroundings. Sinking to the floor, she began to weep. Pascal, surmising the cause of her outburst, quickly drew the drapes concealing the mirrors. When Paulette finally gathered courage enough to take another look at her own image, at what she really looked like, the mirrors had disappeared. Somewhat relieved at the sight of the swaying curtains, she quietly arose and walked in deep meditation to the cabin she had chosen for her grandparents.

Chapter 13

With the instinct of a homing pigeon, Batiste set his course.
Somewhere in the distant west, where the evening sun would sink
slowly into the horizon, was the young man's objective. His parents
and relatives, his friends and neighbors lived there contentedly, within
a friendly atmosphere encircled by the magic of home.

As the first streaks of light were appearing in the east, the
young man left Paulette's trading post. Noiselessly, like a spirit
returning to its daytime haunts, the half-breed slipped past a few early
risers leaving no sign behind to mark his passing. Careful lest dry twigs
and broken limbs extending sharply from parent trunks of small trees
betray the direction of his departure or noisily rub against his buckskin
suit, the young man moved slowly. Once beyond the outer circle of
habitation, he stepped up his pace while noting the direction he traveled
by the bright shafts of light extending high into the sky where soon the
rising sun would appear bright and warm. Traveling north temporarily
and keeping well within the forest, away from the shore of the long
point extending well into the lake, Batiste headed for the range of low
lying hills rising early in the dim light. From one of its many bald tops,
he would survey and choose his route, either along the range amidst

scrub and scraggly pine, or in the valleys where the park-like growth of giant trees offered but little resistance to the traveler.

The morning hours passed swiftly and unnoticed. As the sun hung directly over his left shoulder, he stopped at the shore of a lake that lay across his course. From the tip of a cedar tree, he surveyed a much of the long narrow body of water as he could see. Sliding back to the ground and landing with a thump, he smiled wryly and sighed with an air of resignation. "That water must be cold, but I guess there is no way out...I'll have to swim," he muttered as he searched his surroundings for material to make a small float on which to transport his earthly belongings. Upon two small dry poles securely lashed together with his all-important "tumpline", he carefully placed his bow and arrows, the clothing he wore together with his blanket and a few pieces of well dried and smoked venison. A few lumps of maple sugar that the Indians had brought from Lake Superior, he first carefully wrapped in birch bark and tucked carefully among the folds of his blanket. With several sharp intakes of breath as he came contact with the icy water, the half-breed slipped quietly into the lake and swam out, towing his little raft with its precious cargo, everything he owned in the world.

That evening, beside a small pond deep among the hills of des Pays d'en Haut, the sharp crackling of a campfire, followed by a shower of sparks revealed our young man lying seemingly content on a bed of evergreens. His tall and muscular form curled, rather than stretched out, beside the fire. His sharp, black eyes, gazed intently at the blazing logs while he drummed nervously with a bit of twig. Suddenly sitting up, he crossed his legs before the fire and searched the heavens before fixing his gaze on a bright star attended by a cluster of smaller, dimmer stars well to the east. Tracing their probably path across the heavens to a point near the western horizon, he said, "When you get that far, I'll have to be on my way." Once again lying down, this time stretching out full length and enjoying the heat from the fire, Batiste listened attentively to the beautiful, yet eerie and haunting call of the loon. Somewhere back there along the route he had come, a pack of wolves set up a confused series of wild howls that ended in the lone staccato of barking from the leader in frightened retreat. "If you get that scared when you run across my tracks, what would happen if you saw me?" With that bit of cheerful assurance, he yawned and nestled his head into a hollow spot among the thinly covered boughs thickly laid to serve as a pillow. The young man slept uneasily and fitfully. As the fire died and little remained of the logs save a pile of glowing embers, the sleeper sat up, yawned and hesitatingly arose to replenish the fire. The night was cold and frost glistened on the bushes and branches within the firelight. He glanced at the pile of wood he had gathered and made a wry face at its probable depletion before dawn. Turing around to warm his chilly back, he searched as much of his surroundings as was visible, in the flickering light, for more dry wood. A dead and dry small tree that he might have overlooked, but he had done his work too well, there were none in sight. Oh well, he would get some further back, when the pile was gone.

The sharp whistling snort of a buck deer as it cleared its nostrils of a strange and offensive scent, broke in on the night stillness, its bounding hoof beats becoming fainter with its hasty retreat. "Strange how you can run so fast through the dark without breaking your neck, I suppose the 'Great Spirit' made you that way," his thoughts ran in Ojibwe. He found it easier to philosophize on nature in his mother tongue.

Idly hooking a thumb into the wide woolen sash loosely encircling his slim waist, the young man slowly withdrew the small pearl handled dagger encrusted with the blood of the slain trader Francois. Holding the weapon near the firelight, he examined it closely…then threw it aside as something unclean. Staring long and pensively into the blaze, apparently oblivious of its existence, at times closing his eyes as one in mental anguish, Batiste finally arose and searched about for the weapon he had cast aside. Retrieving the toy-like dagger, he pressed on towards the pond where the stars danced in happy carefree reflections on the glassy surface. Feeling his way carefully stopping to wait while his vision became accustomed to the change from bright firelight to the darkness, he moved steadily towards the water, clutching tightly the little dagger. Upon reaching the pond, without hesitation, the half-breed tossed the weapon out into the lake where it landed with a noisy splash and sank to the bottom, disappearing amidst centuries of rotting branches, leaves and detritus.

Like one having completed the rites of an important ceremonial attendant upon the eternal welfare of a well beloved friend, the young man returned resolutely to his lonely camp. As the cluster of stars traveled on their way across the sky, he noted their progress impatiently. Having piled the boughs of his bed into a comfortable seat beside the fire, Batiste prepared to pass a sleepless night. Between intervals of replenishing the little blaze with added fuel from his diminishing pile, the young man sat in dreamy quiet far into the night as the dark encircled his camp, the dark of night where the trees stood still and silent. In vain, he tried to put away the thoughts that kept creeping back into his mind, thoughts of Paulette, the ragged half-breed, her frank expression of helpless resignation. He thought of how she had startled him with her friendly Ojibwe greeting. He could see her eyes slanting mischievously as though she knew the heartaches they would cast, like a spell, upon anyone who dared penetrate their depths.

Along in the forest, Batiste cast aside the inherited stoical characteristics of his Indian ancestors and allowed full play of his emotions over his face. A worried expression crept slowly into view as he recalled their first meeting. With the unstudied grace and charm born of the great Forest, she moved about with the ease of an unfrightened doe in its native haunts. Pain clearly reflected in memory as he recalled his first sharp disappointment in her marriage, she belonged to someone else.

So on into the dawn, scene after scene repeating unrelentingly over and over as the cluster of stars moved slowly on to the point in the night sky when he would be relieved…relieved of the torment, as sting that only he, a child of the forest could sense to its very depths. Shaking himself resolutely as a furred animal would to rid itself of water drenching its coat, the young man rose hurriedly as the last remnants of memory of the little blood stained dagger faded into the departing night. Stirring up the fire, he hastily extracted pieces of dried venison from his light pack. With a small square of maple sugar, he ate his morning meal slowly and thoughtfully, gone, however, for the time being, were the memories that tortured him the night through. Somewhere in the next few days, he didn't know how many, he would find some familiar landmark, some lake or hill, perhaps an old campsite with the wigwam pole framework of his own making. From then on, he smiled in happy anticipation, the path to home would be short, not over a week at most.

Testing his bow and sinew, he sighted along several arrows that he had weighted during the night to correct some little defect in their line. With his light blanket pack, its tumpline stretched across his deep chest, Batiste stepped out towards the summit of the low range of hills, on his second day towards home.

Chapter 14

Except for the sharply indented outlines of narrow snow paths, the forest rested quietly in the periodic attainment of its highest level of picturesque grandeur. From the very tips of the stately trees that covered the hilltops, along its slopes and flatland below, the first temporary covering of dazzling white lay unblemished and unmarred in the midday sun. Little drops of water dripping with maddening regularity from long glittering icicles, hanging inverted and unevenly from the roof eaves of Paulette's newly acquired trading post, added to the ever growing accumulations of little mound-like piles of ice along the snow-covered ground beneath. Bared patches of the bark covered roof lay glistening wet as the heat from the fireplace melted the freshly fallen snow. Within the large room or studio of the late Francois, artist, trader and raider, the heavy velvet drapes swayed uneasily to the alternate currents of warm and cold air, set in motion at each opening of the heavy log door. At the long shelved rustic table, set diagonally across the room, Paulette sat facing her friend and "man of affairs" Pascal. At oft recurring moments, requiring deep study and concentration with bowed head, the little man's flaming red square cut beard spread fan wise across his chest. With his feet dangling midway between the floor and table top, at frequent intervals, Pascal thumped with his heels, the especially constructed long legs of the stool that allowed him to sit with equal dignity above board.

"But why, Madam, would we make a list of all the goods we got, from Lake Superior?" As was his habit, Pascal rolled his head from side to side in utter perplexity.

"Because Pascal," the girl spoke slowly, there would be no misunderstanding, we are going to pay for them."

It was not so much the words as the note of finality they carried, that shocked the little fellow. The two braids of Paulette's black hair displayed with marked advantage the triple string of pearls that encircled gracefully the classic lines of her neck. The blue of her woolen gown, with the red velvet trim, matched the flowing folds the material draped down her back. The possessive instinct of the girl left whatever ideas of inferiority to her fellow human beings she may have entertained.

"But, Madam," he lingered on the word, while he searched his mind vainly for a convincing array of words "that has never been done before. Pay for the goods, after all the trouble we had to get them?"

The girl smiled. "The goods were stolen, Pascal. They must either be returned or paid for."

The little red man, in evident agitation, attempted to stand on his own two feet that his words might carry more weight. Forgetting, for the moment, his lack of stature, his chin bumped forcefully against the table top as he slid from his stool. Not being satisfied with the new position where his nose barely extended over the table, the little fellow hastily climbed back atop his stool.

Paulette sat unmoved by the antics of Pascal. Since early childhood, her grandmother had consistently preached against open ridicule or criticism of more unfortunate human beings. With surprising ease of controlled merriment, Paulette sat and patiently awaited Pascal's return to his accustomed place.

"Madam," the little fellow spluttered, while as much of his beard within range of his explosive words jerked outwardly in company with slightly exaggerated gestures "that was not stealing, the goods were taken in broad daylight."

"What is your idea of stealing, Pascal?" Paulette interrupted.

The little fellow regarded his mistress for some moments, his round blue eyes becoming rounder with each passing moment. Such ignorance of the "law of New France" and the world must be handled gently and with finesse. Spreading his hands before him in a helplessly pleading gesture, Pascal spoke softly, "Madam, if I were to sneak into my neighbors' cabin in the dark, while he was asleep and take that which belonged to him, that, my dear would be stealing. But, if I meet him out in the open and give him ample opportunity to defend what I want from him, if I were strong enough to take what I want fairly, that, my child, is not stealing, it is fair conquest."

Paulette shook her head slowly, "Where did you get such ideas, Pascal?"

Pascal snorted in disgust, "In France where we came from, in all the world, Paulette, in every country of the world, conquest is recognized as honest dealing with one's fellow man. Great Empires, with powerful armies, are built up that way. Are the returning soldiers accused of stealing something that must be paid for? No, no, Madam, the generals of old get gold medals pinned on their breasts. The soldiers are paraded before the cheering crowds as heroes, not as thieves in the night for they have taken entire kingdoms, its people and all their earthly possessions fairly in open combat. If governments can do these things, Madam, merely take possession without stealing, why should it be wrong for us?"

Pascal's argument had ceased to be amusing to the girl, and in its place there arose within her consciousness a sense of uncertainty, of doubt. If the little man was telling the truth, if what he said was an established custom of the entire world, if it was right to take what belonged to someone else without paying, No! She shook her head decisively… her people, the Indians, never did that, regardless of what their uncomplicated minds believed, they at least clearly defined the differences between what was theirs and what belonged to other members of the tribe. Continuing her reasoning out loud, Paulette said, "What you say may be true in France and the rest of the world, but not here, Pascal. Father Daniel, the missionary, didn't say it was right to steal or take what is not yours."

Pascal exploded with joy and thumped his heels vigorously against his high stool. "Oh! Ho!" he shouted, "So that is where you got that foolish idea about stealing. What does he know? Ask him sometime if what I said is not true. Ask him about the great armies of Europe that take…not steal, Madam, everything they want, if they are strong enough."

Paulette interrupted, "No, no, Pascal, we did not get those ideas from Father Daniel. For long…long before the Missionary came, the Indians had an established code of honesty, it was simple, yes…it did not change from day to day at the wish of individuals, but it was something good, something clean that every child learned and passed along to the next in line. It was honest. Surely, my friend, the civilized white man can do as well as the 'savage'." Paulette arose and with a somewhat disinterested air, her fingertips drumming lightly on the table top, said, "You make a list of everything Francois stole from Monsieur LaChance, get Batiste to help you, he can open the bales and count the items, while you…"

"But Madam," Pascal interrupted, "Batiste is not here. He left before the snow came."

The girl stood staring, seemingly unbelieving, "Where did he go? Has he gone to hunt?"

116

Pascal shook his head, "No, Madam, he took nothing with him, not even the uniform that Monsieur Francois gave him. He went away during the night with only the clothes he came with. Where he went…?" the little fellow raised his shoulders, mush as an eagle would its wings preparatory to instant flight. "No one knows, on the bare ground, he left no tracks. Even the Indians do not know."

The girl's fingers ceased their drumming on the tabletop and lay limp. "Get me the uniform he left, Pascal."

As the heavy door swung noisily on its creaking wooden hinges and its latch had dropped into place, the girl turned excitedly and strode towards the door that opened into the spacious store room…changing her mind and direction simultaneously, with a few quick deliberate steps, she stood before the veiled portrait on the wall above the bed. Not since the day Pascal had unveiled the painting, had Paulette looked up the "Lady in Mist." Somewhere in her mind, she entertained an idea, vague but real, that she could not bear again, a comparison of the lovely portrait and her own image in the mirrors. The mirrors alone, yes, for they soon established a place in her daily life. Only that morning, she had turned away from their reflection satisfied that she was beautiful. How she had emphasized the varied slant in her eyes and studied its effect on her appearance. Over and over, like one rehearsing a part in a play, she memorized many little movements of her slim graceful body in coordination with a mischievous twinkle of her eyes or a subtle shadow of a smile.

"Now after all this" she stood bewildered, "he was gone!" Shrugging her shoulders, she didn't care, after all he could come and go as he pleased, but he didn't tell her he was going. Why? Why? Thoroughly vexed with disappointment to the point of overflowing emotion and for want of something better upon which to relieve an ever mounting emotional strain, she grasped the hanging cords and jerked them into revealing the beauty that was hidden behind their gently swaying folds. With a feeling of misgiving, Paulette hesitated to glance upward at the painting and when she did, the smothered a cry of alarm, for in the painting, she recognized her own portrait. Rushing to the mirrors, she brushed aside their curtains and stood facing two identical reflections before her. As yet not completely satisfied that the painting was of her, she tore the necklace from her neck and loosening the fastening of her dress, she let the garment fall to the floor. Stepping back in alarm as the girl in the portrait actually smiled, then quickly recovering as she discovered that it was her own smile and not that of the painting, sobered the girl somewhat. Paulette studied and compared every line of her body with that of the girl in the painting, it matched with uncanny reality. Save for the excited heaving of her breast and the fiery glitter in her eyes, the illusion of two identical images would have been complete. So engrossed was the girl with the discovery that the painting was a portrait of herself, she was unaware of Pascal's entry. The little man, with the bundled uniform of Batiste securely tucked under his arm, stood as one transfixed, for, he too, saw the remarkable similarity.

Unaware, at first, that the curtains before the portrait had been drawn, the little red man was puzzled by the double reflection of one person. Not until the movement of Paulette quickly gathering her garment about her did he realize that one image was the painting and the other a reflection of Paulette.

After hastily refastening her dress Paulette drew the curtains before the mirror. In a tremulous voice, the girl asked, "Did you see what I think I saw, Pascal?"

The little fellow nodded and shaking his head vigorously in turn, stammered, "Yes...yes...No...no...I can't believe it."

"You can't believe what, Pascal?"

"How could Monsieur paint a picture of you without ever seeing you?" The little fellow walked thoughtfully to his high stool and climbed upon it. Resting his elbows up on the table, he buried his face in his cupped hands.

Paulette strode slowly to the portrait and stood before it. She was not afraid of it now. Somehow, it had suddenly become a part of her, it was herself. She gazed upon it and smiled. She was beautiful, beautiful beyond her wildest imagination. Slowly drawing the curtains back into place, she turned to the little man at the table. In a bewildered voice, like one groping in the fog, she said, "Pascal, my friend, tell me why, I mean, how could it be?" Walking steadily towards the table, she raised one hand to her head. "I…I don't understand, it is of me, yet impossible."

The little man raised his head slowly and spoke reminiscently to someone distantly apart. "Monsieur Francois painted the portrait of the girl he knew he must someday love. He believed that and nothing could shake his faith." Lowering his voice, he continued, "I remember the day when the painting was finished, I was somewhere about when I heard his loud shouts. Naturally, I came running as fast as my legs would carry me. There he stood before the easel, his brushes, paints and pallet scattered about the floor. "Look Pascal! I have created the girl I love, now I must find her, and when I do, I am going to marry her. Is she not beautiful, Mon Ami?"

"As simple as all that, Monsieur," I said.

"Just like that," he said. "Today she walks someplace, tomorrow I will find her."

I asked, "Among the Indians?"

He looked at me with such sorrowful eyes. "Pascal," he said "Why don't you let me dream, why awaken me? I am an artist…an artist, my friend. I live in a fantastic dream world, without which I would whither away and die." Then he turned again to his work and in a voice that I could barely hear, said, "She is beautiful and someday I will hold her in my arms, for she is mine. I know she lives."

At the simple narrative of the little man, Paulette felt she was being inexorably drawn nearer and nearer to the brink of the spirit world, a world where its inhabitants saw clearly into the future, as well as the past. Was Monsieur Francois an inhabitant of that world at times, did he come and go at will, as easily as he lay away or gathered his paints and brushes? She shuddered, the place suddenly felt like her grandfather's wigwam on the nights when he recounted his youthful visions and summoned the inhabitants of the spirit world to fulfill their promises.

Noticing the bundle of black clothing that Pascal had brought back from the warehouse, Paulette was instantly brought back to the present day realities.

"Are those Batiste's clothes?" she asked.

"Yes, Madam," said Pascal somewhat startled back into consciousness. "Yes, he left everything we gave him, except a bow and a few arrows. He had broken them shortly before he left."

"Didn't he take a blanket?"

"He had his own, one he brought with him."

Paulette bit her lip. "Who shall I get to help me in making a list of the trade goods?" asked Pascal.

"Anyone you wish, it doesn't matter now," answered the girl petulantly.

Chapter 15

Ankle deep in the brown, green, crimson and gold of fallen August leaves, Batiste, like one treading upon a fairyland magic carpet, moved slowly and deliberately as the changing color patterns at his every step rustled quietly. The sun, now midway to its noontime zenith, found the young man approaching the windswept dome-like crest of a hill that he intent upon reaching. Though the ascent was easy, with his jacket of ornamented caribou skin carefully placed over his blanket pack, his naked shoulders glistened with perspiration in the unseasonal heat of the sun. The whirring flight of a startled partridge broke the stillness as it sped in and out among the thinly spaced growth of short and thickly limbed jack pine. Batiste stopped and dropped his pack quickly. He barely had time to slip an arrow into place when a hawk, like a wolf following the scent of its quarry, came winging unhurriedly in pursuit of the bird. The young man smiled and his black eyes danced in respect and admiration of the small hunter. "Another time," he thought.

Reaching the dome shaped summit, the half-breed set his pack among the lacy green moss and star shaped gray lichen that adorned the many little depressions in the otherwise solid granite, and sat to rest on a boulder of convenient size and shape. Like the smoke from myriads of campfires in the cold of midwinter, a bluish haze hung suspended over the forest. Unlike the muffling blanket of winter snow, the still Autumn air carried and magnified echoes from range to range of low forested hills and valleys, from far beyond the range of human vision. The oft windswept bald top of the hill, upon which the young man rested, commanded a clear view in every direction, over the surrounding hills of lesser height. Far within the southern valley, the pecking of the great "redhead" in a quick staccato roll reverberated in an ever diminishing succession of echoes. Statue-like, in rapt contemplation of the scene spread before him, Batiste sat in reverent pause before the awe inspiring spectacle of nature at its best. Raising his eyes to where the far distant hills faded into the palling mist-like haze and broken bits of clouds rode the horizon like gulls on a summer sea, the young man without outward expression of inward emotion paid silent homage to the handiwork of an all wise creator.

Somewhere beyond, far beyond the last range of hills wreathed in the bluish purple haze, was the great Lake Superior. He had left home at the first spring breakup of the ice bound lake, and like a lonely pilgrim, set out to visit the waters that, as legend told, extended to the very edge of the earth. But seemingly, the spirits willed otherwise. Traveling from lonely Native habitations to little groups of wigwams clustered village fashion. He was guided eastward until past midsummer when the blueberries had withered or their vines. Beaching his light canoe at the trading post of Francois, making known his intent to visit Lake Superior, the trader received him with open arms. Francois invitingly informed him, "Soon they were starting on a little journey of adventure to the great lake. Surely you can come along." The trader appraisingly noted the young man's broad back and muscled shoulders. He could help a little on the way. In the meantime, he could hunt for the post. On the appointed day of departure, he was given a new outfit of clothing, black woolen britches with jacket to match, along flowing cape of the same material fastened at the throat with a plain silver clasp and a wide brimmed chapeau of beaver adored with a gracefully curving plume. The thin bladed knife lay snugly concealed beneath the fringes reaching well below his knees. He had noted, with some curiosity, that every member of the party, except, the four Indians was dressed alike. Only Monsieur Francois' clothes differed in color. His were blue.

Excited, he bent his paddle almost to the breaking point as he pushed the heavy freighter canoe through the water, satisfied that every lake and connecting portage brought him nearer to his goal. His efforts so willingly rendered, also admitted him into the sacred circle, occupied only by those capable of passing the test of brawn and endurance.

At last the day arrived when most of the great canoes would be cached and the party would go on over the long divide to the great lake. A quiet undercurrent of subdued excitement pervaded the little group, as each prepared, in his own way for whatever adventure lay in store. It was then that Monsieur the trader had called Batiste into his tent. He, of all the party, had been selected to remain behind to guard the canoes and the "little red man" who would be in charge.

"Oh, yes, Pascal would be in charge, but," the trader smiled knowingly, "someone would have to protect him and the cache in case of necessity, after all the canoes meant life or death to the party."

Batiste felt no little pride in the trust suddenly placed upon him and in assuming his responsibility completely forgot his pilgrimage. Strangely the young man felt no regret over the failure of his avowed purpose of seeing Lake Superior. He as a young man and there were many more summers to follow. He had killed a man, it was true…the memory of that episode in his young life carried no remorse. He had killed in defense of the defenseless young girl Paulette.

123

The slow hopping of a red squirrel among the dry leaves brought Batiste alertly to his feet. "Ah! So it's you," he said somewhat relieved. "You can make yourself sound as if you are something important." The little animal, in seeming displeasure at the thinly veiled insult, bounded up the trunk of a small pine to its first limb where it sat chattering noisily. "Well, well, don't get so upset about it, I was only fooling." Advancing cautiously and carefully almost to within arm's length of the furry little beast, the half-breed said, "Little squirrel, you who are wise and see into our lives, could you, would you tell me what it is that makes my heart so heavy? Ever since I found the little bloody knife, something in here, inside of me, like a heavy pack on a long portage, holds me back, holds me down until I feel I must stop and weep like a child. In my youth I dreamt ok you. You promised me that if ever I needed you or your wise counsel, I would need but call and you would answer."

The young man swayed a little as he spoke softly and with eyes closed, while the squirrel ran up to a higher limb from whence he eyed the stranger curiously. "Come to me when I, too, will travel in spirit. Come little squirrel and speak to me of the girl I cannot forget."

As Batiste swung his light pack over his back, he was startled into an extremely cautious attitude by the sound of voiced, muffled voices that were scarcely audible. Quickly stepping beside a great boulder that topped the dome of the hill, he stopped within its sheltering height. With hearing attuned to the slightest sound, he was soon aware of the direction from whence came the sounds. Carefully keeping within hiding from the approaching footsteps now plainly audible among the dry leaves, Batiste smiled as two Indians, one old and gray, another young and alert, approached."

"It was in the valley beyond this hill that I saw many deer," said the elder of the two.

Batiste stepped out from his hiding and laughingly confronted the two. "Do you expect them to be there yet?"

If either of the Natives were surprised, they showed not the slightest sign. The elder one smiled slightly. "If one is hungry enough, it is not difficult to expect anything."

"You are a stranger here?" the younger asked curiously.

"Yes," Batiste nodded. "I am traveling."

"You have come far?"

"Many suns," Batiste answered.

"You go far?" the young fellow was persistent.

Batiste shrugged, "I don't know, the winter is not far off and my home is many suns away." Before the young Indian could ask another question, the half-breed inquired quickly, "Where do you trade your furs, do you have far to go?"

The elderly man shook his head, and with a slight nod of his head with pursed lips toward the west, said, "Not far, on the next lake."

"Many white men there?"

The Indian held up the fingers of one hand, "Not more than that."

"Do they have much trade goods?"

"Very little," The Indian looked off towards the thickly gathering haze to the south and added, "They take away all the furs the Indians can get for what little they have. It is not good, they give us so little and take everything we get."

"Are there many of you?"

"Yes, yes, very many, like the leaves on a small tree."

Batiste studied for a moment, then said, "So many of you and only a few of them, is there no one among your people to teach the white men that this land and the game belongs to the Indian? They are only visitors here, not the chiefs of our people."

125

The Indian smiled knowingly and said more seriously, "They would have all died before the last snows came, but the 'Man in black', who comes by here often, tells us it will not please the Great Spirit if we kill other men."

"Father Daniels," thought Batiste and asked, "Has the good Father Daniels been here?"

The Indians looked up in surprise. "You know him? He is at the post now. We are going there when the sun comes again. That is the day when we do not work, if we are lucky and get enough game today."

Batiste noted the sun's position, turned and remarked, "The sun's trail gets shorter every day. I will see you at the traders when the light comes again."

"You will not stop there for the night?"

"I am not sure, maybe many nights," said Batiste as he turned to leave.

"Be careful and watch the white men closely, they are not good and drink much of the water that makes them crazy."

"I will be very careful," laughed the half-breed as he started off over the boulder strewn granite dome of the hill.

As Batiste approached the little clearing with its usual number of scattered low log cabins, he stopped and standing partly concealed by a pine tree and several clusters of short shrubs, he studied the scene before him. With the practiced eye of an expert hunter, the young man searched every visible portion of the place for anything that could shed some light on its occupants. The trading center or post, he guessed, was the long building located in the center of the clearing. The half dozen smaller flat roofed cabins would be the homes of the "runners" or "Courier du Bois". In the distance beyond the clearing, with its cluster of buildings and partly concealed by the dense forest growth of pine and birch, another log building while small stood much taller, its log walls in contrast to the others of the place were smoothly and carefully stripped of their bark covering.

Batiste stood puzzled, for at best the buildings of all outlying trading posts were but hastily constructed makeshift affairs for temporary use. The place seemed deserted, except for the occasional squeak of a wooden door hinge or the yelp of a cur dog that was rudely kicked off the little narrow path winding torturously between each of the buildings. The setting was more that of a cemetery, than a real live trading post. As the young man stood statue-like, his black eyes flashing eagerly in search of at least one of the inhabitants of this ghostly place, he began to sense a feeling ok nervous solitude. On the verge of turning and continuing on his way over the hills and homeward when a red squirrel ran up the trunk of a tree, directly in the path he must take to carry out his intention, and chattered madly, its little eyes blazing furiously. "Now what's wrong with you Mon Ami?" he asked. It was seldom that the young man gave voice to his thoughts in French when he spoke to the wild things of the forest. First and above all else, he was a Native and as such adhered religiously to the belief of his Indian ancestors that he was but another of the forms of life as created by the Great Spirit and to them he spoke in the common tongue. The squirrel had ceased its wild chattering upon being addressed in a foreign tongue. Batiste laughed and spoke in Ojibwe, "So you don't understand and you want me to stay? All right, I'll stay but remember, if I lose my skin, it will be your fault." The little animal scampered up to the very tip of a long branch, where it sat up, swaying precariously; its little paws held up in defiance of the laws of gravity. "So you have been here a long time and still have your skin…but I make a much better and larger target than you." With the agility and speed of light rays from a flambeau, the little animal leaped nimbly from branch to branch until it disappeared from sight among the broad palm-like boughs somewhere near the treetops. "So I shouldn't stay too long, all right, tomorrow I'll be on my way." The sound of a short muffled chatter somewhere high up amidst the boughs accompanied the young man as he turned and resolutely strode into the clearing.

Past an occasional skeleton-like upright frame of an abandoned wigwam or the bent branches that once held in place the bark covering of a deserted "Sha-ban-do-wan" or lodge, Batiste strode with quiet deliberate steps. His knife hilt within easy reach of either hand, he carried his bow and three flint-tipped feathered arrows lightly and with a natural assurance that, given an even break, the half-breed feared no man. With more curiosity than misgiving, Batiste swung open the heavy door to the store room and entered. Light filtering through the small square of white cloth, serving as a window, added to the gloomy atmosphere of the place.

It was some moments before the lone occupant had aroused himself sufficiently from a dep slumber to notice his visitor. From amidst a pile of trade goods, such as blankets, bolts of cloth and small bales of various items placed conveniently to form a nest-like couch, a black bearded man aroused himself sufficiently to open wide a pair of small round blue eyes to gaze upon, and not without suspicion, the tall muscular young man who stood before him.

"Where did you come from?" the trader attempted to say in Ojibwe.

Tempted, for a moment, to carry on the conversation in his Native tongue, but seeing the man's difficulty in expressing the simplest question, Batiste asked instead, "Vous parley Francais, Monsieur? Je vou comprende pas."

The trader laughed and replied, "You look more like a savage than a Frenchman."

Again the young man was sorely tempted to reply, "For which I thank the Creator,", but said instead, "I am part Indian."

"Oh, a half-breed, there will be many like you some day after the French are gone from here."

Batiste raised his eyes in surprise and asked, "Are they going?"

"I am sure they must someday. A white man cannot live like a savage for very long."

Batiste nodded vigorously, "I understand, Monsieur, neither can a savage live like a white man. This is the Indian's home so the white man must leave…is that what you mean?"

"No! Young man…That is not what I mean. A white man goes anywhere he wishes and stays as long as he likes. If this forest was a fit place for us to live, the Indian would have to go."

"Where?" asked Batiste simply?

The Frenchman shrugged his shoulders impatiently, "I don't know or don't care…die I suppose."

The conversation was interrupted by the entry of another black bearded Frenchman. This one was obviously under the playful influence of strong drink, "Well, well, well," he said thickly, advancing up to Batiste, "look who is here…and see the nice black hair the boy's got. I like nice long black hair too. Give me one of those nice braids, eh, young man?"

Roughly grasping one of the half-breed's braids, he drew his knife. About the time he got the knife into position to cut the hair, he sensed a burning sensation, like the application of a hot fagot in the region of his stomach. The man's knife stopped in midair as the young man's voice, crisp and cool, penetrated his muddled understanding. "Go ahead, your move, we play for keeps."

The Frenchman glanced quickly towards that peculiar feeling in the region of his belt line, and paled at the sight of the knife that had slit his buckskin garment and penetrated enough of his skin to create a very uncomfortable feeling. The knuckles of the hand that held the knife hilt were white and bloodless. The sight of a small trickle of his own blood creeping along the broad flat blade towards its hilt caused the fellow to sway slightly.

"Well, why don't you move, it's your turn."

The knife tip was getting hot. The drunken Frenchman returned his knife to his belt, released Batiste's braid and turned away, sober. The door leading into the living quarters, swung heavily into place behind him.

"You are quick with the knife, Monsieur." The voice was that of the trader who had come from back of his trading table of roughly hewn plank.

"I manage to keep alive…and keep my scalp," Batiste added with a smile.

"You are lucky, young man. Henri is very bad when he is drinking. I was afraid for you."

Batiste's lip curled showing his contempt. "Only a bluff, Monsieur, but I wasn't bluffing. I was ready to slit him open from end to end."

"But, be careful young man, watch out for him" the Trader warned.

"Tell him that, Monsieur, tell him also to step lightly on the thin crust that separates him from hell."

"For a young, man you are sure of yourself," continued the trader as he walked around the half-breed and noted, in open admiration, the young man's muscled shoulders and back. "How would you like to join us, we could use an intelligent young man like you. You speak the Native language?"

"If I did, what would I have to do?" inquired Batiste

The trader replied, "Oh-h, there is much to do around a place like this."

"But, you have no trade goods, and there are too many of you already," noted Batiste.

"True, we do not have much now, but we will have plenty next summer."

"When the other traders get back from Lake Superior?" asked Batiste.

"You are intelligent, something unusual for a Native."

Batiste's eyes flashed dangerously and he remained silent. The trader continued, "Where do you come from?"

"From the east, I was with Francois' trading post."

The trader frowned and regarded Batiste with narrowed eyes, "Far from here?"

"Ten days overland."

"Why didn't you use a canoe?" questioned the trader.

"I do not have a canoe. I am on my way to my home to the west."

The trader nodded slowly, "So...does Monsieur Francois have much goods?"

"Yes, we just landed twenty big canoe loads a few days before I left."

The trader kept up a steady drumming on the table top with the tips of his fingers. "We have a little account to settle with Monsieur Francois. Two years ago he was here and about cleaned us out, a very clever man."

Batiste smiled, "And why is it you want me to join you?"

"Yes, we will need about ten more like you, could you find them for us?"

The young man frowned and pensively studied the embroidery on his moccasins, in a flash, his mind traveled back to Paulette's post where he visualized a number of freshly covered shallow graves...but suppose that Paulette was…No…No!. Looking up quickly at the bewhiskered man, said, "I alone will go with you, in the spring."

"But we want the goods now."

"Too late, you couldn't possibly get there and back before freeze up, some of the smaller shallow lakes are frozen over now, and would you do with the goods anyway?" asked Batiste.

"Trade them for furs, of course" the trader replied.

"Clever white men," Batiste mused partly to himself "Why bother with the goods when you can get the furs?"

The trader's eyes opened wide, "I never thought of that. Francois takes our goods, trades them for furs, then we get the furs…good…good! How many men does he have?"

"Twenty two Frenchmen and as many Indian scouts."

The trader's expression clouded as he shook his head slowly "Too many, I am afraid too many. We have one chance, not much, but still a chance."

"What is that?" asked Batiste with suppressed merriment over the effects of his slight exaggeration.

The trader walked to the heavy door and swung it open and motioned to the young man to follow him. "See that new building over there?" he said pointing to the structure that had puzzled the half-breed earlier in the day. "That, young man, is a church, and the cabin, you see beyond it, is where the priest lives.

Batiste admired the clean buildings standing serenely amidst the tall pines. Not far beyond the glassy surface of the lake, reflected the rays of the sun nearing the western horizon.

"But what has that to do with…?"

The trader interrupted smiling. "When one does not have muscle enough, then the brain must take its place. When we visit Monsieur Francois, mon Ami, we will take the priest with us." Batiste frowned deeply, he knew the good Father Daniels…surely. "Don't make that mistake, young man," said the trader quickly, "what Pere Daniels does not know, will do no harm, he is getting old and we will do all we can to help him in his work, especially among the savages at Monsieur Francois' trading post. When the time comes, we will strike, from the inside." So that was it, those renegades would use the good Father's cassock to screen their thievery. Batiste felt a sudden desire to bury his knife deep into the grinning man. The voice beside him continued to speak. "We went to much trouble and hard work in preparing our plans."

"You built the church for no other reason then?"

The trader nodded. "The good Father needed it. We must get something back for our trouble."

"Yes, yes," Batiste agreed. "I think it is a good idea to take the good Father along, he can say the last rites at your graveside."

The trader started "You think that our plan might fail?"

Batiste shrugged his broad shoulders and raised his eyebrows. "I don't know, but take the priest along anyway. One never knows when he will be needed. I remember hearing him say that we go through life without needing him, not until something happens to cut off our stay on earth, then we want him. By all means take him along. I shall accompany you. I will be here at the first breakup of the spring."

"That is good, and you will have your companions?"

"No, I shall come alone."

The sounds of raucous laughter at the completion of snatches of song coming from within the living quarter of the building, reached the two men. With a slight jerk of his head towards the origin of sounds, Batiste said, "In the meantime, tie up your dogs, you may lose them."

Chapter 16

Autumn days were busy days for Paulette and her little band. With her grandparents well housed in one of the many log cabins, the girl settled into the routine activity of the post. Families from far and near arrived hourly for their usual allotment of trade goods. During the autumn season, only essential goods were given out on credit. Not until spring were the Indians allowed to spend small balances for trinkets, after all the debts were paid. Ever mindful of their poverty stricken days at Lake Superior, Paulette searched every habitation within a day's travel by canoe for the old and helpless. Like a ministering angel, she sought out the aged and orphaned, sending them on to the post for clothing that would protect them against the ravages of the approaching winter.

It was on the return of one of her many errands of mercy, that Pascal approached the girl. "But Madam, we cannot go on giving goods to people who we know can never pay for them, the helplessly old, crippled and very young, that is not good business, it is"

Paulette held up one hand, and the little man, across the long table, sitting atop his high stool glanced uneasily at his Mistress. The girl spoke slowly as though groping for words to express an idea but vaguely formed. "I agree with you, Pascal. One cannot stay in business long if we give away the stock we have, and, and, when we are through, the Natives will also lose, including the old and sick. Surely there must be some way to help them and stay in the trade." The girl turned slightly and glanced up at the portrait that seemed to smile down upon her. "You told me once, Mon Ami, that in the France you came from, it was not wrong to take things not yours if taken by force, if that force is represented by a King or someone like, let us say, anyone with authority whose orders must be obeyed...is that not right?"

Pascal nodded vigorously, the tips of his long beard spreading out in rapid succession over the table top at each nod. "Yes, Madam, that is the custom and a very good custom it is too."

"All right then. Now I, Paulette, am the power or force here. I believe that the strong and able should help care for the less fortunate of the tribe, so you will take the accounts of those unable to pay and divide them equally among those that are. There are many among our Indians who do little else through the summer than boast of being the mighty hunters, to them will be added the bigger share. Those are my orders, Pascal. You will see that they are carried out...and Pascal, we will keep this to ourselves. If our people knew, there are many who might not understand and think that we are not honest."

"God bless you, Madam, I was afraid you were giving away too much...Ah, but now we shall do well." With that, the little fellow slid off his stool and ran to the heavy door leading to the store where the latch was built low for his convenience.

Paulette sat in deep meditation for some moments. "I hope I am not doing wrong," she mused, "but there is no other way, the strong must care for the weak, the young for the aged. Creator, forgive me if I am wrong!"

After replenishing the fire in her fireplace and hanging a kettle of water to warm, she passed out of the building and on towards the cabin occupied by her grandparents. Much to her surprise, there stood, not far from the cabin, a new wigwam, its borrowed pole frame blackened in marked contrast to the new covering. "Must be a newcomer," she thought entering the abode. Paulette stopped, in amazement, at the curtained entrance, and laughed at her old grandparents seated in happy contentment beside the little fire that crackled merrily beneath the funneled opening at its peak. Paulette looked around in pretended amazement. "What is all this?" she inquired mischievously, "Why have you moved in here, don't you like the log cabin?"

"Your grandmother has not slept one night since we camped beneath those heavy logs. She awakens me every night to go out and see if it is still safe, if the logs are still in place. We could not stand it any longer, so I borrowed this wigwam from some people who are moving away."

Paulette looked about the circular abode and tears filled her eyes as happy memories of her childhood flashed before her. "Do you mind if I come and sleep here too, maybe just for tonight?"

The old couple exchanged happy glances. Paulette was still their grandchild, the happy carefree little girl whose toy bark canoes, little bows and arrows, embroidered moccasins, tasseled snowshoes, cold numbed fingers and toes had marked each passing year and filled the hollow fragments of their waning lives.

****

With the autumn trade taken care of, it was time to think of approaching winter, when the ice would cover the lakes and the deep snows come, on the cold wind from the land of Kee-way-din. Soon the canoes would be cached for the winter…and the flat traineau or toboggan, its end rolled like the carved head of a violin, taken down, its rawhide lacing renewed and the bottom scraped and polished. Half-wild dogs must be caught and hobbled or tied securely until tamed enough to do their share of the winter's work. Boys and girls eagerly

136

awaiting the time when preparations of the grownups would be completed and they, in turn, could command, through incessant demands, enough attention for renewed pleas for that new pair of snowshoes or a play toboggan. Fortunate, indeed, were those with grandparents. Grandfather could always be counted upon to make the frames, while grandmother lovingly prepared the rawhide filling and laced the webbed shoes so vitally important in the lives of those who would move about in the land of snow.

At the post, Paulette's hunters and "Courier du Bois" or runners infused with renewed energy viewed with some misgiving the unseasonal warmth of the sun and winds. Native wives of the French, caught in the activity of the season, busily tanned caribou and deer skins as each cache, placed high out of the reach of hungry dogs, was piled with dried meat, fish and makuks of wild rice and blueberries. Every addition to the stored food and clothing supply, brought a sigh of relief and satisfaction to the Native and French alike, for each knew what to expect of a merciless winter that gave no quarter. Mothers with infants searched the highland spruce swamps for the long silky burr-less moss and gathered it in great piles on windfalls high above the ground, necessary for its absorbent properties to use as diapers to swaddle their young offspring.

Paulette, infused with the joy of living and happy in the knowledge that all of the Natives were cared for, excitedly swung open the heavy door to the store or trading room where Pascal sat high above the floor on his stool with its attached steps like the rungs of a ladder. Turning from his accounting records, he was met with, "How many dogs do we have, Pascal?"

The question, unexpected, carried the implication of an impending disturbance in the quiet and peace of the present atmosphere. The little man regarded his mistress with a mixture of alarm and curiosity. Paulette's sudden and impulsive ideas of late, kept the little red man guessing as to what was coming next. With a view to softening what, he was sure, was band news, he asked as casually as the tension of the moment would permit, "Why does Madam ask?"

"It is not why do I ask, Monsieur, but how many do we have…and where are they?"

"I should say about forty, they are kept in a stockade near one of the lake just north of here."

"Do we have any young dogs…say…old enough to break to harness now?"

"Yes, I was to see them a short time ago. We have several litters who will see their second winter."

"Good," the girl's eyes shone in a happy anticipation that added to Pascal's apprehension. "Get me four of the biggest unbroken pups…have the men pick them out from the best litter."

As was his custom, when under a strain of emotion, Pascal jumped from his stool and immediately climbed back again from where he proceeded to strenuously voice his disapproval. "Madam, those dogs are wild vicious brutes, and have to be clubbed into submission…can you do that?"

Much to his dismay, Pascal noted that Paulette had relaxed into a position with her eyes partly closed. That meant, insofar as she was concerned, the incident was closed. "I don't think that will be necessary, Monsieur." Coming a step nearer and lowering her voice, the girl spoke reminiscently, "Ever since my two little fists were big enough to close over a dog's tail or I could reach high enough to bite its ears, I've had and trained many kinds of dogs both wild and tame. I do not like tame dogs, perhaps, I don't know, maybe because half of my blood is that of wild "savage" ancestors that I love the wild things of the earth. Please Pascal, get me the four of the wildest, biggest, most savage young dogs we have and chain each one to a tree near my back door."

"Shall I have one of the Indians come and train them?"

"No! No! Pascal, please, Monsieur, they will be my dogs and no one else must go near them. I selected one of the traineau with the laced leather sides from the warehouse and four harnesses. You will set them aside. No one else must take them?

"Madam's wishes will be carried out," The little fellow hesitated and the girl interrupted him, "You wish to say something else, Mon Ami?"

The little man beamed joyfully, it was not often she addressed him as "my friend". "Please, Madam, don't do this wild thing, I fear you do not know what you are doing. I know these wild dogs, they are worse than wolves. They are savage and cannot be trusted."

"I am glad you can recommend them so highly, Monsieur. Now, I know I want them. Get them here as soon as you can, the lakes will soon freeze over and I will need them, and please don't worry. I think I know what I am doing, after all, I am Lake Superior Ojibwe."

139

Chapter 17

Far into the night, the two men sat beside the small fireplace while fitful flames darting into the smoke opening made grotesque shadows over the clean white walls of the cabin in their passing. Father Daniels shifted his position uneasily on the squared end of a log originally meant for firewood. Batiste reclining lazily on a many colored mat of cedar bark, pilfered for the occasion from a cache left by some Indian family, sat up quickly. "But you cannot winter here, Mon Pere. Dry firewood is scarce and what will you do for food?"

The white haired missionary turned his head towards the young man with some effort, he could not chance removing his elbow from the little table, that, like a carpenter's brace, held him upright on his precarious seat. The missionary spoke reminiscently, "I came to this country with some of the first white traders, I was a young man then and set about my work with an absolute faith in divine guidance and protection. In the years that followed, I have grown old, my hair is white. I am getting feeble and as it must to all men, soon I will, in God's good time, pass on from this life. Now as I live from day to day, I have but one fear and that is, in my old age I may forget to beg daily for grace to maintain, unshadowed and unshaken, that faith in God and his divine protection. True, I have been severely tried at times," here the kindly old man drew from his sash the black ebony cross with its silver figure of his Master and continued, "one cannot be unmindful, Batiste, of that fateful day when the Son of God from the summit of Calvary's hill cried out in bitter anguish, 'Father, why hast thou forsaken me?'" Fondling the little crucifix tenderly in his wrinkled hands, he returned the cherished emblem to its accustomed place. "While it is true I am getting old, I am still active. I can get wood enough and as for food, well, I must admit it is more of a problem." He smiled, and for a moment with enjoyment over some secret accomplishment. "I have not lived all these years among the Natives without learning some of the tricks of living." Arising from his wobbly seat, that immediately fell away and rolled over the uneven earth floor to the opposite wall, he opened a black brass bound box and extracted a carefully wrapped ball of rabbit snares, lengths of twisted strands of nettle thread and, lest an unfortunate bunny decide on eating the cause of his demise, plentifully covered with distasteful pitch from the balsam tree. Batiste laughed outright. A look of pained uncertainty clouded the good Father's countenance. "Why do you laugh, Batiste? What is wrong?"

"Oh, nothing, nothing at all Father," the young man quickly assured the priest. "It just struck me as being rather funny, you snaring rabbits."

"Is that all? For a moment I was slightly worried."

"Sitting beside your campfire knowing that your next meal depends of when that rabbit makes up its mind to stick its neck in your snare, is not nearly as funny as it might seem."

Batiste had quickly lapsed into a more serious mood. "Forgive me, Father. I understand it all too well, as does everyone who tries to live in the wilderness. Is that the only trick you acquired?"

"Oh, no, I also have some plain uncoated snares for catching the spruce hen and I have had many, many times sat beside a rocky cave until the porcupine decided to come out."

"Do you snare those too, Father?"

"No, Batiste, I have had to employ other means to kill them."

"But, you can snare them."

"I didn't know that, I guess one is never too old to learn."

"Did you ever get any big game, Father, such as a deer or caribou?"

"Only once, that was a long time ago when I first came. You see, Father Moran was sent further west when I was to take his place here. Before he left, however, we traveled together for one summer, to acquaint me with the country and the language. Father Moran thought he was woodsman enough to dispense with a guide, so we started out alone. Everything went well enough, until we reached the sugar bush country along the divide near Lake Superior when we ran completely out of food. Search as we would, there was none to be had and no Natives to help us, for it was long past sugar making time and they had returned to Lake Superior, a good four days travel away."

A light breeze from the west that blew the ragged blanket door curtain inward, fanned the little fire into a whirling cloud of acrid smoke and filled the cabin with a thick haze. "I intended to weight the door down today. I must remember to do that tomorrow."

"Not tomorrow, Father," admonished Batiste as he returned to his mat after piling some firewood on the lower edge of the offending blanket, "tomorrow is Sunday."

"Yes, yes, for the moment I had forgotten. As I was saying, Father Moran and I searched the countryside for partridge and rabbits. We set out several snares in the little rabbit trails deeply indented in swamp moss. With each one of our snares, something always went wrong. Either the rabbit traveled other paths or jumped over or crawled under them. Father Moran, having boasted so much about his ability to travel and procure food unaided, was, to say the least, on trial with our lives as the stakes. We found may caches of sugar making equipment, stacks of 'akikozens' or bark containers for catching the sap from the sugar maple, complete lodges carefully dismantled and laid away for future use but nothing that could help us get food. It was while following a well-worn deer path that I nearly fell into a deep pit. If the little animals had not worn their trail around it, I surely would have tumbled headlong into it. Being a newcomer, I was attracted by the piles of sand and gravel t either side of what looked to me like a huge grave, perhaps the length of a small canoe and the width of a paddle length. After Father Moran had thoughtfully encircled the pit at least twice, he said, 'Father, this is the answer to our prayers, this is a pit dug by the Indians for catching deer.'" The good Father had retrieved his log and resumed his seat, while the half-breed added fresh fuel to their fire. "I looked down into the thing and I am sure it was the depth of twice the height of a tall man."

"How," I asked, "do you propose getting the animal out if we do get one, and suppose a bear tumbles in instead of a deer?"

Father Moran looked puzzled, for a moment then replied, "It is not a question of getting it out, Father, but how can we get it in? As to Mr. Bear, I am sure if we give him a little, very little assistance, he will gladly climb out of his own accord."

"I have often and still do, admire Father Moran for his resourcefulness, he was a very observing man, for, when he had the pit covered it was so deceivingly clever, that any animal might have walked into it. First he placed small rotted poles across the top of the pit, then a light covering of boughs. Over the boughs, we carried dried leaves and earth. To make it all the more realistic, Father Moran dug up hoof prints from the well beaten deer path and placed them carefully over the pit until the whole thing looked as if the unbroken path led right over the pit. That night, we retired to our shelter full of hope and not much of anything else." Batiste had sat up and with eyes dancing with merriment, restrained with some difficulty his ever mounting curiosity. The good Father turned and gazed pensively into the fire. "I don't recall when we did get to sleep that night, but it seems like I had slept but a few minutes when I was rudely awakened by Father Moran. With suppressed excitement that, I am sure he was having a hard time to control, he said, 'Come! Come! Father we got one!' Got what Father? I wasn't quite fully awakened and in my short sleep I had completely forgotten about the deer pit."

'A deer...A deer!' he continued in a loud whisper, 'We got one, come get up.'

When consciousness fully returned, I must say that I was as excited as he was. Our two days without food had left us somewhat weakened, but that was forgotten in the rush to get to our trap. Sure enough, there was a big hole in the covering of the pit where the animal had fallen through. The as we stood, each with his own thoughts, beside the grave-like pit the one question, I am sure, occupied both our minds. 'What next? How are we going to get the animal out?' At last, after what seemed hours, Father Moran broke the silence and in a somewhat subdued tone, said, 'We got it in, now...' his voice died away, but I understood fully.

'You are the woodsman, Father,' I said, 'surely you can draw on your experience to solve this problem.' He glanced at me rather quickly with a meaningful expression that made me feel that I'd better use tact rather than ridicule...After all, he was my superior and he could order me to get that thing out of there. The first flush of excitement having quickly subside, we were left calm and collected enough to plan a course of action. First we would uncover the pit, but it was still too dark to see what we had captured, so we returned to our camp for an ax, knife and tumpline. In the meantime, I had given up

getting back through the curtained doorway, the blanket was ragged and persisted in catching the sharply protruding ends of the wood, he said, "I have decided to remain here for a few days, Father, and gather some firewood for you, and you could use some meat too."

"But, Batiste, you have a long way to go, snow will soon be here and you have no snowshoes."

The young man laughed "If you can live here alone, Father, I shouldn't have too much trouble, I am at home wherever I build my campfire, it takes only a day to make a pair of snowshoes."

"You know, Batiste, now that I have arrived at a time in life when I can look back over the years that stretch out like a beaten path through the forest, I sometimes wish that I had acquired a little more knowledge in the art of living in the wilderness. You people are so independent, you, as you say, are at home wherever you are, with us who have come so far from another part of the world, are interdependent and cannot live except through the activity of units bound into large groups. Some make clothing, while others specialize in food and other necessities that go to provide for the mass as a whole. But out here, it matters not whether a family lives by itself, cut off from other families or whether it is one of several families grouped in a village. They continue to live individually independent of others of the tribe. I noticed that particularly in their pagan beliefs, their religion is individual, not collective. Each man or woman earns for themselves alone the right to call upon the Spirit world and when that person dies, the knowledge or claims to certain prerogatives end and are not passed on to the living."

The young man nodded understandingly, "Father, tell which way of life, since they are so different, do you prefer?"

The priest smiled, "There is no choice, Batiste, if man is to improve his station in life, his mode of living, his thinking, that can only be brought about through group or mass existence, the transfer of knowledge acquired by a few to the many, among rising generations, but that is no farther than the span of an individual life, it leaves nothing that this offspring do not know or upon which succeeding generations can build for the future knowledge of mankind."

"I think I understand, Father, though sometimes it is difficult for an Indian to grasp the reasons the white man advance for his strange actions. When I was at a trading post in the east, I heard much talk about it being right to raid other posts. I heard white men tell of great armies of soldiers that raided countries and captured entire nations, they say that is not wrong, but merely fair conquest. They take whatever they want from one another because they are stronger, and they are doing the same thing in this country. I don't understand that, Father, it is not what you tell the Indians."

The Missionary had turned to face the square of white cloth pegged securely into an opening in the wall, the flames from the fire revealed a pained expression. "The right or wrong in human behavior, my son, is never determined by the actions of one's neighbors. The laws of God apply equally to the strong and the weak, the man alone in the wilderness and immense armies of Europe. There is no distinction, implied or otherwise, in the commandments, 'Thou shalt not steal, thou shalt not covet thy neighbor's goods." It is true that earthly heroes have their names blazoned across the pages of history for no other reason than that they were successful in the looting and pillaging of weaker states. One wonders to what degree of importance the angels have assigned them in the book of eternity, the only record that determines the ultimate fate of each individual."

It was not often that the two men lapsed into meditative silence. At intervals, however, they sat each with their own thoughts. From his position on the ground, Batiste gazed with mixed admiration and a curious urge to know what passed beneath the classic lines of the good Father's forehead. To the half-breed, he seemed like one so near, yet alone and apart, far beyond the bewildered circle of humanity. It was hard to collect one's thoughts and arrange them in orderly sequence concerning the good man. His clear blue eyes, set well apart, looked out upon the world with a depth of feeling, unlike the Native, but reflected his every heart felt emotion for the wayward and the good. There were times, however, as now when an expression of pain mingled with the swiftly darting shadows cast by the flames of the fireplace, over his sallow and thinly wrinkled features. Often, while on some lonely trek in the great forest or beside a cheery campfire, the half-breed visualized the good Father as standing alone, with eyes shaded against the glare of worldly pleasures and superstitions, midway along a straight forest path. Oblivious of his immediate surroundings, his gaze fixed at one of either end, the one the beginning, the other the conclusion, the accomplishment of his life's self-imposed task. And now, after all the years spent in a labor of love, the renegade French traders would use him as a shield to cover the crime of thievery. They would break his heart and hasten his end. The young man involuntarily reached for his knife, it would be so easy to pick them off one by one as the moved about the post. No! That would not do, the good Father was safe until spring and he would be here. They would never use the good man for a decoy, not so long as his good right arm lasted.

While thus occupied with his plans, Batiste detected the sound of approaching footsteps. Arising to his feet as nonchalantly as possible, yet moving surprisingly quickly, the young man stepped to the corner of the cabin occupied by the priest's bed or bunk of saplings covered with boughs and moss. Partly concealed by the shadow cast by Father Daniels' position near the fire, the half-breed waited. With the hilt of his knife protruding from beneath his sash and within easy reach, Batiste noted that he had not aroused the Missionary's suspicions. Soon the blanket curtain covering the doorway was thrust aside and Monsieur La Duc, the trader, entered.

149

"I did not know that our young friend, the half-breed, was still here," he said in a vain attempt to appear surprised.

"Baptiste has very kindly offered to gather some wood for me in the next few days."

"If Monsieur will let me use one of his large canoes," added Batiste.

"By all means, young man, I shall send one of my men along to assist."

Batiste shook his head rather decisively and smiled, "I always work alone, Monsieur, and your men are busy."

"You are right, and we will be one less tomorrow."

"Yes?" Father Daniels quickly inquired.

"Henri had an accident, he has swollen around his belly, he was slightly wounded somehow."

Batiste's eyes narrowed. Monsieur La Duc was a little too casual. The French were rather easily excited in matters of that kind.

"I shall come and see him at once," said the priest arising.

"No, no, Father, he is not that sick, tomorrow perhaps, that will be time enough."

"But, are you sure, Monsieur?"

"Yes, I am sure, Father."

Batiste eyed the trader closely. The man was lying. The story about Henri being sick was only a cover, at least not that sick. "I was telling Father Daniels that I shall be here in the spring to accompany you, to Lake Superior if necessary. If I am not here on time, you will wait for me...yes?" Batiste groped for a way out.

"Yes, yes, my friend, we will not leave without you. I am glad you have not changed your mind as so many young people do."

"Do not fear, Monsieur, I shall not change my mind, nothing but death itself could stop me. I intend to see Lake Superior next summer."

"Then I shall sleep better tonight, without your assistance, our venture might have failed."

"I shall sleep well, too, Monsieur, now that we understand each other," said the young man knowingly. So that was it, mused Batiste.

"Now I shall bid you Bonsoir, Mon Pere…Bonsoir Batiste." The blanket door dropped back into place and billowed slightly inward.

"He said Henri was wounded," said the priest.

"Bruised, perhaps, that happens often," replied the young man as he turned his head away. "Or perhaps he drank too much. They were all talking quite loud when I came by there."

Father Daniels shook his head sadly and said, "Too bad, too bad, and they are such good men, but they will drink too much at times. Henri is a fine fellow when sober."

Chapter 18

Cold…bitter cold, floating in from the north on a breeze that, scarcely moved the great palm-like frozen branches of the pine, held the naked limbs of the birch and maple pointing stiffly upward. Beneath the blue sky an occasional grayish mist moved lazily southward with its burden of snow.

The flat traineau, or toboggan, ground the snow, along the frozen trail, into queer little screeching sounds as the four wolfish dogs strained at their traces. At a sharp command from the lone rider, the brutes came to a sudden halt and immediately dropped to the trail and proceeded, with sharp teeth, to tear off little balls of snow and ice from between hairy toes. The lone traveler completely wrapped in a fur trimmed garment of grayish woolen material extending well below the knee, its attached hood of the same material, more luxuriously trimmed with flowing fox tails, hid the owner's face with the exception of an occasional gleam of one eye. The girl, Paulette, advanced quickly to the lead dog, who, immediately sprang to his feet and nuzzled her outstretched hand affectionately.

"Down, Pierre, down, take good care of your feet, we have a long way to go." The animal, however, remained standing unmindful of the girl's admonition. "Come…come let me look at those paws." So saying, she picked up each one of the animal's feet and examined them carefully, extracting little bits of accumulated ice from deep within the hairy foot pads. Pierre shook himself thoroughly and proceeded to examine, minutely, the distant shoreline of the lake, holding its head high and sniffing the air. "All right, Kai-aushk, your next, let me see those paws." Kai-aushk, a beautiful animal, its neck and shoulders encircled by a snow white band bared its fangs and growled throatily. "Bi-zaan, be quiet, you growl just to hear yourself making a noise, up with that paw."

Kai-aushk, or the "gull", shut up and licked the girl's hand as she patted the huge paw. Next, came Mai-ingan, or the "wolf", a huge brute standing with its back on a level with the girl's hips. "If I get tired listening to you fellows, always growling, and you don't mean it. Come now, let me see those paws." As she reached to pick up the animal's front foot, Mai-ingan snapped at her hand without hurting it. Making no effort to extricate her hand from the animal's mouth, she said, "Well I didn't know you understood French, come now, let go." Teasingly Mai-ingan would release its hold slightly, only to close down again as the girl attempted to withdraw her hand. For a few moments Paulette stood undecided. Mai-ingan was tricky and moody. One never knew what he would do next, his eyes rolled dangerously. "Listen boy, I can't stand here all day because you want to hold my hand, let me go or else." Mai-ingan growled ominously. Placing her free hand over the animal's muzzle, she pressed its upper lip against its fangs with all her strength, Mai-ingan twisted his head in evident distress and opened its mouth. Instead of freeing her hand, she grasped its tongue and held on until the animal gave up its struggle and stood quiet, its growl stilled. "Try that again and I'll make a nice robe from your coat, now up with those paws". After examining each hairy paw carefully, Paulette patted the animal's broad head and rubbed its sharply pointed ears. Mai-ingan growled its pleasure.

153

"Come, Koko-ko-oo, we must hurry, the sun is moving fast and we have far to go." Koko-ko-oo, as big and powerful as the rest, though not blind, was near sighted. From puppyhood, it had developed the habit of staring fixedly at some distant object hence it had earned the name "owl". Nest to Pierre, the leader, Koko-ko-oo was her favorite, partly because of his handicap, but mostly because he was dependable. He never ran away, at each opportunity, like the others. When free, he would lie beside the toboggan and guard it day and night. Whenever his four white paws needed attention, he, however, like the others, resented too much familiarity and growled as loudly as the rest. If Paulette ever had any misgivings about the others, she had none concerning the "owl". She loved the big brute and she surmised, in his wolfish way, he displayed some affection for her.

"If you ever quit growling at me, I'll get worried. I'll think you are sick or something, so just go ahead and enjoy yourself, but, up with those feet, we must keep them clean. You could do this yourself, if you knew enough, I suppose you would." Chattering incessantly, the girl finished her task of inspection and returned to Pierre, the leader. Rubbing the animal's pointed ears and patting it shoulders, she continued to speak. "Soon now, Pierre, we will rest." Shading her eyes against the frost dimmed rays of the sun's reflection against the glittering snow, she, searched the distant shore for signs of human habitation. The sun now midway from its noontime position to its setting, would give them barely time to reach the far shore of the long lake and make camp before dark. While busily scanning the distant shoreline, the girl noted the heavy growth of pine, their wide tops seemingly interlaced over the valley that extended away to what, she felt sure, would be the next lake.

Somewhere in that valley, flanked on either side by rugged hills, their forest covering gracefully reflecting with perfect simplicity each little rise and fall of the granite slope, would flow a small connecting river where the clear icy water, tumbling noisily down and down along its banks with glittering icicles hanging intermittently, the sleek coated otter would slide into the open water of the rapids with scarcely a splash or even a ripple, its beady eyes every alert in search of an unwary fish. Maybe along the bank, the clear imprint of and Indian's snowshoe would lead them to its owner's wigwam, snug beside a granite cliff from whence little trails in the snow radiate in many directions, little threads that bind one to the magic of home. "A likely looking spot for a family to camp," she mused in a loud whisper. "I have enough to feed you tonight, tomorrow we will have to stop and hunt for more. We have been lucky so far, Pierre, if it doesn't storm too much," she stopped suddenly and noted the sudden stiffening of the dog's muscles, its sharp ears pointing motionless in the direction ahead. "So there is someone there. I wonder if our search will end here." Pierre whined and stirred impatiently, seemingly as a signal for its mates to be on the alert. The girl worked her way cautiously back to her conveyance while watching the animals for any sign of premature departure. Grasping firmly the heavy rawhide thongs attached to the toboggan and serving as traces, Paulette, without mishap, settled herself snuggled within the flat traineau's leather sides. In a voice scarcely audible to the leader, the girl spoke gently, "Easy, Pierre, come boy." The animal, with ears still pointed stiffly and muzzle sniffing, stepped ahead enough to tighten the traces. This time the girl spoke sharply, "On avon…Marche."

The huge dogs bounded forward as one, the light traineau swung dangerously from side to side over the snow, as the girl laughed gleefully and urged the animals on. Knowing they wouldn't go far at that speed and would soon settle down to a steady trot, she held her head down to protect her face from the flying particles of snow kicked up by the willing animals. Soon the leader feeling the slackening paces of its mates, settled to a fast trot. From within the securely laced packs at her back, the girl unwound a long lashed well-oiled whip of braided caribou hide. With a short heavy handle safely tucked beneath her knees, she re-coiled the trailing lash. The girl hated the thing, but there were times when approaching human habitations and tantalizing little cur dogs, the hissing and sharply cracking whip over the heads of her dogs was seemingly the only sounds they would obey. With her hands warmly tucked in white fur mittens, she brushed the accumulated snow from her moccasins and drew the blanket robe over her lap.

"Mai-ingan! Mai-ingan! Marche!" Wolf turned his head quickly and bared his fangs slightly. "All right boy, I won't use the whip, move along now." Mai-ingan tightened his braces and laid his ears back. The girl loved her dogs more and more as each day she came to know them better. With pride and no little satisfaction, she recalled how everyone at the trading post said that she could never handle the brutes. Day by day, Pascal had, not without misgiving, watched the girl tame Pierre, the most vicious of the pack, until the animal would actually watch impatiently for the girl's coming that he might snuggle his cold muzzle into her warm hand. At the time when the first light snow covered the ice bound lakes, she started training them to work in harness. Three were easy, taking to their work in ready response to her gentle coaxing. Mai-ingan, whose black tipped gray hair earned for him, not only admiration, but his name, was stubborn. In vain did the girl work with him for several days until she had completely exhausted her patience. Mai-ingan would not learn. "There is only one way left, Mai-ingan. I'll make you work or I'll kill you trying." First tying the animal's mouth securely, she chained him to a tree, then cutting several bushy switches, she worked on him until he gave up all attempts at struggling for freedom and laid down and whined pitifully. There were tears in the girl's eyes as she released the beautiful animal and wiped the blood from his mouth. Not daring to release its powerful jaws from the grip of the thongs that bound them together, Paulette led the animal back to its harness and the long flat traineau where it submitted willingly to being hitched. Patting the dog's head and rubbing its ears, the girl noted, with no little satisfaction, the animal's immediate response, its ears pricked up and it shook itself thoroughly. Mai-ingan had learned its lesson for life.

In the others, including Pierre, the leader, she had complete confidence, but the wolf growled and bared his fangs at the slightest provocation, she knew that when the occasion arose, he, with the others, could be depended on to defend her to the last.

As the traineau sped over the snow, the distant shore loomed out of the frosty air clearly. The girl was in strange country and had been for the last four days. Lake after lake, over portage trails often marked only crooked little wolf paths, Pierre had led them on into the west. Two nights out of the three, she had camped out. With a blazing fire against the butt end of some fallen tree and the dogs chained some distance away, each beneath his own tree. Paulette passed the nights comfortably despite the bitter cold. With naught to disturb her thoughts, except the usual thumping of a rabbits long hind feet as it sped over its well packed snow path or the gliding landing of a flying squirrel on a nearby stub of a dead tree that it might better survey its chances for a thieving raid on her food supply, the girl was left to concentrate on her mission, to survey the surrounding country and its trading possibilities. In this she was highly successful. In wigwam after wigwam, some singly and others in small groups, she had spread the word of her enterprise. To the amazement of the Natives, she recounted the story of her husband's death "Yes the post would continue. Beaver is the most wanted of all the furs, when the lakes open up, bring all you can get to the post." Everywhere she was greeted as one of "them". In this, her fluent command of the Ojibwe tongue, along with a thorough knowledge of customs and superstitions, proved of immense value. To many, the girl appeared as a spirit of healing from the other world. A little advice on the care of a sick child, a bit of maple sugar to add to grandfather's sacrificial offering to the Great Spirit brought lifelong gratitude and friendship. Acting on the popular belief of the time that an Indian "Never forgives an injury or forgets a favor," Paulette made friends wherever she passed. Her dogs and equipment, her clothes and the way she braided her hair made interesting conversation and set many an example for the forest maidens. Her manner, an air of good fellowship, and rare beauty, excited many a sigh from within hopeful Native breasts.

With her dogs well fed and cared for the night, the long flat traineau with its curled and rawhide sides and lacing lay safely high above the reach of hungry dogs. From the square opening at the top of the low oblong "Sha-ban-do-wan" of bark, the smoke rose and hung heavily at treetop level. From the crackling fire within showers of sparks, rose no higher than the frosty night air that hovered with depressing intensity throughout the great forest. At frequent intervals, half-wild little dogs howled in response to related offspring of wild ancestors. Like the rest of the family, whose hospitality she was enjoying, Paulette sat facing the fire. The sound of approaching footsteps, the creaking of frozen snowshoe lacing, an unceremonious lifting of the curtain doorway, the neighbor's critical appraisal of the stranger, the sudden lifting of the eyebrows in surprise at the sound of his Native tongue…"You speak our language, I thought you were of the log builders."

"No, I am from Gichi Gamee, my mother was Native."

So on into the night, questions and answers pass around in rapid succession. News of the welfare of other families and relatives along the way, the lone traveler has come, in welcome indeed. The maiden of the family finding courage in the kindly smiles of the stranger, moves nearer and strokes her fur trimmed and brightly colored garments tenderly. Paulette's eyes momentarily fill with tears as the simple act brings back poignant memories of her own childhood.

Soon the visitor departs and others enter, mothers with impish youngsters, other maidens closely pursued by suspiciously jealous swains, crowd within the glow of the firelight. At a lull in the conversation, Paulette, with quickened breath and a slightly tremulous voice asks the one question for which she has traveled many days.

"Did anyone see a young stranger pass by here before the snow came? He is tall, long black braided hair, speaks Ojibwe and French, he is a half-breed too."

A hush fell upon the assemblage while Paulette's breast rose and fell rapidly, her eyes, almost closed as she stared at the mat before her, to hide the emotion that caused her hands to tremble slightly.

"No, no one can remember seeing such a person. The only stranger to pass was the man dressed in black. He carried a cross tucked in his wide sash."

"Who was with him?" Paulette asks quickly.

"Only an Indian boy who lives beyond the next trading post, two day walk from here."

The girl struggled desperately to hide the disappointment, she sure her features must betray. She is not helped any by the rapid fire questions that are flung her way. "Who is he, a relative, a friend, where was he going, trapper, hunting maybe, what kind of clothes did he wear? No, no one saw him."

Paulette raised her head quickly, "Did someone mention a trading post near here?"

"Yes, it not very near, not very far either, only two sun's walk when the snow is not too deep."

"Do they come this far?" Paulette asked anxiously studying the face of the master of the family who was giving the information.

"No, they don't, there are not enough of them to spread out much in their travels. But the ones that are there are very bad, that is why we camp away from them."

Paulette was not only disappointed in finding no trace of Batiste, but her journey west was ended, now, she must return. She had no desire to become entangled with more traders, not at the present time. Perhaps at some later day, she would return, with a suitable bodyguard. Aside from the traders, Paulette was troubled. What had become of Batiste? Where did he go? Surely someone along the way where she had inquired of everyone she met, must have seen him or some sign of his passing if he had come this way. It was not easy to pass through a country overland and not leave some sign of one's passing. As the fire died away and the smoke cleared to a thin vapor in the opening of the lodge, Paulette pulled her fur blanket closely about her and watched the stars that peeped in at the sleepers. In the morning, she would start back, but not the way she came. To the north there must be other Natives, she would cross one or more divides if necessary, there were other lakes to lead her back home. At any rate, she had Pierre, she could always get safely home. All she had to do is point his long slim muzzle towards the east and tell him to go home.

There were other lands far to the east and north…maybe…Batiste lived there, she would find him, surely he couldn't pass out of her life so easily, merely because he willed it, who was he anyway, she was Paulette. She unconsciously pulled the blanket closer about her head. The night was cold.

Chapter 19

Like two pendulums swinging frantically, Pascal's two long arms beat the air in unison with his two short legs that thumped the frozen path in rapid succession. His two round blue eyes gleamed wide with excitement from behind the curtain of flaming red hair covering his head and face. Midway from the lake to the trading post, the little man stopped short by grabbing onto a small birch tree and spinning completely around the smooth trunk. Losing, momentarily, all sense of direction in the unexpected suddenness of about face, the little fellow blinked his eyes furiously while the hair covering his mouth in turn pointed stiffly outwards and retracted with each panting breath. Recovering quickly, he focused his gaze towards the tip of a long point extending well out into the lake far to the west. Rocking his head slowly from side to side, he was about to retrace his steps, when he again spied the black object, wormlike, rounding the point. Without further waiting, "little red man" instantly took up where his doubts had prompted him to verify the glad news. After a dull thud against the heavy log door of the store room, he lost some time in doing what he should have done in the first place, raised the latch before trying to swing it open.

The three bearded men, sitting idly about on bales of trade goods, sprang to their feet in alarm as the little fellow stood panting and speechless. Pointing shakily in the direction where he had seen the objet approaching, he managed to whisper between deeply drawn breaths, "She is coming! She is coming!"

The three men, unable to grasp his meaning immediately, looked at one another quickly. Disappointed for the moment at the cool reception of his long awaited "glad tidings", and fearing lest the looks of doubt in the eyes of the men turn into downright suspicion of his sanity, the little fellow dashed back out through the open door and, plowed into the snow waist deep. With one hand pointing at the approaching object, he waved frantically with the other to, "Come see! Come see! She is come!"

****

Out on the lake, Paulette dug her heels deep in the snow on either side of the traineau. Again and again she commanded the four half-wild dogs to stop. With muzzles held to the trail, they continued to strain at their traces. Little by little, the girl managed to slow the animals down to a walk and finally to a complete halt. Springing up from the nest-like seat on the conveyance, she hastened to the head of Pierre. Turning to the others, like one making an important address on the eve of some game, she said, "Now listen to me you fellows. We have to do better than just crawl along on the way in. See all those people waiting for us. Grandfather and grandmother will be there, we got to come in with a little speed. Lie down now and cool off...down Pierre...you too Mai-ingan...come Koko-ko-oo. I'll look your feet over while you are resting." Pierre was uneasy and shook himself repeatedly, his sharp ears pointed sharply at attention. Paulette came quickly and stood beside the animal and patted its shoulders and shaggy head, "Good old Pierre, you did well for one trip, let me see those paws." For once the beast forgot to growl and meekly submitted his hairy feet for inspection. Giving the animal a light tap on the nose with her mittened hand, she commanded, "Down! Pierre! Down!" Reluctant, but obedient, Pierre stretched his long body out on the trail and proceeded to lick its paws.

From where she stood, the girl could see an ever growing crowd of people gathering around the door of the post. "I think we should have waited until night to come in, but I want Pascal to see the dogs," she muttered audibly, more to keep the dogs quiet than to express her thoughts. Just so long as she kept talking, the easily excited animals would lie quietly. Nothing aroused the suspicions like extreme quiet on the trail. "Take it easy boy," She continued, "We have more trips to make, it will be harder next time, I wish it wouldn't snow anymore, maybe someday we'll find where he went, when we do, maybe won't mean anything, but we will find out why he went away."

Koko-ko-oo was snoring loudly, he was getting tired, as the "pole dog" or last on the string next to the traineau, his was the hardest task. On short bends of an overland trail, his was the task of keeping the conveyance on the path, often against the combined pull of his mates ahead of him. For that reason, Paulette never urged him on, but gave him every opportunity to rest and relax, even while trotting along over the ice. She watched Pierre closely now, he was getting restless. The girl patted the sleeping dog gently on the head. Koko-ko-oo yawned lazily and slowly rose to his feet. Paulette straightened its harness, ran her hand around its collar and straightened the fur lest it become knotted and cause friction. Pierre got to his feet, also, and shook himself free of particles of snow that clung to its silver coat. Mai-ingan yawned and rested its muzzle on its two paws placed close together, while watching every move the girl made. Kai-aushk now arose and lifted one its hind legs back between the traces and sniffed the slowly moving air.

"I ought to tie your mouths up, but if I did, they would say that I was afraid of you. I'm not and if you fellows don't behave, I'll skin you alive."

Paulette worked her way back slowly and settled quickly into the traineau. There was too much slack in the traces, a sudden jerk with the combined weight of the huge dogs could leave her sitting on the ice. With her heels, she pushed the wide toboggan back and spoke to Pierre gently. "Pierre, move up a little." The animal obeyed and moved enough to tighten the traces. Paulette grasped the heavy braided thong that encircled the upper edge of the traineau, "Marche!" With surprising coordination, the animals bounded as one, Paulette hung on. She had passed the first test, that of remaining seated after the first quick jerk, she smiled happily. She watched the leader for signs of letting up speed, its traces were slack. Pierre was having a hard time keeping out of the way of its mates. "Pierre Marche!" she commanded sharply. Pierre glanced back quickly over its right shoulder, bared its fangs slightly at the surprise command, laid its ears back tightly to its head and settled down to a long lope that quickly tightened the slack in its traces. Paulette smiled a crooked little smile so common among the people who inhabited the great wilderness. She was proud of her dogs.

In ever growing numbers, inhabitants of the post gathered about the store building. Rapid, but hushed whispers, mingled with the high pitched voice of an elderly woman as she chided her semi-naked offspring shivering in the cold and snow. Giant bearded Frenchmen puffed excitedly on stone pipes, long since burned empty, while voicing suddenly acquired assurance that the girl would return safely. From all this, Pascal had worked his way step by step along the frozen well beaten path to the lake where Paulette and her rapidly approaching dogs would pass. Seemingly unconscious of his movement along the trail, the little fellow son verge of tears, continually wiped away the incessant gathering of mist obscuring his vision. While he felt sure that the approaching traveler was his mistress, there was always the possibility that it might be someone else. A kind fate, however, intervened for the moment as his vision cleared and he recognized the broad white band around the neck and shoulders of Kai-aushk. With a glad shout, arms waving high above his head while his long red hair flowed straight out, the "red man" bounded down the short hill to the lake.

As Paulette approached the landing swiftly, she uncoiled her long lashed whip. She felt no little concern for the people especially the children gathered about the store. The girl felt some apprehension over the behavior of the dogs. Driving them among a small crowd of people for the first time, might excite them beyond control. She regretted not having muzzled the brutes. Watching the reaction of the leader, Pierre, intently, she was relieved to note its slackening pace as with muzzle pointed high, its ears fixed rigidly forward; the others followed their leader's example. She must try and stop them before getting too near. One snap of their powerful jaws, and sharply pointed fangs would tear the muscles from the leg of the stoutest man. Nearer and nearer the shoreline approached, only a little way further and she would halt the animals, if she could. When her heart sank, standing directly in the path, but a short distance away, was Pascal, his long red hair and flaming red beard moving slightly in the breeze. Not daring to shout to him to move away from the trail lest the dogs mistake her cry as a signal to attack the queer looking creature, the excited girl did the only thing she thought best. Somewhat reassured over the behavior of the dogs in not evincing any burst of speed toward the little fellow, Paulette grasped the thongs holding the curled end of her toboggan and digging her heels in deeply into the soft snow beside the path, she spoke gently to the leader. "Easy Pierre…E-a-sy boy, whoa boy." With her heart pounding rapidly, she almost shouted with joy as the huge animal reacted to the soothing tone of her voice and slowed to a trot, then a walk and finally to a complete halt.

Pascal, on seeing the girl and her dogs come to a stop but a short distance away, reacted to a natural impulse, to rush over and not only bid the girl welcome back, but to see the dogs. As the little fellow approached, Paulette quickly wound the whip lash around Pierre's head and faced the animal in the opposite direction. Like a frightened doe warning its fawn to hide, Paulette in an impatient gesture at the little man's evident intention, stomped her foot creating a little flurry of light snow that settled back and covered the silk and colored quill embroidered decorations of her moccasins. Pierre moved uneasily, the sensed a stiffening of his muscles as she attempted to turn his head towards the little man.

"Hurry, Pascal! Don't' run, walk fast! I'll try and hold them here until you get back, go on Pascal. Please, Monsieur, don't run! Tell the others to stay back as well."

The huge lead dog attempted to push the girl aside, but Paulette resisted and held the animal's head firmly. With its shaggy head and black pointed ears raised on a level of the girl's breast, the dog growled throatily. Paulette placed her mittened hand over its eyes and she felt or rather sensed the animal's muscles relax. While speaking continuously in Ojibwe, she watched Pascal reach the rest of the small gathering who stood near the open door to the store.

The girl breathed a sigh of relief. In spite of Pierre's continued low rumbling growl, Paulette's assurance of the brute's good behavior returned rapidly. She knew the others would make no move except in response to the leader's example. With her every sense finely attuned to the dog's least reaction, she loosened her grip on its head. Was it a natural reaction in the lives or minds of the living things that moved about the great forest to enter into for self-protection if you will, this feeling of savage passion permeating the animals about her? Was it the momentary reversion to a primitive urge to kill on the part of the girl that found ready response in the behavior and held in strict obedience the semi-savage brutes she so ably controlled?

Mai-ingan rose quickly to his feet and shook himself thoroughly and pointed his ears shoreward. Pierre again attempted to turn his head in the same direction, but Paulette with all the force of persuasion at her command, yet finely balanced with a subtle gentle tone induced the animal to relax completely and nudge her with some show of affection.

Paulette breathed a sigh of relief and adjusted her hood. Carefully unwinding the whip from Pierre's head, she led him back to his position. "I'll walk ahead of you," she informed him, "and if you try anything funny, I'll brain with this whip handle. I hope you understand." Pierre rolled his eyes, his breath came evenly and quiet. Paulette stepped ahead of him on the trail, the dogs followed, each in its own place.

Paulette led each dog to their designated spot near the trading post and once the animals were securely chained she returned to the traineau and gathered her pack and belongings. One of the Native men graciously offered to take care of the toboggan and store it until it was needed again Paulette smiled and replied, "Milgwech" or "Thank you" in the Ojibwe language. As she neared the trading post the door was opened for her by one of the people who were waiting to welcome her home. Walking in amongst the waiting throng, welcoming comments and warm sentiments were expressed in both the French and Native language. Soon the crowd began to dissipate and she moved to her accustomed position at the long table. Pascal was seated atop his stool waiting to address his mistress. There was a small brass kettle steaming, full of wild rice and venison stew, and a cast iron pan with warm freshly baked wheat bread or "lug", a word contracted from the French word for bread "legolet". Pascal informed Paulette, "Your grandmother has prepared food for you and requested it be sent over, now you must eat."

After Pascal had dished up a small wooden bowl of the stew for the girl, he climbed back up to his stool and inquired, "Was your trip successful, did you accomplish what you set out to do?"

Paulette thought for a moment then replied, "Why yes, Pascal, I traveled to a few villages and informed the inhabitants that our trading post was in full operation and to come and trade in the spring." The girl was careful not to show her bitter disappointment in the failure of her true mission, to find news of Batiste.

Pascal's eyes sparkled with the excitement and relief he felt that his mistress had returned unscathed and apparently in good health. He said with heartfelt emotion, "I am filled with relief that Madam has arrived in good spirits, now you must rest, it must have been long and tiresome days for you. Any news can wait and I will bid you adieu until tomorrow". With that Pascal stepped down from his perch and quickly exited the post.

Paulette ate the food lovingly prepared for her by her grandmother then made preparations for the night. After putting on her night clothes she gratefully climbed into her bed and quickly fell into a deep, exhausted sleep.

Chapter 20

Light feathery snow swirled in fitful little puffs and settled unevenly in the wake of Batiste's snowshoes. The young man glanced up at the sun and stepped up his pace. The far shore at the end of the lake was several miles away and it would be a race to reach its heavily timbered shelter before the head of the sun melted the snow into a wet soggy mass that would cling to his webbed shoes and make further progress arduous and tiring.

Since long before daylight or when the sky cleared and the stars came out and the snow ceased falling, the young man had pushed his way eastward in keeping with his promise to the good Father Daniels and the trader Monsieur La Duc. All through the last moon, from its first faint outline like a crescent shaped jewel of pale gold mounted on a field of blue, he had watched it nightly fade to a silvery hue as it grew and grew until seemingly its rim must give way and break open to release a shower of stars.

Impatiently he would lie awake and, through the smoke opening at the cone shaped top of their wigwam, watch the procession of stars as they floated across the heavens, some in advance, others following in the path of the moon. After an arduous day of chase or the more laborious and less exciting task of gathering and packing firewood for his widowed mother, he would sit by the fire of the village sage and philosopher listening attentively to the white haired friend's recent discoveries of probable reasons why the spring should be early or late. At the end of every visit, the young man came away with the depressing advice, "Wait until the crows come back, then travel will be easier, the days longer."

Day after day, the weeks dragged on into the time of another moon, first the "midwinter moon", when the cold bore down upon the inhabitants from the land of "Keewaydin", the home of the North Wind, depressing the spirit until the Natives wondered in fear if it would ever end. Next came the moon of the "North Winds" when the days lengthened amidst the welcome warmth of a sun following a path higher and higher in the heavens as the days wore on.

One day the moon of the "crusted snow", shaped like the prong of a buck's horn, appeared in the western sky and sank quickly beyond the horizon long before the sun set. It was then the old historian of the tribe gave his word to the young half-breed to prepare for his journey to the great lake that lay on the edge of the earth. "Soon, my son, the crows will be back from their home in the land of the "Shawano" the South Wind, marking the time for your departure."

One night, after sleeplessly tossing on his bed of boughs, he had recalled little incidents of his experiences of the summer before and on the autumn when the leaves changed their color and fell to the earth. Gazing up through the smoke as it sped away into the clear cold night air, he was startled by the appearance of a furry red squirrel. The little animal eyed him closely when suddenly from beyond its perch atop one of the poles that pointed in many directions, a voice deep and clearly audible, said, "Follow me." Without power to resist or effort on his part, the young man arose and passed on and into a shower of sparks that floated high into the air beyond the tree tops. Not far in advance, the little squirrel seemed to be running or hopping swiftly over a pall of smoke extending southward beyond his vision. Without knowing how or why, the half-breed followed closely. Without warning or slackening its pace, the little squirrel, or "Ajidamo" in the Ojibwe language, hopped onto a dry tree that suddenly loomed up out of the smoke. Climbing nimbly to the first branch extending over what now appeared as earth, the voice again sounded, "You asked me to tell you why you were sad, behold what you see ahead." The smoke upon which they had traveled cleared away and in its place appeared a broad beach. It was a strange place and the young man was puzzled by the sound of waves washing upon the sand. Waves in rhythmic regularity, broken only by the sound of an occasionally larger and noisier wave washing upon the sand with a display of white water only to return exhausted and spent. Batiste sensed a feeling of impatient curiosity and turned to the little animal who apparently was the cause of the strange experience. Sitting quietly at the junction of the limb and the trunk of the tree where it had first settled, Batiste noticed that its gaze was sharply focused towards the eastern end of the beach. The young man turned his gaze in the same direction and saw a young woman leisurely approaching. Stopping at short intervals to shade her eyes, she searched the forest surroundings. Nearer and nearer she came and at each step the enveloping mist cleared. With an inarticulate cry, the young man unsuccessfully attempted to extend his arms to the beautiful creature as he tried to cry out the one name that had been locked in his heart ever since he retrieved the bloody dagger at the camp of Francois. Nearer Paulette approached swaying gently as she walked, dressed in a gown of blue velvet with a sash of many colors, its fringes barely touching the sand, a string of pearls around her neck that glowed pale, lustrous and iridescent against her dark Native complexion. Searching intently the sands at her feet where nothing marred the smooth trackless surface save that of her own delicately embroidered moccasins of white caribou. Often her eyes would flash in fruitless search of the forest that lined the shore of the lake. Coming abreast of the young man, who had by now realized that he was powerless to attract her attention, she stood gazing helplessly in his direction. With a mighty effort, he vainly tried to break the bonds of his soundless existence. As the girl looked steadily in his direction, he realized in dismay that he was also invisible. Overcome by her fruitless search, the girl settled slowly to the sand and there, as a thing crumpled and cast away, she wept bitterly. In vain, the young man turned again and again to the little squirrel, sitting so jauntily and unconcerned on its perch seemingly above the trials of earthly mortals.

Again the unearthly voice sounded from somewhere beyond the little animal. It said, "I am powerless to give you voice or substance, for I, too, must look beyond the horizon for the power to fulfill our promise to you. I have answered your request, you will come here again and when you hear my voice, you will know that your journey has ended."

Batiste awoke gradually, sat up and placed more wood on the fire. Searching among his meager belongings, he withdrew a small stone pipe and filled it with kinik-kinik while thoughtfully gazing into the fire. As the fragrant smoke ascended and mingled with that of the wood fire, the young man in compliance with an age old custom of his mother's people, offered the pipe to the spirits of the four directions, the earth, sky and lastly to his dream friends, beyond the horizon. At the opposite side of the fire, his mother stirred uneasily from a deep sleep, sat up and asked, "Your dream?"

The young man nodded and recounted his experience. At the finish, his mother smiled knowingly. "That is right. I, too, was there, I followed you. I never let you out of my sight, you will go and fulfill the duty fate has decreed for you. Rest now and when the day comes, I will help you prepare for your journey."

172

The firelight faded, the long darting shadows played over the circular walls of their wigwam as the mother and son returned to their slumber each satisfied and happily content in the faith of their ancestors.

****

The sun now passed its noontime zenith in the sky. Batiste with a sigh of relief, stepped ashore and after worming his feet from the snowshoe hitches, dropped to rest on a bit of ground, bare of snow. The young man noted the welcome sounds of thawing snow and tiny rivulets that starting on their long way to the great salt ocean, brought back memories of other springs in the days of his youth, memories of frenzied preparation for the spring trapping of beaver and otter. His father deceased for the past two winters. Batiste's gaze fixed on the red bark of a pine. Strange how he seldom thought of his father, would his relatives and friends forget him so completely when his turn came to pass on to another life beyond the horizon? Having rested, the half-breed carefully removed the wet snow clinging to his snowshoes, examined the webbing carefully for signs of breakage in the rawhide lacing and hung them up to dry. For the rest of the afternoon and part of the night, while the wet snow froze and hardened sufficiently to make travel easier, he would camp and sleep before starting on the third lap of his journey.

As the sun sank beyond the cloud banked horizon, the young man picked a large star and set its position midway its nighttime path as the proper time for departure. Too many times in his impetuous youth, he has mistaken a short evening nap for a night's restful sleep and as a result spend the entire night traveling and waiting for daylight. Now that he was older, in experience if not in years, he had learned the value of rest, even though he was anxious and equal to the demands of a long sleepless trek. With his bed snug against a fallen tree trunk, Batiste started a small fire the proper distance away. After an evening meal consisting of one roasted rabbit, the young man stretched out comfortably on the springy bough bed. The dark was closing in rapidly as the chill night air dropped to a freezing temperature. Overhead the great horned owl cam to a noisy landing among the heavily branched top of the pine trees that stood row upon row, each rising higher and higher along the hill, sloping gently upward from the water's edge. As the evening progressed into night, there came more clearly the steady sound of falling water broken only by a noisy splash following the resounding slap of a beaver's tail upon the swiftly moving water. Thoughts of the short overland trail along the stream that would lead him to the next lake stretching away into the east, gave the young man some concern as he yawned sleepily. "I should have camped at the other end of the portage, it will be difficult to follow the dark…take time…I must wake up about midnight…hope it stays cold tomorrow…wonder what Ajidamo meant, 'the journey will be ended'…will camp with some Natives tomorrow night…cold…cold nights."

The young half-breed shivered a little and unconsciously stretched his thin woolen blanket dangerously near the ripping point. The pine tops stood quiet and hushed as the increasing cold of the night stiffened their branches against the occasional breeze that rolled upward into hilltops where the wolf pack sniffed the campfire smoke of the lone traveler.

The flickering blaze of the little fire suddenly died to a small mound of glowing embers. The dark rough bark of the pine that, but a moment before, joined in the mad dance of the shadows that springing, like crazed small furry denizens of the forest, to the snow where, after darting frantically back and forth only to return and madly dash over the rounded form of the tree, now melted into the surrounding blackness, quietly and in its own still way panting in happy memory. The sleeper, oblivious of the activity of his surroundings, lay restfully awaiting his lode star to reach its destined point in the heavens when he would awaken, for another day was approaching beyond the eastern horizon.

Chapter 21

The arrival of the crows from their southern retreat, the first harbingers of spring, awakened renewed activity at Paulette's trading post. Under the ever increasing warmth of the sun, bared patches of earth appeared amidst the timbered hills. Paulette's dogs lay gaunt and shaggy, their eyes rolling ominously at each passerby that followed the little path skirting well beyond the length of the chains that kept the animals confined within a limited reach. Within the long low walled building, Paulette stirred the contents of a small brass kettle that hung over the fire. The fragrant aroma of boiling venison with wild rice filled the room and caused Pascal to sniff the air in hungry but happy anticipation. At the near approach of high noon, black smoke poured from the many chimneys of log buildings surrounding the main store. Native mothers of light complexioned children hastened the preparation of the noontime meal lest their offspring's ceaseless clamoring in the language of Old France drive them to distraction. Black bearded "Courier du Bois" arose tired and sleepy, scowling at the insistent and merciless commands to "get up and eat." The many nights and days of forced travel throughout the winter after weary dog teams, left big strong men but shadows of their proudly vaunted strength, they neither swaggered nor stepped boldly along the little paths joining the buildings, but moved cautiously as one wary of stumbling over an unseen object.

On a large skillfully woven reed mat before the fireplace, Pascal and Paulette sat and sipped fragrant black tea sweetened with maple sugar from Lake Superior.

"This maple sugar is good," remarked the little man between self satisfying smacks of his lips from somewhere within their heavy covering of red hair.

Paulette nodded, "It is the only thing we have that keeps me from getting too lonesome for the big lake."

"Does Madam plan to travel any more this spring?"

The girl glanced over her uplifted cup before setting it back on the mat. "I wouldn't know where to go Mon Ami. I have covered the country to the west, the north and the east."

Pascal raised his penetrating blue eyes slyly and in a voice that inspired confidence asked simply, "And you found nothing?"

With her hands resting idly on her lap and eyes downcast, the girl shook her head. "Nothing, everywhere I asked, but no one has seen even a trace of his passing. Strange how anyone could travel for days through a country and not leave some sign, that the Natives might even suspect."

With deep wrinkles creasing his brow in perplexity, the little man asked, "But Madam, what is the answer, surely there must be a reason. Did he meet with an accident?"

Paulette shook her head decisively, "The Natives would have found him if anything happened. There can be but one reason, he wished to pass out of our lives entirely. This is why he was so careful not to leave any trace of his passing. Travelers in this country do not avoid our people unless they do not want to be seen."

177

"But why, Madam, what did we do?"

Paulette shrugged, "If I knew the answer, Monsieur, my dogs would not be so tired and weary, poor animals."

At the mention of the dogs, Pascal's eyes lit up and he shook his head wonderingly. "The brutes love you, Madam. I am sure they worked willingly."

The girl nodded, the reflection from the fire played on the strings of pearls encircling her throat and neck, the little red and crimson flashes attracted the "red man". "Yes, I think, at times, they enjoyed traveling about the country, it is their nature, yet, on our second trip to the north after the deep snows came in two storms, I had to push them along over the three divides where the snow was so deep they had to swim through it for days. It was there on the last divide that Mai-ingan laid down and quit. I had to punish him for the second time in his life."

"Shall I send them back to the stockade for the summer, Madam?"

Paulette opened her eyes wide in alarm. "What did you say, Monsieur? Send my dogs back to the stockade? Never! I would kill them first, one by one, with my own hands!" The girl's eyes flashed. At each trembling expression they seemed to close narrower and narrower until her long black lashes covered their lower lids. "We shall keep them here and feed them well until they have regained their strength, then they shall be released, free to go where they please."

"But Madam, will it be safe?"

"I think so, they will all leave, except perhaps 'Koko-ko-oo'. He has become attached to his harness and traineau, he may not leave. I shall muzzle him and keep him here, he is almost blind and should he lose his sight, we must kill him. If he were free, he would be killed by others."

Pascal held out his teacup for more tea. Paulette filled it and dropped a small square of maple sugar into the black liquid where it fizzled, sending tiny bubbles to the surface. The little man made no further suggestions and drank his tea with a loud slurp after each sip, carefully parting the heavy mustache and beard lest some of the precious liquid be wasted by clinging to the bushy growth.

"What are your plans for the spring, Madam?"

Paulette studied the queer patterns of the woven mat and sighed uneasily. "As fast as the younger Natives come, I shall choose enough of them to post lookouts day and night."

"But, why Madam, we never did that before?"

"Perhaps not, Monsieur, but that was when this post was a raiding post, everyone feared Monsieur Francois. It is different now. We are not raiders or victors anymore. We could be victims instead. If we get all the furs I have been promised, we cannot handle all of them. We will have more furs than any two or three posts in this country. We could lose not only the furs, but have our throats cut besides. We will head for Lake Superior as soon as the ice breaks up."

"But all the Indians will not be in by that time."

Paulette shrugged, "For those that are left, we will leave word to follow on. We are taking every family we can to Lake Superior. We will need many scouts and packers."

"No one but scouts and packers ever accompanied us before."

"I know, Pascal, but this time it will be different." The girl smiled mischievously and continued, "All the winter I have invited every family that I could reach and many more beyond, to attend the big spring festival at Lake Superior. You know the Indian's weakness for a celebration of any kind. Lake Superior and Monsieur LaChance are due for a surprise, a big surprise."

The little red man held out his hands in a helpless gesture. "Do you still intend to pay for the goods we took away from Monsieur LaChance?"

"Oh, yes, Monsieur! That is the first thing we must do. It is no less right to pay our account now than it was the day we arrived here."

Pascal let out a great sigh of resignation and merely shook his head. The girl looked at Pascal rather severely. Pascal drew back, he had heard enough for one day and now there was more to come. She always looked at him like that when she had something really important to say.

"Tomorrow you will start making preparations. Bale the furs we have on hand and start some of the men repairing the canoes. I shall tend to the scouts and look to our defense. Every man that can handle a musket will be furnished with powder and load. We may have to fight, but we are not going to be taken by surprise and Pascal, I must tell you something else." The little man looked bewildered. The girl, by way of appeasement, poured more tea into his cup. "During the winter, I invaded the trading grounds both to the east and west of us. Many, many families who trapped for the other traders are coming this way, for the big festival at Lake Superior. We are not going to be liked by the other traders for that. We will have to be 'engarde'."

Pascal's eyes had opened wide as he sprang to his feet and roared with laughter. Tears ran down his cheeks until the girl began to think the little man was stricken with some form of insanity. Like the sudden bursting of a dam to relieve a heavy pressure of water, the pent up feeling, owing to Paulette's decision to pay for the goods stolen from Monsieur LaChance, left the little fellow on the verge of a nervous tension bordering on collapse. The idea was insane, for never in the history of the French gentleman trading into "Du Pays d'en Haut" had such a thing been dreamed of. It was not only downright crazy, but extremely dishonorable. But…how this slip of a girl with her team of wild dogs had evened up all accounts that might be charged to her stupidity, by stealing away, single handedly, and in broad daylight, if you please, the trappers upon whom the traders depended upon for their very existence. A gala celebration at Lake Superior! Again and again the "Little Red Man" burst out in uproarious laughter until at long last he stopped with a few last spasmodic grunts as he traced the tears along his whiskers and wiped them away, leaving a quite noticeable streak down each side of his nose.

Paulette felt relieved as Pascal relaxed and settled back to his seat on the mat. For a moment, she had stared at the man with a growing feeling of apprehension. She couldn't detect anything humorous in what she said and refrained from asking for fear of precipitating another paroxysm of laughter. During her childhood, she had heard Grandfather tell of someone who had laughed himself to death. For a moment, she feared for the wellbeing of her faithful friend and servant.

"You will hurry with the preparations, Pascal. We must be ready to move when the ice breaks up."

"Yes, Madam, your wishes shall be carried out. I understand now why we must move quickly."

The girl noticed a slight tremble in the region of the little man's midsection. She spoke rather severely, "Everything I have said, you will keep to yourself. Do you understand?"

Pascal frowned and his blue eyes, once dull, now glistening clearly after their bath of tears, opened wide. He had pictured, the sensation he was going to create among the French population with his latest bit of news, how Paulette had tricked the neighboring traders, how she, all by herself, of course he could never admit to any part in the plot, but, if the public jumped to any conclusions in regard to his activity behind the scenes, well, there was nothing he could or would do about it. Modesty would naturally prevent his taking any of the glory away from his mistress, especially in a country where glory was scarce. Now he stood staring, frustrated. "But why, Madam, would it not be better to explain to the men why we must make all the unusual preparations?"

The girl shook her head decisively. "Tell the men we are in danger of attack, it is not necessary for them to know why. They must be prepared to resist from now on."

The little fellow nodded his head slowly. His mistress could be so unreasonable. After the latch to the heavy door had dropped into place at Pascal's departure, Paulette shot the wooden pins into place that prevented the opening of the doors leading to her living quarters. After clearing away the remains of their meal, she rolled up the grass mat and placed it beside the mud plastered fireplace. Drawing back the hanging before the mirror, the girl stood for a moment gazing intently at her reflection. She frowned and shook her head in decisive disapproval. "No, no! I don't like your looks, your face is dirty, your hair is not braided right, I don't like the color of your dress, your pearls, yes, but wash your neck first, they will look much better. If I were a man, I wouldn't take a second look at you." Glancing down at the reflection towards her feet, she continued to think in an audible whisper, "Just look at those legs, ashes and soot from the fire. Moccasins could be whiter and cleaner too." Roughly drawing the drapes back before the mirrors, Paulette turned away with a look of determination. Three strenuous months on the trail, hunting for food, for her and the dogs, camping out in extreme cold, often breaking snow trails ahead of the brutes in waist deep snow left the mark of its inevitable results on the girl.

Naturally slim and of medium height, she now appeared willowy and taller. Once away from the heavy snow laden webbed frames that made travel over the deep snows possible, she stepped about lightly with a grace of movement bestowed by nature only to those having gone through the heart breaking torment of days, weeks and months of travel by snowshoe. She stood squarely on her two feet, erect in a posture that nature planned and intended. Later, as the sun shone warm and brightly through the skylight and the shadow of the long table crept upward towards the scenic murals along the light drenched timbered walls, Paulette again drew aside the curtains before the mirrors. Facing the reflection bravely, with her eyes in a dreamy pose, she turned slightly and gazed over her left shoulder upon her imaged figure. Gowned in woolen material of subdued scarlet, with sleeves that hung midway down her arms, the girl moved slightly and noted the gracefully flowing folds and the wide blue trimmed hem, encircled with small pearl stars skillfully and painstakingly made from the shells of native mussels. The stars held in place with crimson thread of silk reflected iridescent light with the girl's every moment. Her gaze moved downwards towards her feet in the reflection, she smiled approval of the skillfully embroidered and shaded flower patterns decorating her moccasins and matching leggings of smoke tanned buckskin. Raising her arms above her head, the little stars of shell adorning the blue trim of the short sleeves flashed with white and pink. A long sash of blue and red geometric patterns gathered the garment into folds resting gently around her slim waist while its fringed ends extended well below the hem of the dress that ended above her moccasin tops.

Paulette frowned thoughtfully for moment before hurrying to the farther end of the long table and returned quickly with her short slim bladed knife covered with a fringed buckskin sheath. Once again standing before the mirrors, she carefully adjusted its protruding hilt, bending over slightly, to properly adjust the razor edged blade in its sheath. Turning to various poses before the mirrors, the beautiful young half-breed sighed contentedly. She had mercilessly criticized her appearance and was satisfied. Walking quickly to the farther end of the long room, she unhesitatingly drew back the curtains from the portrait of the "Lady in Mist". She needed but little imagination to nod in response to the Lady's smile of approval at her appearance. Kneeling before the mirrors, Paulette marveled again at the exact of her appearance, and that of the portrait directly above her. To make the likeness more real, she quickly unbraided her long glossy black hair and let it fall about her shoulders, arranging it like that of the portrait. Her eyes immediately filled with tears as memory of the man who had envisioned her likeness and who she may have loved had fate decreed otherwise, passed before her. Resting lightly back on her heels canoe fashion, she meditated over the incidents leading up to her present position, until her memory brought up the image of the half-breed Batiste. Was it the Indian blood that flowed through the veins of the young man that compelled her love, or was it the call of her "savage" ancestors that prompted the girl to reach for the cords and quickly draw the curtains, shutting from view a life that "might have been" the life of a people from another world.

Paulette arose and deftly re-braided her hair pensively. Without sympathy for the doe and fawn, she glanced from time to time at the painting above the fireplace. She admired the powerfully muscled and deep chest of the wolf and shared its feeling of pride and the satisfaction that accompanied the successful conclusion of the chase. With an ironically twisted little smile, she turned her back upon the painting and drew the drapes that curtained the "Lady in Mist".

Chapter 22

Warm south winds rippled the icy water, ankle deep, over the lake ice. A look of pain clouded the weather beaten features of Batiste as he walked steadily on. His feet and ankles ached unmercifully as he glanced about for a mound of ice or snow where he might get temporary respite from the penetrating cold that numbed the very marrow of his bones. For two days and nights, the warm winds had melted the snows. Tiny rivulets turned into sizable streams overnight, pouring water into the thousands of lakes that, like an intricate lacework pattern, covered the land known to the French trader as Du Pays d'en Haut. Truly it was the "height of land". From its forested hills, the water flowed in many directions to great salt oceans known only to daring "Voyageur" and intrepid "Courier du Bois". The sounds of falling water cascading over granite cliffs or tumbling tortuously through boulder strewn gorges, attracted the young man as he stopped form time to time to hold each of his feet in turn above the water to relieve the agony that was creeping to his knees. At such times, he would, as usual, search his surroundings for some slight upheaval in the surface of the ice where, like on an island of refuge, he might rest and regain courage to continue. Both of his moccasins, now twice their original size flopped about at each step and proved somewhat of a hindrance to this steady progress. Often he was tempted to run to the nearest shore and there beside a fire bask in the warm spring sunshine. Not far to the north, where the sun poured its golden warmth over the rising foothills, the bare ground looking so clean, dry and inviting, all but broke the half-breed's resolution of keeping on regardless. He was nearing the first objective in his journey. Somewhere nearby, possibly tomorrow, he would find the trading post of Monsieur La Duc and the cabin of Father Daniels. The country looked familiar, on each connecting portage, the winter traveled trails were more apparent and of recent use.

Recalling tales of endurance of his mother's people, he stepped out feeling no little satisfaction that, come what may, he would not subject himself to ridicule for lack of endurance either in his own knowledge or that of anyone else. Fixing his attention on the far end of the lake where a ravine or depression plainly marked the course of water flowage that would lead him to his destination, the young man with determination, stepped resolutely along. The water in little eddies closed smoothly after his every footstep only to resume its rippled way before the breeze that dried the beads of perspiration dotting the young man's brow.

****

At the trading post of Monsieur La Duc, the warm winds brought the usual activity attendant on preparations for the spring movement of furs to the market at "Ba-wi-ting," the outlet for Lake Superior. On a floor of boughs piled deep lest the priceless bales come in contact with the damp earth, the traders worked feverishly. For here were the fruits of their ambitions wandering from the security of homes in Old France. Here was the price for which they dared the little known dangers of the Atlantic, the path from Quebec to Superior strewn with the unburied skeletons of less fortunate predecessors equally brave and daring. In the bales of beaver, otter, mink and other pelts, lay wrapped the accumulated agony of bitter cold, hunger, strained backs and muscles, the torture of insect pests, the ever present danger spiraling over every post, like death on motionless wings, the raider. Somewhere in the ever mounting pile of baled furs could be counted the un-inventoried labor of Native trappers, men and women who in the rapid transition from the old to the new way of life suffered the usual agony of travail common to these unfortunate creatures existing in the path of what was to be known in later years as the "path of progress". The accumulated bales on the bed of fragrant boughs, brought to Monsieur La Duc of indulged visions of his beloved France…and what Frenchman could think of France as something apart from Paris? Its cathedrals, bridges, gates, towers and palaces of Kings long since relegated to the role of markers amidst the pages in the book of time. Its cafes and markets, convents and chapels, carelessly exposed beside the fortified St. Martin's, the spire of Notre Dame towering over the lesser, St. Denis du Pas or Saint-Pierre-de-Bœuf. How often in the long nights of winter, Monsieur the trader after considerable effort would return to reality from a swaggering promenade along Rue St. Martin or Rue St. Denis. And now as he placed his hand lovingly upon the baled wealth, he trembled with emotion at the nearness of a realization of his dreams. His review was rudely disconnected as his attention was keenly focused on the stranger who, until his near approach to the shore, had escaped notice.

Three of the men quickly slipped into the part of the store room set apart as a block house or fort. The sound of heavy pegs being withdrawn from peepholes or ports accompanied the ramming home musket wads made of hornet's nests.

Batiste happily oblivious of the hurried preparations for his reception should he prove to be other than a welcome guest, stepped ashore where he immediately sat down to relieve his aching ankles. The trader motioned Henri to "go see who he is". The half-breed turned quickly at the sound of approaching footsteps and was greeted with, "So it is you again. We thought you were afraid to come back."

Batiste raised his eyebrows in surprise. "Afraid? Monsieur, why should I be afraid, I promised Monsieur La Duc I would be here to accompany you on...should one say...a trip of adventure."

"It is well, 'Mon Sauvage,' that you have some excuse to be here, or I would finish you now."

The young man arose and stared at Henri. Forcing a smile that he knew would aggravate the Frenchman, said, "Save your words, Monsieur, they are only for cowards who can use nothing else. You talk of finishing me, go ahead, you make the first move."

Henri's assumed look of ferocity wavered. "Monsieur La Duc needs you so I am forced to bid you welcome. I am sure everything we have shall be at your disposal."

"At least I shall die happy, in such delightful surroundings, and in your, shall we say...presence."

Batiste laughed good-naturedly as Henri turned to retrace his steps but not until he had flung a few parting words. "When this venture is accomplished, you and I will settle this little matter between us."

Batiste shrugged his shoulders in an attitude of unconcern, "At your pleasure Monsieur, sooner, if you wish."

As the half-breed followed the narrow path leading past the channel to Father Daniel's cabin, he felt no concern over this personal safety, Monsieur La Duc would see to his protection until the raid was carried out. Many, many things could happen before that venture was accomplished. Batiste smiled ironically as he approached the open

188

doorway to the priest's cabin. The young man felt like shouting as the tiny wisp of smoke escaping the mud chimney of Father Daniel's cabin caught his eye. The good Father was alive and at home. That, in itself, was enough to make the young half-breed forget the aches and pains from wading through the water. Unconsciously he raised his head higher and extended his chest. He understood why his mother's people had boasted of endurance on the trail. He, too, was proud, proud that he had not failed, proud that he had the courage to resist temptation, it would have been easier, it is true, but shame and not pride would have been his reward, a shame that would have lingered and like an unexpected ghost haunt his every time he faced a fellow man.

Like drops of white paint scattered about carelessly from an artist's brush, little patches of snow lingered in the shade of closely knit branches of the pine that dotted the landscape; persistent reminders of the passing of winter. Near the lake where its banks sloped sharply to the waters' edge small groups of men watched the ice as it moved before the fitful gusts of the west wind. On the rocky islands dotting the eastern part of the lake, mounting piles of the honey combed ice glistened white in the glaring sunlight. The ice pack moved relentlessly steady, carrying away everything movable along the shore where the tinkling sound of candle shaped particles of ice crumpled against the trunks of trees resisting its force or huge boulders remaining immovable, reluctant to leave their beds of frozen clay and sand. In the wake of the moving ice field white capped waves broke steadily over the retreating and fast crumbling ice that gave out sounds as of some far away stringed musical instrument. In the varying density of the warm west wind, the musical sounds came as in obedience to the fickle moods of the artist. Now loud and clear, then suddenly faint and seemingly from beneath the depths of the crystal clear water always in perfect time with the overall rhythmic wash of the waves.

The missionary, Father Daniels, and his half-breed friend, Batiste, stood apart from the other groups and silently watched the movement of the ice and the display of power it carried in its weight. Despite the many obstructing islands and points of land jutting out into its path together with narrowing shores of the lake, the main body or mass of ice moved steadily on, leaving glistening piles where it failed to move obstacles. Father Daniels stood bareheaded, his long white hair flowing freely in the stiffening breeze.

"If this wind keeps up, we should be able to move real soon."

The half-breed nodded, the bead band of tanned caribou encircling his head held the stray strands of his black hair in place. "We could go tomorrow, or as soon as this wind storm is over."

"Is Monsieur, the trader, ready?"

Batiste shrugged, "I don't know, they should be. They have had plenty of time to get ready,"

"A wonderful wind, is it not?"

Both the priest and his companion turned quickly to face the trader who had come upon them unobserved. The half-breed frowned in self-disapproval. It was not often that he allowed anyone to come that near undetected, a Native, perhaps, but a clumsy white man. That made his carelessness double offensive.

Quickly recovering from the shock of the Native's first rule for self-preservation in the great wilderness, he was able to answer the man quite casually. "Yes, Monsieur, a good wind. When will you be ready to leave?"

"We are ready now. I came to ask you the same question."

Batiste smiled, "I am always ready, Monsieur. Father and I will leave in the morning."

Monsieur La Duc frowned. "I supposed you were to travel with us."

"I shall, Monsieur. I shall wait for you on the portages, but I must go on ahead to pick the way, you have no scouts. Will you be heavily loaded?"

"Not so much from here," he looked at the young man meaningfully. "We expect to collect some debts and trade a little on the way. By the time we reach Lake Superior, we should be well loaded."

"I shall not accompany you any further than Lake Superior, Monsieur. I would be of no use to you on the big lake."

"I am sure we shall greatly appreciate your company that far, Mon Ami, beyond that, we shall manage without you. Au Revoir, Mon Pere, I am glad that you will be in good hands."

"Oh, yes, Monsieur Batiste is a very capable young man. Stop by my cabin and see all the meat he has dried for the trip. He brought me several pairs of new moccasins." The old missionary's eyes lit up happily like some youngster with a new toy. "I shall not cease to thank God for the blessing of this young man."

Monsieur La Duc turned away with a smile, a twisted smile tinged with irony.

That night the young half-breed pondered long over the trader's words "We shall manage without you" and decided that he would be doubly cautious when the time came to part. He smiled as he rolled over on the hard ground and drew his blanket closely about him.

Chapter 23

Lac Superieur! Like a bird long confined now freed from its cage to soar, at will, even to the dizzy heights where specks of clouds moved lazily across the field of blue sky, Paulette stood barefooted where the wash of waves played about her ankles. Forgetting for the moment the bustle and hustle about her, the launching and loading of canoes as willing helpers stood waist deep in the clear cold water, holding the frail bark craft clear of the pebble strewn bottom, the girl let her gaze wander far out where the clouds rested, like gulls on the rim of horizon. She thrilled to the freedom the broad expanse of gently undulating water implied. The girl smiled broadly as she noted the subdued air of activity, the hushed voices of youngsters long given to boisterous shouts and laughter. She missed the sound of childish quarrels and fights, the loud wailing over a broken toy, the high pitched scolding voices of mothers threatening their offspring with dire punishment should they continue in the pranks. Sharing the feeling of awe and veneration the great lake inspired in the minds and hearts of more than one hundred families of backwoods Natives who seeing Gichi Gamee. The girl felt a glow of pride in her heritage.

Little gusts of wind, rustling fitfully the first leaves of spring, no larger than an average thumbnail, set tiny ripples outward over the incoming waves. As Paulette strolled slowly along the beach, she overheard many expressions of wonderment, how could the waves roll in against the wind? Over and over, to intensely interested Natives, the girl explained that the waves of the "big water" never ceased to roll. Dressed in a simple gown of gray with a low cut yoke and sleeveless, trimmed with black velveteen and cut a short ankle length, her black hair severely parted and braided, glistened in the sunlight in keeping with several strings of beads of varying colors that adorned her neck. As naturally as the calm in the wake of a storm, the girl, without either her will or consent, had assumed the sole place of authority in the lives of the people about her. Due partly to her activity in promoting the mass migration for the spring ceremonial festival, the Natives and mixed bloods had without one dissenting voice fallen in line with her leadership. Older men long accustomed to wielding authority, jealously guarded, submerged their identity for the time being and cast their lot into the swaying influence of "Wi-sa-go-de ikwens" or "Little Half-breed woman", obeying her without question her suggestions for their mutual protection and wellbeing. This signal honor rode lightly on the shoulders of "Little Half-breed Woman" as she was known to her mother's people and one would have found it difficult indeed to single her out as holding the power of life and death over the party, both white and red. Never raising her voice above the ordinary conversational tone, Paulette displayed a latent talent for leadership in the flash of her eyes that registered disapproval, in pointed pins of fire, any infraction of instructions given for the welfare of the party. Slow to praise, like her savage ancestors, she felt that knowledge of a thing well done

193

carried its own rewards. Idle expressions of praise were both unwanted and withheld.

Refusing, decisively to ride at ease in one of the large freighter canoes as befitting one of her rank and position, she used one of her own choosing, one scarcely larger than the play canoes of her childhood. Consistently refusing assistance on the long portages, she packed the light craft while grandfather and grandmother came slowly along with the rest of their belongings. Only one item she entrusted to Pascal, her small bale of personal apparel, prepared for the occasion, during the days and nights of spring. Upon threat of having his heavy red paint brush beard taken out by the roots, the little man was admonished to protect the package with his very life of necessary. With her grandparents safely tucked away within the narrow confines of her little canoe, Paulette, with the willing help of the old couple, moved in and out among her flotilla of canoes, at will.

That morning as the first streaks of light began to show in the east, she fired the shot that called in the scouts posted at strategic positions some distance from the camp. After a hasty cold meal prepared the evening before, "Little Half-breed Woman" walked slowly through the camp and selected eight fresh scouts. Four canoes, two men to each craft would paddle far in advance, skirting the shore. Next in order a number of families or brave men and their sons proudly filled the position of advance guard. Following the heavy fur and supply laden canoes, would come the main body of highly nervous and dubious Natives riding Superior's waves for the first time. The difficult task, however, was the selection of young hunters for the day, young men tried on the field of experience. Traveling with the advance scouts or lagging far behind, with eyes trained to detect the slightest movement in the forest, their arrows furnished the food to supplement that carried by each family in well protected bundles. She had to disappoint many ambitious young hunters each day, willing and capable young men nervously anxious to display their prowess. A nod and a promise that "tomorrow will be your turn" would suffice to dampen the most ardent candidate. Without stopping to listen to veiled comments on her selections or the barbed jibes of young wives, belittling the capabilities of husbands on the chase, in the hope that "Little Half-breed Woman" would overhear and reconsider her selection, allowing friend husband to stay nearer his family in the trying hours ahead on Superior's waves, the girl passed on, stopping only to inquire the health of a newborn infant's mother, or pat the head of a prized pup, securely hobbled. Once out on the broad expanse of Superior, the girl relied considerably on the keen memory and judgement of her grandparents with their knowledge of nature's storm warnings. Only on one or two occasions did grandfather question her judgement as she sent the heavy canoes across deep bays and ordered the smaller family craft to skirt the shore in safety. The old man could see no reason they should go the long way around when their objective was so near. I took much explaining to convince the old fellow, ably defended by her grandmother, that the "Sa-gwaan-dago" or backwoods Indian was not accustomed to "Big Water". The waves and wind "out there" gathering in size and momentum could easily cause panic among the simple people who lived out their lives in the comparative peace and quiet of Du Pays d'en Haut.

In passing the lead canoe of the freighters, Paulette burst out in joyous laughter. Atop the forward thwart of the broad beamed canoe, Pascal sat waving his arms frantically to his mistress. Like some wood sprite from another world, with beard and hair silhouetted as a red patch against the brown canvas makeshift sail, the little fellow, with some effort, let his bare feet touch the cool water as it lapped the sides of their canoe. With scarce a worry except for the welfare of those he loved, the carefree little man was most excitedly happy. Beside his light paddle, set aside for the time being as the wind moved them along in

195

keeping with the smaller canoes, a loaded musket protruded, its muzzle and hammer lock carefully wrapped against the spray that might render it useless when needed.

As the days wore on and the fleet of canoes neared their destination, Paulette kept a sharp lookout for landmarks that like old friends would be the first to send the blood rushing excitedly through her veins. While grandfather pointed out several places along the shore and recounted stories of connected happenings, it was not until they rounded a heavily timbered point that she first recognized a huge dead pine that, standing on a bit of raised ground, spread its skeleton-like limbs protectively over the smaller green trees surrounding it.

"Look grandfather!" the girl cried, excitedly pointing her dripping paddle, "I remember that old dead tree. That is where we came to fish in the stream. Remember when the fish went up the creek to spawn and we built a dam of stones near its mouth?"

Grandfather shaded his eyes while grandmother merely glanced up and nodded quickly. "Soon we will be home again," and in a lowered voice continued, "I wonder how many came back from the winter camps."

Every spring it was the same question that lay uppermost in the minds of the Natives, "How many?" With renewed effort brought on by the sight of the old landmark, Paulette's light canoe surged forward. It was not a matter of days and nights anymore, but each paddle stroke, like the wash of the waves over the sands, marked the passing of time when she would again beach her canoe on the sand of her native shore.

The girl let her mind wander aimlessly about the old village, in and out of the log cabins of the French quarter, along the winding paths that held the wigwams of the Native quarter as one. With a start, she remembered the great maple tree laying across the path and her encounter with Napoleon LaChance, the trader's son. Her face flushed as she concentrated her attention to the madly swirling water in the wake of her paddle strokes. With eyes partly closed and unmindful of the course of her canoe, Little Half-breed smiled an ironically dangerous little smile. All too vividly the picture of the selfishly smug trader passed before her. Shaking her head like one dislodging clinging cobwebs, Paulette brushed aside, for the time being, thoughts of the only very unpleasant memories of her youth and quickly brought the canoe sharply back to its course, its prow pointing homeward.

Chapter 24

The uneven markings on his canoe, not unlike a turtle's shell, glistened wet in the midday sun as Batiste quietly pushed the light craft among the tall rushes along the lake shore. An occasional boulder ominously poked its head above the surface of the water, the young man with surprising ease, guided the frail bark canoe skillfully out of harm's way. His black eyes, ever on the alert for the trading post of the late, Francois, that he knew was located in the vicinity.

One day's travel "back there" where at the junction of the east and west water shed with its chain of lakes, and the beginning of the trail to Lake Superior, he had left the trader La Duc and his party. In a camp of his own and some distance away from that of the trader, the good Father Daniels awaited the return of his young friend. After examining the portage carefully, the half-breed had informed Monsieur La Duc that hundreds of people both Natives and white had migrated to

Lake Superior, having passed several days since. Selecting several boot shod foot prints, the young man tried to convince the would-be raider that a trip to the post was useless as they would find no one there. But the trader, having visualized so many times the successful outcome of his plan to rob the post of its furs, found it hard to adopt himself to the new turn of events. Clinging desperately to his original plan and hoping against hope that the signs belied the facts, the man finally induced the half-breed to "go and make sure" that his deductions were correct.

As Batiste stood in the strange quiet beside the clustered log buildings, the gently swishing sound of long swamp grasses fluttered rain-washed from the clay binding of the chimneys, like tattered raiment of some ghostly skeleton. Satisfied that the girl Paulette and her stock of furs were safe for the time being, the young man turned and strode away in search of some Native family. Everywhere empty cabins and the vacated frames of wigwams intensified the awesome loneliness of the place. The atmosphere of complete desertion was overpowering and he felt an urge to run away, but, thoughts of Paulette held him, as if he were drugged beyond recognition of his surroundings. This place was hers. She had trod the little path he now followed. He searched unconsciously the well-beaten trail that wound so gracefully in and out among the pines, for one little moccasin foot print on the bare possibility that it might be hers. As he walked steadily along, his reverie was broken by a low ominous growl, clear and unmistakable, a note of warning. Stopping in his tracks at the first sound, his hand unconsciously resting on the hilt of his knife, he uttered an exclamation of surprise and admiration as Kai-aushk, Paulette's half-wild dog rounded a bend in the path and stopped but a few steps away. The animal seemingly aware of its beauty, carried its head high, its black tipped ears pointed sharply forward. With a sudden desire to pet and stroke its snow white head and shoulders, the young man stepped forward, but the dog's bared white teeth and low ominous growl again stopped him. "I see you are particular who you make friends with," Batiste spoke in Ojibwe. An immediate change in the animal's attitude became quite apparent as it took a few steps forward. The young man squatted on his heels and extended a hand. "Come boy. I wish I knew your name, let's see. I you were mine, with that white band around your shoulders, you remind me of a gull riding the waves. I'd call you 'Kai-aushk'." The animal cocked its head sideways and took another step forwards. "I think I made a good guess. Come on Kai-aushk." The huge beast warily advanced, slowly and suspiciously put its cool muzzle into the outstretched hand of the man who would be its friend. Batiste happily rubbed the animal's ears and patted its head and shoulders all the time keeping up a steady chatter. "Is anyone living around here besides you? I wonder who you belong too? If you weren't so big, I would like to take you with me. You are well taken care of, so fat and sleek, let's go and find out. Somebody must live where you came from." Batiste arose and passed on beside the animal, which eyed him carefully and turned to follow closely. They had walked but a short way when the welcome sounds of a woodchopper's axe broke in upon the stillness. The young man stepped up his pace closely followed by this newfound friend.

The old man looked up quickly, gave out no sign of surprise and said simply, "Boozhoo," and continued to gather into a convenient armload the pieces of firewood he had broken into convenient lengths. "Where do you come from? I have never seen you before."

Batiste ignored the question and asked in return "Do you live here?"

"Yes, my wigwam stands nearby." Seeing the big dog come up and nudge the half-breed in a friendly fashion, continued quickly, "That dog never makes friends with anyone, and you are a stranger." As though seeing the half-breed for the first time, he eyed the young man intently and continued, "You are welcome, young man, to enter my wigwam. Come, we will go, my woman will prepare some food for us, come."

The half-breed quickly gathered the remainder of the wood the old fellow had cut and followed along the path. All the way to this wigwam, the kindly white haired man kept up a steady unintelligible muttering.

Later that afternoon, reclining restfully on the lavishly bough covered ground beside the outdoor fireplace, Batiste learned of Paulette's activities throughout the winter, of her team of wild dogs, the mass migration, at her invitation, to Lake Superior for the seasonal festival. Strange Natives from far beyond the hills, where seemingly only the echoes of the girl's voice must have reached, had arrived during the first days of the breakup, with canoe loads of furs and fervent requests to join the party. Strangely the young man thrilled with satisfaction at the news of Paulette's wellbeing, he seemed to recall that somehow he never doubted the girl's ability to survive and prosper. It was with a light heart and many thanks that he left his host's abode.

Reaching the landing where he had placed his canoe well up on the bank, he was surprised to see the friendly look of the dog nearby. Reaching up among the branches of a small pine where he had cached his sack of dried meat, Batiste sat on the trunk of a fallen tree, called Kai-aushk to his side and generously divided his meager supply with the animal. "I don't have much, Kai-aushk, but I can get more along the way," The animal looked up and came very near to being the first of its kind to wag a friendly tail.

Chapter 25

The smoke from two hundred campfires hung heavily, like a ceiling at treetop level, obscuring many of the young leaves of the birch and poplar. Great pines and maples generously interspersed with hemlock entwined their wide spreading branches in friendly embrace.

Lake Superior, not to be outdone, lay in comparative quiet, the ceaseless roll of its waves in keeping with the prevailing whim of nature muffled its tone to a low whisper. Despite nature's unusually calm atmosphere, the Natives milled about in what could seem a useless, pointless activity. Over and above the usual sounds of village life in the early morn, an unusual tension seemed to permeate the little groups gathered about various village campfires. Usually one of the groups talked in excited tones while the rest listened with mounting interest. "Yes, the missionary and his half-breed companion arrived first. Later the four strange white men were captured by the "Little Half-breed Woman's" men and securely tied. "They say the Frenchmen are traders, some of our people should recognize them, no one knows what will be done with them, some say they will be shot, others say the Little Half-breed Woman will decide what to do." And so it went, gathering momentum as it rolled along from wigwam to wigwam, from group to group until the prisoners had been shot, hanged, burned at the stake and tied to a tree and left to starve, for what reason? No one knew.

Emerging from the oval Sha-ban-do-wan, or lodge of her grandparents, Paulette quickly turned her steps towards the sand beach and the lake she loved. Walking knee deep into the cool water and scooping up the refreshing fluid in her cupped hands, she drank deeply more in token of happy reunion with childhood memories. Yes, it was here she floated her first toy canoe and shot her first arrow far out into its turbulent waters and sat to wait patiently for the great lake to return it. Starting, like one guilty of some inexcusable oversight, or the willful neglect of an important duty, the girl glanced uneasily towards the cliff-like shore beyond the ravine. Over there, where in her childhood, the little old men had come up out of the earth, out the caverns beneath and danced and wrestled in carefree abandon. She smiled in happy memory at the many colored beards and the long funny looking gowns, the little round mischievously sparkling doll-like eyes, how she loved the little cavern folk. True, they always left some wild flower to mark the place where they disappeared into the earth, and their garments were of the color of the flower that stood unconcerned, it was so aggravating, as though ti didn't know. And the bits of maple sugar she begged from grandmother and tobacco from grandfather, placed so carefully and secretly beneath the dead leaves near the roots of each flower stem. Tonight, after the moon comes and casts its golden streak across the water, she would visit them if, and this was serious, if they were at home and not out racing about on that golden pathway. Upon reaching dry land, she was met by her right hand man and confidante, Pascal. I spite of a sleepy and work look, he could not hide an excited expression.

"Madam, listen to me before you go back to your camp. There are some men waiting to see you about those four men, they want to know what you are going to do with them."

Unhesitatingly the girl answered, "Nothing, Pascal, tell them that. Nothing until we know more about them. They are to be held until noon, see that they get plenty to eat and drink. After dinner remind me again."

With his feet thumping the ground in rapid succession, the little man sped away at what was to him a fast pace. He enjoyed his position as messenger to the Little Half-breed Woman. When the girl arrived at their lodge, the committee had left and all was quiet, but she had a busy day ahead, the site for the ceremonial lodge must be selected, another for the games, feats of strength, foot races for men, women and children, gambling, moccasin games and canoe races. The selection of hunters for each day, some of the youth were beginning to tire of the daily hunt and complained of some imaginary ailment that they might take part in the more exciting festivities instead. To these, the girl used her seldom employed biting sarcasm. "The men of Lake Superior are good and willing hunters. Were the men of Sa-gwan-da-go like old women crippled with sickness and age?" That was severe medicine for the proud Natives steeped in the tradition of his ancestors. It never had to be administered but once.

There was bark to be gathered for the roof of the great lodge and men selected to do the work, saplings must be cut for the framework and other men and young women to gather wood for the fires, not only for the nighttime festivities, but for the old and helpless. She had also her own private affairs to attend. There was the little matter of Monsieur LaChance and his rat of a son Napoleon. She frowned deeply at the thought. The hours sped by rapidly as it does to all people busily engaged.

Pascal, ever at the side of his mistress, darted in and out carrying a stout staff to ward off vicious little dogs that came snapping at his heels. Greeted with ill-concealed smiles, not meant in ridicule, the little man spread cheer, in his own particular way, among the Native villagers. Working her way from group to group to the farther end of the village, Paulette greeted and visited a few moments with each of her people. Among those of the backwoods whom she had visited during the winter, she gathered the history and an account of the activities of the four prisoners, by noon she was well equipped to pass judgement.

News of Paulette's intention to dispose, publicly, the question of "What to do about the four captives," spread rapidly. Soon groups of men, women, and children gathered about the abode of the girl. Black bearded Frenchmen stood shoulder to shoulder with semi-naked Natives and borrowed a "little fire" from long stemmed stone pipes. Mothers with infants securely strapped to Ti-ki-na-gan, or cradle boards, chattered ceaselessly on various social problems of the day, the coming festival, the run of fish up the streams, what possibilities for a good blueberry crop, did many of the newcomers get seasick on the way, the woman living alone by the lake hoarding maple sugar and wild rice, always complaining about starving to death, and on and endlessly on.

Eager eyed young hunters and maidens impatiently waited for the excitement to begin, "I hope she has them shot, I never saw anyone killed, some say they are dangerous and have many lives and cannot be killed, maybe better if Little Half-breed had nothing to do with them, one never knows what strange power they might possess." The steady hum of noises rose in volume as more and more of the inhabitants ceased their allotted tasks and forgetting the long looked for festival, hurried with undue haste along the sharply indented path leading to the supposed place of execution. Within her lodge, Paulette listened to the drone of voices like an approaching swarm of bees, and turning to Pascal who sat near the entrance nervously awaiting his mistresses' orders. "Tell our men to bring out the captives, they will lead them to the cleared spot by Monsieur LaChance's post, and Pascal, first tell Henri LaClair to gather together all his men and arm them. The prisoners must be protected, go now quickly."

Like a flash, the little man was well on his way before the weighted door curtain had clattered noisily into place. Little Half-breed Woman, dressed in a red gown trimmed with the little shell stars and gathered at the waist with a wide band of black beaver fur, her hair usually braided, now lay in two large rolls one on each side of her head and gathered loosely at the back with a narrow strip of white ermine, red tipped, gazed reminiscently into the fire and with a short twig of burnt sapling, toyed with some of the embers that rolled dangerously near the woven mat of marsh grasses. Suddenly oblivious to all else, save her thoughts, as she traveled back along memory's pathway to the time when grandmother had placed her high upon a platform among the trees to fast, in keeping with Native custom. The girl struggled for a moment like one tugging at a long line to loosen its end entangled somewhere along the path, and at last successful, she smiled at the vista that opened up to her in memory.

It was on the third evening of her fast, she remembered now quite clearly, that she dreamt of following a lonely path, narrow and strewn with many obstacles. Struggling on, she came to a spot where it widened somewhat and turned sharply upward towards the hills. Following on more easily, she came to another bend and saw four strangers sitting by the wayside securely bound. Directly opposite, a large crowd of people gathered. They seemed antagonistic and eagerly watched her untie the four prisoners and sent them on the way she had come with instructions never to return. Over and above, like the wind sighing in the pine tops, she had distinguished a low melancholy song, its words forgotten, yet the melody lingered in her memory. With the bit of twig, Paulette kept time in rhythmic beats, as she hummed the tune. Grandmother cast a knowing glance at grandfather who nodded understandingly, little puffs of tobacco smoke arising from his pipe bowl in time with the girl's imaginary drum beats. As the song ended, Pascal thrust aside the curtain door and entering said, "The men are on their way, wear the cloak, Madam, the wind has shifted and is coming from the north."

Paulette searched among her belongings and brought out the blue cape with its silk lining of many colors. Stepping out into the cool air, she was surprised to find herself calm and collected. Fastening the silver clasp that held the garment securely and wrapping its folds about her, Paulette worked her way among the assembled people towards the place selected for the trial.

Standing in the opening among the trees, surrounded by twenty white men with loaded muskets mistakenly supposed by the Natives as guarding the prisoners, the four men looked as dejected as mortals could. Fastened in pairs to the birch pole lying across the back of their necks, much as a yoke for oxen, and tied securely with many turns of rawhide to their necks, their hands uplifted as one in shocked surprise, but tied to the pole beside their shoulders, the men touched a sympathetic cord in the heart of the girl as she said, "Untie the men, surely so many of my white brothers can guard so few without the added torture of being tied like wild animals."

The girl walked slowly before the captives, releasing her hold on the folds of her cape, the breeze blew half of it over her shoulder where its bright silken colors changed rapidly with her every movement. Stepping about noiselessly, her plain tightly fitting moccasins of white caribou in marked contrast to the brown of autumn leafs, left no imprint on the springy soil. "Which one of you is the leader?" she spoke in a quiet even tone.

"I am, Mademoiselle. I am Jean La Duc begging to ask why my men and myself are treated like animals."

"Because you are criminals, Monsieur La Duc"

"But, Mademoiselle, we have not killed anyone, except perhaps in fair combat."

"One does not have to kill his fellow man to be a criminal, Monsieur, unless you can produce someone to speak for you, to convince us that you are not thieves and raiders, you will be taken back into the hills and shot."

Like a gust of wind rustling the leaves of a birch, Paulette's words caused an excited wave to pass through the crowed. Excited translations by the Native wives of the French men, passed quickly from group to group.

Near the prisoners, the crowd parted as the white haired missionary, Father Daniels stepped quickly forward and stood before the girl and looked upon her with increasing emotion as he noted her calm and collected attitude. With some difficulty, Paulette controlled her expression of surprise at the sight of the good man lest it betray her inward emotion. With all the willpower she could command, she asked rather saucily, "Does the good Father wish to speak for the prisoners?"

"Not for the prisoners, my child, but for you. What is this terrible thing you think of doing?" The priest, with tears of compassion glistening in his brown eyes and voice filled with emotion, continued, "Know you not that for the crime you are about to commit, you, in turn, will be judged and punished by Almighty God?" Drawing the black ebony crucifix, with its silver figure of his master from his wide sash, like one drawing a dagger in defense of his life, his tall frame now bent with age, yet ever ready to do battle for the right as he saw it, said, "In the first place, you are only a child and can have no right either from God or man to pass sentence upon your elders."

The girl interrupted, "Perhaps I have no right, Mon Pere, but if I order them shot, they will be shot, whether or not I have a right to do so. I have two hundred braves and twenty of your kind to carry out my orders. Have you more to say?"

The old man bowed his head and with gaze fixed upon the little crucifix, prayed silently. This was not the first time that he was at a disadvantage. In his long years of battling with, in his belief, ignorance and superstition, rooted deep in the minds of the Native people, he had often wept bitter tears after a retreat for want of endurance to continue the battle, yet in the loneliness of the great forest, he had prayed much as his Master in the garden of Gethsemane on that fateful night. With renewed strength fortified by his belief in the promise handed down through the ages "Ask and you shall receive," he would return to the battle and invariably win. The hushed crowd, like the calm before a storm, sensed that they were standing on the eve of something momentous; they knew not what, as they watched intensely, scarcely daring to breathe as the white haired man bowed in prayer. Looking over the assembled Natives, in the distance a glimpse of the great lake flashed among the trees, little waves reflected like jewels the rays of the sun now well on its way past its noontime rest. Changing from French to Ojibwe and holding his precious crucifix high so all could see, he raised his voice in a fervent plea, not for the prisoners, but for his children. "There was a time, my children," he began and pointing a trembling finger towards the upraised symbol, he recounted the oft told story of the birth and crucifixion, of the thieves, the Master's words, "This day thou shalt be with me in paradise. Who are we to judge our fellow man, judge not lest you be judged." Turning again to the girl as she leaned against a great hemlock in an attitude of mild disdain, he said, "Again I plead with you, my child, do not do this

209

terrible thing, I will concede that you hold the power of life and death over these men, do not, for one moment, my child, forget that Almighty God holds the fate of the world and all his people in the palm of his hand. His angels in heaven shall weep bitter tears over this act of yours, should you persist in committing this terrible sin. There is not much I can do except to pray, 'May God in all his goodness, have mercy on your soul.'"

The kindly man, as one bearing a heavy burden, one, too heavy to bear, turned and slowly walked away and disappeared among the people, his lips moving in silent prayer. Paulette remained silent for some moments as all eyes were turned toward her; eagerly awaiting her next word.

"The good missionary should have preached to these four thieves before they became criminals, it could have saved them and us a lot of trouble and pain."

"But, Mademoiselle, they are Christian gentlemen, born and educated in the faith of Old France." Father Daniels had quickly returned and again faced the girl.

Paulette smiled that crooked little smile. "Mon Pere, you do not know it, but these crooks intended to rob this post and were using you and your cassock as a cover to get on the inside, not only of the post, but into the confidence of the people."

The good padre, with eyes widening from shock, evinced his doubt of the girl's statement by steadily shaking his head. "I cannot believe that, my child. You have been misinformed."

"Ask Monsieur La Duc, Father, and let him tell you."

Father Daniels turned to the trader and said, "Tell me, my son, that this is not true, that I do not hear right, this girl was misinformed."

The trader, with a feigned look of innocence, said in a hurt tone, "Mon Pere, it is not true. My only motive was to help in the good work of spreading the gospel among the Native children of God."

Before the priest could say anything, Paulette sprang forward and for the first time, raised her voice in anger. "You liar..! You thief! Unless you can produce someone from this gathering who can truthfully say that you have ever done any act of kindness to anyone, it is my will that you and your men shall be taken back among the hills and shot. You will be buried where only the wolf pack can find and howl over your graves!" A forward surging motion among the crowd of Natives, who, not understanding the girl's words, surmised that something was amiss. Paulette held up one hand and the crowd quieted. "My people, you will not take any part in this proceeding. Remain where you are, that is my word."

A murmur of approval reassured the girl that she was still in command. Monsieur La Duc and his companions quickly huddled with their heads close together in animated though subdued conversation. While waiting, the girl glanced over the assemblage and started at the sight of Monsieur LaChance and his son Napoleon. If she had any reason to experience a feeling of satisfaction over the proceedings, it was in knowing that the trader and his son were spectators.

"Soon it will be your turn," she thought. "I have a score to settle with both of you." Once again giving her attention to the prisoners, she said in her natural tone, "It seems, gentlemen that you are having some difficulty in finding what you most desire at this time, maybe I can help you." The men looked at her blankly, hope for a reprieve having been lost completely. Turning to the Natives grouped nearby, she said, "Is Wa-sa-gii-shik, the one from the blueberry country beyond the hills, here? I am sure he is here somewhere, someone find him and bring him. It is my will."

A slight movement among the spectators some distance away from the front line, a tall Indian scantily clad came forward, a lone eagle feather tied in his long hair swayed gently. Muscular and actively alert, the middle aged man stepped proudly as one on a mission of great importance. Standing before the girl, the Indian waited for her to speak.

"Will our relative tell what these four men did for you when your mate was sick and you were unable to leave her side?"

Without hesitation, the man started on a long discourse, beginning with the winter before the last one, it was during the cold of the midwinter moon, that his woman was taken sick, dwelling at some length on the probable cause, he continued to relate how these men had come by his wigwam and seeing his plight, gave him blankets and warm clothing. They also cut much dry wood, enough to last until his mate got well so he could get back on the trail and hunt for food.

At the end of the man's narrative, Paulette asked, "Have you given them anything in exchange for what they did?"

"Oh, yes, I got many beaver every spring and gave all to them."

"How many more winters did they say you would have to work to pay them for what they gave you?"

The Indian held up one hand signifying five more winter.

"That is all, you may go my friend." Turning once again to the four men, she said, "A high price for mercy, gentlemen, and don't say it was all done in the name of God." Monsieur La Duc and his companions looked at the ground at their feet and remained silent. Paulette bit her lip in silent study before speaking. "One cannot ignore the kind interest of the good Father Daniels. His words are heavy with wisdom. It is with a lighter heart, do I say that these four men shall be turned loose upon the waters of Lake Superior. They shall be given back everything that was taken from them except guns, ammunition and knives. With one knife and sufficient food to take them across the lake, they shall leave this shore, never to return. If they do return, it shall be the duty of any man or woman, both, White or Native, within the sound of my voice, to kill them on sight. If they should escape, then

212

they will be hunted as one hunts for wild animals until their bodies are safely buried where they can never be found by their kind. That is my wish. Take them away." Raising her hand for the Native's attention, she repeated the statement in Ojibwe and added, "These men have done some good among our people and for that they must be allowed to go unharmed. If any of you do them harm, you shall be brought to me and you, too, may know what it means to leave home, never to return."

Paulette quickly returned to her Sha-ban-do-wan and threw herself upon the grass mat. She was tired and for the first time in her life, she felt an ache about her temples.

Chapter 26

Buckskin sacks of various sizes filled with sand for the packing contest bowed the platform of saplings upon which they were piled. Other sacks, with convenient hand holds of wide thongs for the carrying contest, lay by. Pascal's eyes blazed with excitement as he darted about like a hummingbird from flower to flower, clearing the path over which the contestants would prove their strength and endurance. The bursts of laughter followed by a more subdued tone from the men engaged in erecting the framework of the ceremonial lodge, its bent saplings securely tied with strips of basswood bark, reached Paulette as she busied herself about the fire preparing their morning meal. With the villagers well organized, each in an allotted task, the girl, in this clear sunny morning, had little to do other than see that the hunters did not shirk their part in the affairs of the village. Ordinarily each family would shift for themselves, but this gathering was different, the villagers had to work as a team. The girl moved about the inhabitants gathering information on the previous day's take and its distribution. Upon the suggestion of a youth that some of the hunters spend their time in taking the fish that were spawning in the many streams flowing into the great lake, Paulette asked with well-directed sarcasm, "Would the brave young hunter from the hills show his prowess by doing the work of women and children of the village?"

Soon several canoes, with young women and insistent boys and girls, rolled gracefully over the incoming waves as they pointed their sharply upturned prows, some west, others east, in quest of fish for the village. Ever on the alert for, at least a glimpse of, the man she wanted most to see and whom she knew was somewhere nearby in the great forest. Paulette moved about with ever increasing fear that Batiste would take it upon himself to leave without seeing her. The must be some way to find him and at least attract his attention, was he at the trial of the four men? She didn't see him. Why did he remain hidden away? If he persisted in acting like a child...she...yes, that was it, she had two hundred scouts, she could have him brought to her. He was hiding, why? Was he purposely shirking his duty as a member of the village, she would find out.

Paulette smiled, but the smile was short lived. She stopped and held her breath as Batiste, standing but an arm's length away, said, "Bon Jour Madam, you are a person hard to find. I have been searching for you all morning."

"Bon Jour, Batiste," Paulette managed to say without too much show of excitement as suddenly her surroundings seemed to blur and move about in a dazed confused way. "The man who saved my life," she thought, "What shall I say?" She reached out and rested her hand against the tree that stood beside her, she wanted to lean against its stout trunk, she needed support as with mounting fear, she felt her knees tremble and weaken. "Where have you been, Mon Ami? My grandparents have often asked for you. You never gave them an opportunity to thank you for saving my life, and theirs." To Paulette, her voice had sounded far away and surreal, the words she uttered seemed to come of their own accord, without thought of effort on her part. Before the young man could speak, she continued hastily, "Won't you come now to our lodge? It is but a short distance, whatever your errand, you may speak there."

"I really have not time to visit, Madam, but Father Daniels"

"We are still young, Mon Ami," somehow she could not help calling him "my friend," "time is not of much importance except to the aged. Come, must I command you?" she asked with a mischievous glance that made Batiste's heart falter. She was the most beautiful creature alive! The narrow band of brown otter fur with its little clusters of red jasper and white quartz skillfully worked into slender birdlike figures hanging at her temples, gave out a subdued tinkling sound as she moved her head with a captivating upward tilt. Several strings of colored beads lay snug against her neck and throat filling the low cut yoke of her gown of blue. The young man hesitated then turned and preceded her along the narrow path.

"I stopped by," he nearly said "your", but somehow it wouldn't sound right, "the trading post," he said. "I met your dog 'Kai-aushk'."

Quickly the girl reached out and grasped the young man's arm, stopping him. "Tell me, Batiste, how is he? Was he friendly…can he still see…how did you know its name?"

Batiste laughed, "Easy, Madam, one question at a time."

Paulette bit her lip impatiently. "Do hurry and tell me. I want to know."

"Time is plentiful only to the young," he teased.

Her eyes flashed and she made a stern face. "Besides being stubborn, you are…what is it they say…impossible."

"I'll tell you all about Kai-aushk if you will first tell me how you knew so much about those four men yesterday."

"We could bargain the other way around, but to save time, I have many, many scouts and I traveled about last winter. I was very near, too near their post and camped with some of their Natives. Monsieur La Duc had tried to get some of our people to join his raid, we were waiting for him."

"Why did you want them to be shot?"

"I didn't, I was only bluffing. It did no harm to let them know what will happen if they ever come back."

"You had poor Father Daniels worried sick."

"I know. I nearly broke down. I wanted to cry, he is such a nice man. Oh well," with a little shrug, she continued, "Monsieur La Duc is on his way back to France and Father Daniels preached a wonderful sermon to many people at one time since he has been in this country."

Batiste stood staring at the girl and involuntarily his head moved slightly from side to side in a gesture of admiration. Summoning all the inherited powers of resistance and self-control of his mother's people, he let his arms hang listlessly at his side and turned to move on.

"Wait, young man," the sharp commanding voice caused him to whirl in his tracks and again face the laughing girl. "What about my dog?"

"I'm sorry Paulette," he said sincerely.

A slight frown emphasized the slant in her eyes at the sound of her name, it was the first time he had ever mentioned it and it was the first time in her life that she thrilled to the sound of her own name.

Within her lodge, Batiste sipped the sweetened tea from a small bark container, the little fire crackled merrily beneath a kettle of rabbit stew to which Paulette added wild rice.

"That smells good," the young man remarked.

"If you will wait, you may have some."

217

"Oh, no, I must get back to Father Daniels."

"I was going to ask, where do you stay?"

"We have a log cabin. One of the couples moved out and doubled up with another family."

"What does the good Father do? I must go and talk to him about yesterday."

Batiste smiled and said, "The last time I saw of him, he was sitting on a stump outside of our cabin. He has all the children of the village gathered about him. Strange how he can hold the children's attention."

"What was he doing?"

"He was telling them stories. It is not what he says that holds their attention, but the way he tells them the story. He seems to put all the kindness of his heart into every word."

Paulette nodded, "I remember, he used to gather us about him, he was younger then, but just the same as now."

"I didn't know he had been here before."

"Oh, yes, several times. I must not forget to see him." For a moment, the silence was disturbed only by scraping sound of grandfather's knife as he piled more red willow bark tobacco by his side. "Did you know that the knife throwing and archery contest will start this afternoon?"

Batiste shrugged, "Does it matter? It is not for me."

Paulette showed her disappointment as she offered him more tea. "That is not the way to talk, my friend." Setting the small kettle back on its wooden hook near the fire, she continued, "Our village had divided itself into two rival camps. On the one side, are the people from the backwoods who are against us who live by Lake Superior. Now we think we are so much better than you Sa-gwan-da-go, we are going to prove it. If you think enough of your people, Batiste, why not join in the fun and let us see how good you are?" Paulette flushed with embarrassment and shame at her words and hastened to add, "Please Batiste, I do not mean it that way, can we ever forget to thank the Great Spirit for your skill with the knife? I…I…it was very thoughtless of me to say it that way. Will you forget it?"

"I shall take part in the contest, Mademoiselle, if you will also try the archery," he said smiling.

"You are very kind, Mon Ami. I do not deserve forgiveness so easily. I will also try the knife throwing. I used to be good when a child, maybe I have not forgotten. I never owned a knife of my own but I remember borrowing grandfather's often."

"Shall we compete as a team?"

Paulette studied the patterns in the grass mat and then slowly shook her head. "That would not be fair. I belong here and you from beyond the hills. I shall compete against you both with the knife and the bow."

"Very well, Madam, as you wish, lucky for you it is for sport and not for keeps."

Paulette found it difficult to tell whether his words were in jest or was he serious, those backwoods Indians had good control of their facial expressions. "You are very sure of yourself, Monsieur." The young man bowed. "You may not have the conceit to take back that you brought from the back country, but tell me, Batiste, what was the errand that sent you in such haste?"

"Father Daniels sent me to tell you that tomorrow is Sunday and he wishes to have mass before the ceremonies begin."

"Tell the good Father that he can do so before the activities tomorrow."

"Always the woman has the last word," Batiste smiled as the weighted curtain fell into place with a clatter behind him.

Paulette sat with face flushed as she poured, with shaky hand, a cup of tea for herself and removed the kettle of stew with wild rice from its wooden hook and set it beside her aged grandparents, saying "The sun rides high, grandmother. Grandfather must be hungry. He can't live on Ki-ni-ki-nik alone."

****

One of the happiest days of the waning years in the life of the good Father Daniels, was coming to a close. Standing before the altar of saplings, its spotless linen cloth glowing white in marked contrast to the back drop of evergreens with boughs closely intertwined. Above the grotto-like tabernacle, the good Father's ebony crucifix with its' silver figure, radiated its message of sacrifice to humanity. At the foot of the altar, cedar boughs piled deep by the village maidens, gave out a peculiarly fragrant odor not unlike incense, adding an air of quiet reverence about the place. Above the vaulted roof of the lodge, chickadees flitted about the wide fronds of branches of the pine and hemlock, their little wings folded in reckless dives from high above to the rounded roof below. One more curious than its mates flew daringly through the open sides of the structure and came to light upon the silver rail of white birch, its little head restlessly turning in many directions, while tiny claws held it firmly to its perch.

The final psalm in the good man's daily prayers, taxed his eyesight in the waning light as he read on in sincere gratitude. At last, he closed the leather bound book and quoted from memory:

"Laudate, pueri Dominum: laudate

Nomen Domine.

Sit nomen Domini benedictum:

Exhoc nunc, et usque in saeculum."

The wash of Lake Superior's waves, the sighing of the breeze, the red squirrel's scolding, and the whir of a partridge's wings passed unnoticed as the kindly Father continued to quote from the psalmist's beautiful thoughts of praise.

"From the rising up of the sun

220

Unto the going down of the same:

The name of the Lord is worthy to be praised

The Lord is high above all nations

and his glory above the heavens."

At the customary ending, "Blessed be the name of Lord forever more," he removed the crucifix from its position above the tabernacle and placed the attached narrow strip of black ribbon about his neck and tucked the emblem carefully beneath his sash and slowly passed through the opening left in the framework of the lodge beside the altar. As the priest wended his way along the dim path he thought of the morrow when the pagan rites would be observed within the same enclosure where he had offered the sacrifice of the Mass. He had no misgivings. Years of patient labor among the Natives had taught him to respect their faiths. He smiled happily. Today he thought he had driven a wedge into their beliefs in pagan Gods. He would pray that the seed he had sown would take root and bear fruit. Tomorrow he would wander among them and view with charity their quaint and harmless pagan ceremonies. He was a kindly man, a patient man, a wise man. His narrow face and deep forehead reflected thoughtful asceticism.

****

Throughout the morning, a light fog settled over the land, voices sounded muffled and distant in the stilled atmosphere. At intervals, the sun, appearing dull and moonlike, its rays in vain attempts to penetrate the enveloping mist, like arrows spent in midair, fell useless and unguided. The wild echoless cries of the gulls, heard distinctly over the sounds of Superior's ceaseless wash, the sudden staccato drilling of the woodpecker or the blue jay's insistent call for rain and more rain fell upon the dampened villagers unnoticed.

Native scouts in war paint and feathers, scantily clad in breechclouts that ill-concealed the wearer, moved about in ghostly fashion; in proud but quiet step. Amidst this subdued atmosphere, the girl Paulette wound her way in slow determined strides towards the establishment of Monsieur LaChance, the trader. The cloak of blue velveteen that she held close about her, hiding its lining of silk, imparted a feeling of warmth and brought back memories of a similar visit to the domicile of the crafty trader and his son. Within his store room, the trader was in high good spirits and frequently rubbed his hands together seemingly to dull their itching palms, an omen among his kind, of impending good fortune. As the girl entered quietly and unobserved, the darkened interior of the place rendered even gloomier by the mist without, she stood by the high table and took a quick inventory of the trader's stock. In his accustomed corner, Monsieur LaChance turned from his rustic desk and stared upon his caller. At last, after what seemed like time enough to boil a pot of tea, the trader leaped from his high stool and extending both hands towards his visitor, exclaimed, "Ah-h, Mademoiselle, at last you have come to honor us with your presence. I was about to come to you. The expressions of gratitude I owe you, my dear, could wait no longer. Last night I did not sleep lest I seem ungrateful for your kindness."

"Kindness, Monsieur? You recollect the word and speak not from the practice of its meaning."

The trader, taken aback for moment by the girl's quiet and resolute attitude, changed his bubbling expressions of gratitude to a more subdued tone. "But, my dear, I would be ungrateful, indeed, did I not tender some sign of our sincere gratitude for the fourteen bales of fur you sent in payment for an account that you were not in duty bound to pay."

"Fair exchange, Monsieur, does not rest upon duty alone. It is fair exchange that I come to speak of, not duty."

Monsieur LaChance, having worked his way around the end of his trading table, now stood before the girl and extending his hands, palms upward, said emphatically, "Say the work, Mademoiselle, and everything we have is yours, take and do as you please. I am but your servant."

Paulette threw back the left half of her cloak and rested her hand upon the knife hilt protruding from beneath a fur belt. She laughed loudly at the trader's words. "I take it, Monsieur, that your words are spoken in jest."

"I swear it, Mademoiselle! Never in my life have I been more serious. In his excited movement, the trader's long buckskin jacket, its collar and cuffs once gaudily embroidered in many colors, slipped its fastenings revealing a hairy chest not unlike that of a bear.

"Careful, Monsieur, you use the language for sound alone and disregard its meaning."

"Ah, but no, Mademoiselle, I was never more serious in my life, say the word and I obey."

"Thank you, Monsieur LaChance, you have indeed made my errand simple…very simple."

"It is not what you can do, but what you have done that matters."

The girl stood still, ominously still, as the trader worked his way back to the inside of the table. The man looked about like one searching for an exit. Perhaps he had said too much, but it was only a polite expression meant only to convey his good will. Surely she must realize that. The girl's next words came upon the trader like a thunderbolt out of a clear sky. With her eyes partly closed, yet enough to hide the sparkle of tiny lights flashing on and off, she spoke quietly in a tone that conveyed a meaning of planned determination.

"You will immediately prepare to leave this country, your clothing and personal belongings of you and that rat your call your son, and nothing else, except of course what food you will need for yourself and as many that choose to accompany you."

The trader's eyes had widened at the girl's every word until now he stood speechless, a sickly pallor had crept over his features. "But, but Mademoiselle, I did not mean"

"You heard what I said, do not wait too long to obey my orders and carry out your part of the bargain."

Monsieur LaChance recovered from the first shock rapidly and after gulping several times, said, "Mademoiselle Paulette, you are a sensible girl. Let us talk of this matter over quietly."

Little Half-breed Woman laughed silently. "I think you have talked too much already. I shall send some men to take over what you are going to leave."

The trader was not one to give in so easily and persisted, "You are being unjust. You are taking advantage of me."

"That, coming from you, sounds funny. I do not have more time to waste on you. I have already given more of my time than you gave me of yours last autumn."

The trader's face flushed as he recalled his abrupt dismissal of the ragged girl on the flimsy excuse of a lack of time. Paulette leaned slightly forward and lowered her voice. Her next words were for he alone would understand their meaning.

"Monsieur, do you know that I hold your life, not in the palm of my hand, but on the tips of my two fingers, the ones that are on the string of my bow? If I were to order a stout stake driven into the ground beside your door and that son of yours tied to it securely and roasted over a slow fire, with tied to a nearby tree so you could not miss one single note of his screams, what do you suppose would happen?" The girl carefully spoke each word carefully spaced.

Like one in a trance, the trader heard the voice of the girl and before a bursting dam, there was no way out, asked quietly and in the same tone she had used, "How much time do I have to prepare for the journey?"

"Be out of here before sundown tomorrow."

The girl turned abruptly and with a slight shrug of her lift shoulder, the long cape settled back into place as she wrapped its folds about her before stepping out into the mist and fog. Reaching her abode quickly, she found Pascal patiently awaiting her return.

"I would have found you if I had known where to look, Madam," the faithful little man said with a note of apology.

With her mind too full of the recent happenings, Paulette merely nodded to her friend and poured a cup of strong tea. For several years, she had dreamed of this day and now at the apex of its achievement, she felt as one after a fitful night, weak and tired. Between sips of the hot brew, she said, "We have just taken over the stock and trading post of Monsieur LaChance."

Pascal aroused from his listless occupation of drawing patterns in the ashes and burnt earth beside the fire, suddenly dropped the partly charred twig. Paulette smiled in anticipation of the little fellow's excited antics. "Did I hear Madam say something in jest?"

"No Pascal, it is true. Now go and find Henri LaClair and tell him to come here."

Much to her disappointment and surprise, Pascal rose quietly and without comment, left the lodge. Listening intently, the girl laughed as sounds of the rapid thumping of "Little Red Man's" feet faded in the distance, his reaction had been slow.

Later in the day, the girl, in passing the post building, was startled by the sounds of chopping coming from within the store. Hastily swinging the heavy door open, she was met by the timed flashes of a new well sharpened ax being swung by someone in back of and below the trading table.

"What is going on here?" Paulette asked in alarm.

The chopping ceased and a pair of round blue eyes rose scarcely above the level of the table. Pascal's nose, as if by predetermined arrangement not unlike a marker, rested on the side of the sapling covered top.

After a moment of ill-controlled merriment, the girl again asked, "What are you doing with that ax?"

Pascal disappeared for a moment, and then unexpectedly appeared around the end of the table, he had been standing on tiptoe. "The legs are too long Madam."

"And, are you making them shorter?"

"Yes, Madam, I will have to chop them down, a little, Madam."

Paulette turned and left the building. As the door closed, the chopping continued where it had left off.

Chapter 27

In the gathering dusk, Paulette, in the days of her childhood, carefully picked her way along the trackless forest. The sound of water rushing past jagged rocks guided her straight to the old crossing where, as a child and not too long ago, she would leap with agility from boulder to boulder until reaching safely the opposite bank, utter a sigh of relief, after the slippery and hazardous footing. Nearing the chosen spot, the girl found the wildly rushing water too swift for a crossing. It was still early spring and the interior swamps let their winter's accumulation of icy moisture out slowly. Rolling her skirt and cloak well above her knees, she made one unsuccessful attempt. Without hesitating, the girl followed along the swiftly moving water to a spot below where it tumbled into a pool covered with foam once white, now stained with specks of brown. Quickly launching one of the many canoes that lined the bank in safety from the lashing of Superior's stormy waves; now lying still and enticing like a siren's beguiling smiles.

Drawing the light canoe and carefully placing it on the opposite bank, Paulette climbed the steep hill forming the west wall of the ravine and disappeared into the dense forest of giant pine, birch, pale and hemlock standing at the very brink of the hill and on into the flat land beyond. The fog, that obscured the sun throughout the day, had lifted enough to let a few stars peep through the remaining mist that, like a gossamer veil carelessly cast across the sky, reflected the sun's rays from somewhere beneath the western horizon. Like sheets of golden lace edged in rose and gray and studded with gems of priceless worth, the remaining mist floated leisurely southward across the face of the waning rays that, like spear points, withdrawn by an unseen hand to strike another time, slowly disappeared into the unknown beyond.

The girl stood listening to the low rumble beneath her feet as she neared the cliff lined shore and thrilled to the trembling touch of a great pine standing erect and proud, its top bathed in semi-darkness. Seemingly not satisfied in her search, she passed on to other trees standing in stately array until she came to another pine with giant roots, stripped of bark and exposed, about its trunk, aged in ageless glory. Paulette moved about cautiously as she neared the edge of the low cliff and gazed for some moments at the small waves passing in rapid succession to dash themselves into the cavernous depths beneath. Satisfied, she returned to the old pine and reclined restfully on the ground between two of the exposed roots. Resting her head back against the rough bark, she started humming a wild unmelodious air-like, and yet unlike, a pagan chant. She sat motionless with eyes partly open, her hands rested listless on her lap. Without apparent purpose, the wordless humming continued, not idly following fancy's dictate, but in a predetermined pattern, now high in pitch, ever in even tone, always audible and softly soothing. For some moments, the humming continued then slowly diminished in volume like one passing out of sight into a darkened room. Little Half-breed sat still, her eyes glazed in a semi-hypnotic state. From amidst a little patch of blooming trailing arbutus, a little figure of a man poked its head above the ground cautiously and glanced carefully about. Apparently satisfied that the coast was clear, he arose to the surface and stomped a tiny foot. The girl felt the giant tree quiver at her back as her lips moved in smiling approval. Instantly several more of the tiny figures, no taller than a rabbit sitting upright on its haunches, appeared, as if by magic. Then, as usual, the fun began. Their long hair and beards of colors to match the wild flowers and long gowns speckled with the pink and white of the arbutus patch streamed in the breeze. The madly increasing tempo of seeming confusion as the little men raced, danced and wrestled amidst a whirling exhibition of calisthenics, went on and on in tireless abandon.

Then as suddenly as they began, the mad gyrations stopped and the little men gathered in a circle. From amidst them, a wisp of smoke arose from little stone pipes, some black, others red. The pipes emitted puffs of fragrant smoke as the tobacco that the girl had secretly buried about the flower stems, burned with a faint reddish glow. Into pouches carefully tucked beneath narrow belts carelessly knotted, the little men returned their pipes. Coming closer together, their sharply pointed caps bunched in many colors forming a beautiful flower. The girl unconsciously frowned. The flower was new, strange and confusing. Her eyes felt tired as she tried to trace each color. The little men separated and the one, the girl recognized as the first to appear, hopped up to a low hanging limb of a small birch near her head. Sitting precariously at the very tip of the limber branch where it swung gracefully up and down, up and down in happy carefree enjoyment until at last it came to rest beside the girl's head; it's tiny sandals barely caught by his toes kept snapping against the little heels. The little man in his gown of many colors leaned far over from his springy perch and whispered in the Ojibwe language, "Walk the sand this time tomorrow night. Fear not." Paulette stirred and looked about her as one after a long restful sleep. Arising quickly, she rubbed her eyes and smiled and repeated in Ojibwe, "Walk the sand this time tomorrow night. Fear not."

The girl noted the light in the eastern sky where the full moon showed its pale gold rim. Tomorrow night it would rise later. She must not forget, lest whatever fate had in store should pass her up.

****

With brow beaded with perspiration, Pascal stood by and dutifully enforced the rules in the knife throwing contest. Shoulder high to the average man, the target hung on the side of a thick pine tree; a smoothly hewn square of soft wood, upon which was drawn a black circle not larger than the head of a full grown beaver, carefully traced with charcoal around an inner circle the size of a duck's head stood out enticingly. The rules were simple. From a position outside the birch pole fastened between two trees a good ten steps away, the contestant threw his or her knife. If the knife stuck into the target anywhere within the circle, it remained there until, if and when, another contestant stuck a knife point nearer the inner circle. When a knife hit the inner circle, the contest, up to that point, closed and started over. The winning contestant became eligible for the play-off the following day. On a tiny ladder, with rungs closely spaced, the little man raced up and down the day through, judging the position of each knife point fairly as it quivered after its speedy passage through the air and came to rest with a soft thud. As the day wore on, only one knife had reached the outer circle splitting the line. After a moment's hesitation, Pascal awarded the tall bearded contestant the right to leave his knife as a mark for the others to beat. At infrequent intervals, a passerby would stop and, with careful aim, throw his knife that invariably whirled through the air, striking the target with any part but its point.

As the sun shone full on the target and the sounds of wild drum beats and excited shouts from the ceremonial lodge where painted warriors and shy maidens and their mothers, their cheeks and foreheads

230

marked with spots of blue or vermilion, joined in the dance from time to time as the ceremony progressed. The dancer's movements represented hunting and battling an enemy. Several items worn by various dancers represented their own personal story and feats of strength and experiences. They wore items such as: A breast plate made of long beads fashioned from animal bones or a shell for protection against arrows; neck chokers for protection against knives; ankle bells or deer hooves; and a shield made of hide with their Clan and Nation designs added to them. Members of clans, other than the one occupying the lodge, amused themselves by occasionally shifting their positions to keep within the shade of the heavy treetops and continue the gambling or moccasin game in comfort. A not so simple game of "now you see it, now you don't" as each side took turns in hiding the lead musket ball under one of four pads representing moccasins placed at evenly spaced distances on their team's end of a blanket carefully spread over the ground. Employing a system of "if you find it, the hiding team pays, if you don't your team pays" with small carved sticks representing points, the point value depending on how many guesses the team takes to find it. While guessing, a small hand drum was beat with special songs meant to confuse the team guessing under which moccasin the lead ball was hidden. The game often rose to such intensity of interest as to strip a player of all his earthly possessions including his blanket, wigwam and canoe.

On various days of the carnival-like celebration, different sports would take place, a day for feats of strength and endurance, men's lacrosse, or the women's version of lacrosse called the double ball game, where a bola of small sand filled leather pouches connected by a leather thong was thrown from player to player using a stick about the height of each player. Other games included the awl game where women caught deer toes in the shape of small cones on a string attached to an awl and the dish game where game pieces were tossed in a carved

231

wooden bowl and depending on which way they landed in the bowl determined the point value. But, regardless of what day or its purpose, the ceremonial dancing continued and the moccasin game went on accompanied by its intermittent drum beats and the short gambling songs. Regardless of whether one danced in the circle of the ceremonial lodge, bet his home or canoe on his ability to hide the little ball successfully or stood proudly erect as the champion archer, both men and women, boys and girls talked and dreamt of little else than the real testing of endurance on the last day and saved some part of their belongings to place as a wager on their favorite one of two inevitable contestants.

On a cleared spot, stood a low oval shaped, Sha-ban-do-wan or lodge, barely large enough to comfortably seat two men, provided they sat on the ground facing each other. The small lodge, minus its customary opening at the top, was constructed so there were no openings large enough for an insect the size of hornet to pass through. Two naked volunteers entered the lodge and became comfortably seated with a real live hornet nest between them. The opening to the lodge was sealed immediately and the plug confining the maddened insects was pulled releasing them to do their worst. In the meantime, the pile of traps, blankets and prized articles mounted as each Native added his bit to the community wager on the side of the favored contestant.

The steady hum of voices outside of the enclosure added to the hum of the hornets inside, punctuated only by the steady series of grunts accompanying each telling sting from an angry hornet. The self-imposed torture went on until the loser, unable to longer endure the punishment, with a loud crashing of bark and snapping of small saplings, burst forth from the small lodge closely followed by the winner.

****

Paulette as a member of the clan now occupying the ceremonial lodge, in a subdued spirit, her eyes listlessly and lazily watching the dancers in their intricate and complex footwork, athletic leaps and dizzying spins, and flashes of color reminded the girl of her experience of the previous evening, took note of the sun's position and quietly arose and left the enclosure. Standing, for a moment, at its entrance, the sound of an excited shout coming from the direction of the knife throwing target, caught her attention and recalled her promise to Batiste to take part in the sport. Again taking note of the sun, it would be shining full on the target, she wondered if he had tested his skill. She would soon find out.

Paulette went straight to Pascal and inquired, "What is all the shouting for?"

The little man pointed to the target where two knives stood out stiff each point buried deep barely within and at opposite sides of the outer circle, leaving the inner circle free with considerable space.

"Whose are those?" she asked.

"Batiste, one with each hand," the little man replied proudly.

"Smart and stubborn," she muttered. "Not satisfied with one, he must show off with two."

Quickly walking around to the barrier as Pascal held up a warning hand for quiet, Little Half-breed dug deep beneath her wide sash of brightly hued wool and tossed a small dagger into the air and caught its point neatly between the thumb and forefinger of her right hand. Resting lightly against the pole waist high, Paulette smiled a crooked little smile. The bystanders, some with eyes fixed on the target, other on the girl, presenting a figure of self-assurance, stood as one not daring to breathe lest her aim would be spoiled. Paulette took a quick glance at the target and with its position indelibly fixed upon her consciousness. The white object sped through the air followed closely by a soft thud. Hardly had the weapon landed, when a great shout rent the air followed closely by a tensely subdued atmosphere as Batiste came forward from somewhere among the closely packed spectators. With quick strides, the young man went to the target and withdrew his two knives, leaving a small pearl handled dagger sticking neatly into the very center of the inner circle. The young man stood as one transfixed at the sight of some frightening object, his eyes seemingly ever widening and unable to break away from the sight of the little weapon. Paulette, after seeing her dagger hit the target and Batiste's approach, nonchalantly turned and walked towards her abode. She was happy for two reasons. The knowledge of having won the contest so far was of minor importance, but, and here she raised her chin a trifle higher, she was partly avenged for the half-breed's arrogant display of not only his skill, for which she was thankful, but his absolute disregard for her.

Batiste, unmindful of the bystanders and their admiring comments of the skill of "Little Half-breed", continued to stare at the dagger. At last summoning Pascal to come near, the young man whispered in a husky shaking voice, "Did…did you ever see this knife before?"

Pascal nodded, "Yes, Jacques, he have two like that. I think that is one. I don't see for a long time, not since he died."

Pascal cast a significant glance at the husky man and wondered if he had said the right thing and continued as the half-breed stared now slowly shaking his head. "Yes, Jacques have two, he brought them from France, he had a very nice leather case, it was lined with purple velvet."

Batiste gritted his teeth, the muscles of his jaws stood out. "And he had to bring them all the way over here. What a fool! What a fool! Why did he have to do that? So I could make a fool of myself, too" he said to himself under his breath.

"Did you say something, Monsieur?"

234

Batiste shook his head. He started along the path to the cabin occupied by Father Daniels and himself. The bystanders wondered at the young man's behavior as with bowed head and shoulders sagging as one extremely tired after a hard day on a long portage. He shuffled rather than walked.

****

Following the sun's glorious passing at the end of a busy day, the villagers each happily satisfied with the exception of the losing gamblers, wended their homeward way. The oval roofed lodge stood vacant, save for a few youngsters playfully imitating their elders. Paulette stopped and watched the children and laughed at their antics. She remembered so well, but a few summers away, when she, too, waited impatiently for the passing day and her turn at the make believe drum or the circle dance. Dusk was falling fast and she had a rendezvous with fate. Despite her carefree mien, the girl experienced a feeling of inward turmoil, not unlike that of a freshly dressed deer. She had often watched the quiver of its muscles long after it was dead and wondered if that was what she was like, inside, now. She felt no fear, she had the assurance of the little people, and walked steadily along the path leading among the trees that stood beyond the reach of Superior's wildest waves. She would go some distance to the east and on her way back, she would "walk the sand" as she was told. She hoped that nothing would happen in the village demanding her attention. Continuing along steadily and quietly, the girl hummed a song, her clan song of the gull.

A faint glow appeared along the eastern horizon, she must turn back. With resolute strides, she stepped out into the open upon the sands of Lake Superior's beach and started westward.

At the cabin of Father Daniels, Batiste hurriedly prepared the good Father's supper. Everything he did was without thought or plan, he moved about as habit dictated seemingly unconscious of his present

235

surroundings. Luckily he was well versed in the art of living in the wilderness and accomplished his task without mishap. Everything he touched brought to mind the little pearl handled dagger. So Paulette did not kill her husband, Francois. What a fool he was for, ever thinking that she could have done such a thing. Jacques had two such daggers. It was Jacques who killed the trader with one of the daggers. He must have dropped the other. The young man poured himself a cup of tea, it tasted flat and strangely bitter, a bite of cooked smoked venison, he couldn't swallow it. A bit of maple sugar lay temptingly on the grass mat. He hastily picked it up and put it back into its container, who cares for maple sugar! He couldn't stand the stuff!

What did Paulette think of him, his foolish disappearance last autumn, without so much as a farewell. Suddenly he squared his broad shoulders and stood erect. At least he could go and tell her.

"I am going out for a while Father. I'll try and be back in time so I won't disturb your sleep."

Father Daniels smiled, "Don't worry about disturbing me. One can always go back to sleep, it does seem much nicer to fall asleep the second time, don't you think?"

"I don't know, Father. I seldom have to take the second sleep after I get started on the first one."

"I notice that, Batiste, it is said that only those with a guilty conscious sleep fitfully. It is probably God's way of warning us.

Batiste hastily gathered their few utensils principally composed of bark containers. He emptied and rinsed their two small kettles, one for tea and another used to cook meat. Looking about the dimly lit interior of Paulette's lodge, the young man felt keen disappointment at her absence. Grandmother quickly volunteered the information that her granddaughter was somewhere along the sand beach and "if you wish to see her, you will find her there." The old woman turned to her task of patching a worn moccasin without further comment. The young man left the abode and hastened towards the beach. Becoming more or less accustomed, since his arrival, to the ceaseless wash of the waves they sounded distant and vague. Peering through the thin evening mist drifting eastward along the beach, Batiste searched in vain for the girl. Not having been to that part of the beach before, the man felt it strangely familiar. Somewhere, sometime he had seen something very much like it. The sound of the waves puzzled him, he had never been anywhere in his life where the waves were spaced so far apart. In his homeland among the thousands of smaller lakes, the waves were small and broke over their shores in rapid succession. Here the waves took advantage of endless time and rolled lazily and well-spaced. He decided to wait awhile, until the moon rose above the pale glow that shone along the eastern horizon. The mist gathered thickly and the half-breed rested against a small dead pine. He wondered why no one had cut it down for firewood. A limb, just out of reach, stood straight out from the trunk. He looked at it long and searched his memory in vain for some recollection, but, he shrugged his shoulder, why worry about a tree, he had seen many trees of all shapes and sizes. Why worry over one, he couldn't remember them all. From out of the misty light, a young woman appeared. Walking slowly, she stopped and peered into the forest. She searched among the many canoes lying carelessly about the beach. They must belong to the newcomers. The Native Indians knew better than to leave their canoes within reach of Superior's sudden fits of temperament, she must send out word tomorrow. As she resumed her walk, the young man watched the girl intently. Coming near, she stopped directly before him. With a cry of joy at his recognition of Paulette, he sprang to her side and gathered her in his arms. Paulette scarcely had time to breathe the one word "Batiste" when the loud chattering of a red squirrel broke in upon the misty night air.

237

The young man suddenly relaxed his hold upon the girl. The memory broke in upon his consciousness like the sudden drawing of a curtain, across his mind flashed the words, "your journey has ended." Hand in hand, they moved slowly, step by step towards the water's edge. The great lake in benediction, subdued momentarily the wash of its waves over the sand, giving way to its distant sounds as of rolling thunder.

The full moon rose slowly casting its lengthening golden shadows across the water until it came to rest at the feet of the boy and girl. Like a carpet of jewels cast in a pale yellow light, the undulating pathway to the moon, in obedience to a rising breeze sparkled into a band of fire. The two children of the forest gazed out along the lighted way to where the moon rested on the rim of the horizon and beyond where the stars turned to silver specks against the dark.